SAEMUND SIGFUSSON

THE ELDER EDDAS OF SAEMUND SIGFUSSON; AND THE YOUNGER EDDAS OF SNORRE STURLESON

SAEMUND SIGFUSSON

THE ELDER EDDAS OF SAEMUND SIGFUSSON; AND THE YOUNGER EDDAS OF SNORRE STURLESON

THE ELDER EDDAS OF SAEMUND SIGFUSSON;

AND

THE YOUNGER EDDAS OF SNORRE STURLESON

By Saemund Sigfusson

CONTENTS

THE ELDER EDDAS OF SAEMUND.

Völuspâ. The Vala's Prophecy.   1

The Lay Of Vafthrudnir.   7

The Lay Of Grimnir.   13

The Lay Of Vegtam, Or Baldr's Dreams.   19

The High One's Lay.   21

Odin's Rune-song.   31

The Lay Of Hymir.   33

The Lay Of Thrym, Or The Hammer Recovered.   37

The Lay Of The Dwarf Alvis.   41

The Lay Of Harbard.   45

The Journey Or Lay Of Skirnir.   51

The Lay Of Rig.   55

Oegir's Compotation, Or Loki's Altercation.   59

The Lay Of Fiolsvith.   67

The Lay Of Hyndla.   73

The Incantation Of Groa.   77

The Song Of The Sun.   79

The Lay Of Volund.   85

The Lay Of Helgi Hiorvard's Son.   89

The First Lay Of Helgi Hundingcide.   95

The Second Lay Of Helgi Hundingcide.   99

Sinfiotli's End.   105

The First Lay Of Sigurd Fafnicide, Or Gripir's Prophecy.   107

The Second Lay Of Sigurd Fafnicide.   113

The Lay Of Fafnir.   117

The Lay Of Sigrdrifa.   123

Fragments Of The Lay Of Sigurd And Brynhild.   127

The Third Lay Of Sigurd Fafnicide.   131

Fragments Of The Lay Of Brynhild.   137

The First Lay Of Gudrun.   139

Brynhild's Hel-ride.   141

The Slaughter Of The Niflungs.   143

The Second Lay Of Gudrun.   145

The Third Lay Of Gudrun.   149

Oddrun's Lament.   151

The Lay Of Atli.   155

The Groenland Lay Of Atli.   159

Gudrun's Incitement.   169

The Lay Of Hamdir.   171

THE YOUNGER EDDAS OF STURLESON.

The Deluding Of Gylfi.   173

Gylfi's Journey To Asgard.   175

Of The Supreme Deity.   177

Of The Primordial State Of The Universe.   179

Origin Of The Hrimthursar, Or Frost-giants.   181

Of The Cow Audhumla, And The Birth Of Odin.   183

How The Sons Of Bor Slew Ymir And From His Body   185
Made Heaven And Earth.

Of The Formation Of The First Man And Woman.   187

Of Night And Day.   189

Of The Sun And Moon.   191

Of The Wolves That Pursue The Sun And Moon   193

Of The Way That Leads To Heaven.   195

The Golden Age.   197

Origin Of The Dwarfs.   199

Of The Ash Yggdrasill, Mimir's Well., And The Norns   201
Or Destinies.

Of The Various Celestial Regions.   203

Of The Wind And The Seasons.   205

Of Odin.   207

Of Thor.   209

Of Baldur.   211

Of Njord.   213

Of The God Frey, And The Goddess Freyja.   215

Of Tyr.   217

Of The Other Gods.   219

Hodur The Blind, Assassin Of Baldur   221

Of Loki And His Progeny.   223

Binding The Wolf Fenir   225

Of The Goddesses.   227

Of Frey And Gerda.   229

Of The Joys Of Valhalla.   231

Of The Horse Sleipnir.   233

Of The Ship Skidbladnir.   235

Thor's Adventures On His Journey To The Land Of The Giants.   237

How Thor Went To Fish For The Midgard Serpent.   243

The Death Of Baldur The Good.   245

Baldur In The Abode Of The Dead   247

The Flight And Punishment Of Loki.   249

Of Ragnarok, Or The Twilight Oe The Gods, And The Conflagration Of The   251

Of The Abodes Of Future Bliss And Misery.   253

The Renovation Of The Universe.   255

Ægir's Journey To Asgard.   257

Iduna And Her Apples.   259

The Origin Of Poetry.   261

Odin Beguiles The Daughter Of Baugi   263

THE ELDER EDDAS OF SAEMUND.

VÖLUSPÂ. THE VALA'S PROPHECY.

1. For silence I pray all sacred children, great and small, sons of Heimdall, they will that I Valfather's deeds recount, men's ancient saws, those that I best remember.

2. The Jötuns I remember early born, those who me of old have reared. I nine worlds remember, nine trees, the great central tree, beneath the earth.

3. There was in times of old, where Ymir dwelt, nor sand nor sea, nor gelid waves; earth existed not, nor heaven above, 'twas a chaotic chasm, and grass nowhere.

4. Before Bur's sons raised up heaven's vault, they who the noble mid-earth shaped. The sun shone from the south over the structure's rocks: then was the earth begrown with herbage green.

5. The sun from the south, the moon's companion, her right hand cast about the heavenly horses. The sun knew not where she a dwelling had, the moon knew not what power he possessed, the stars knew not where they had a station.

6. Then went the powers all to their judgment-seats, the all-holy gods, and thereon held council: to night and to the waning moon gave names; morn they named, and mid-day, afternoon and eve, whereby to reckon years.

7. The Æsir met on Ida's plain; they altar-steads and temples high constructed; their strength they proved, all things tried, furnaces established, precious things forged, formed tongs, and fabricated tools;

8. At tables played at home; joyous they were; to them was naught the want of gold, until there came Thurs-maidens three, all powerful, from Jötunheim.

9. Then went all the powers to their judgment-seats, the all-holy gods, and thereon held council, who should of the dwarfs the race create, from the sea-giant's blood and livid bones.

10. Then was Môtsognir created greatest of all the dwarfs, and Durin second; there in man's likeness they created many dwarfs from earth, as Durin said.

11. Nýi and Nidi, Nordri and Sudri, Austri and Vestri, Althiôf, Dvalin Nâr and Nâin, Niping, Dain, Bivör, Bavör, Bömbur, Nori, An and Anar, Ai, Miodvitnir,

12. Veig and Gandâlf, Vindâlf, Thrain, Thekk and Thorin, Thrôr, Vitr, and Litr, Nûr and Nýrâd, Regin and Râdsvid. Now of the dwarfs I have rightly told.

13. Fili, Kili, Fundin, Nali, Hepti, Vili, Hanar, Svior, Billing, Bruni, Bild, Bûri, Frâr, Hornbori, Fræg and Lôni, Aurvang, Iari, Eikinskialdi.

14. Time 'tis of the dwarfs in Dvalin's band, to the sons of men, to Lofar up to reckon, those who came forth from the world's rock, earth's foundation, to Iora's plains.

15. There were Draupnir, and Dôlgthrasir, Hâr, Haugspori, Hlævang, Glôi, Skirvir, Virvir, Skafid, Ai, Alf and Yngvi, Eikinskialdi,

16. Fialar and Frosti, Finn and Ginnar, Heri, Höggstari, Hliôdôlf, Moin: that above shall, while mortals live, the progeny of Lofar, accounted be.

17. Until there came three mighty and benevolent Æsir to the world from their assembly. They found on earth, nearly powerless, Ask and Embla, void of destiny.

18. Spirit they possessed not, sense they had not, blood nor motive powers, nor goodly colour. Spirit gave Odin, sense gave Hoenir, blood gave Lodur, and goodly colour.

19. I know an ash standing Yggdrasil hight, a lofty tree, laved with limpid water: thence come the dews into the dales that fall; ever stands it green over Urd's fountain.

20. Thence come maidens, much knowing, three from the hall, which under that tree stands; Urd hight the one, the second Verdandi,—on a tablet they graved—Skuld the third. Laws they established, life allotted to the sons of men; destinies pronounced.

21. Alone she sat without, when came that ancient dread Æsir's prince; and in his eye she gazed.

22. "Of what wouldst thou ask me? Why temptest thou me? Odin! I know all, where thou thine eye didst sink in the pure well of Mim." Mim drinks mead each morn from Valfather's pledge. Understand ye yet, or what?

23. The chief of hosts gave her rings and necklace, useful discourse, and a divining spirit: wide and far she saw o'er every world.

24. She the Valkyriur saw from afar coming, ready to ride to the god's people: Skuld held a shield, Skögul was second, then Gunn, Hild Göndul, and Geirskögul. Now are enumerated Herian's maidens, the Valkyriur, ready over the earth to ride.

25. She that war remembers, the first on earth, when Gullveig they with lances pierced, and in the high one's hall her burnt, thrice burnt, thrice brought her forth, oft not seldom; yet she still lives.

26. Heidi they called her, whithersoe'r she came, the well-foreseeing Vala: wolves she tamed, magic arts she knew, magic arts practised; ever was she the joy of evil people.

27. Then went the powers all to their judgment-seats, the all-holy gods, and thereon held council, whether the Æsir should avenge the crime, or all the gods receive atonement.

28. Broken was the outer wall of the Æsir's burgh. The Vanir, foreseeing conflict, tramp o'er the plains. Odin cast , and mid the people hurled it: that was the first warfare in the world.

29. Then went the powers all to their judgment-seats, the all-holy gods, and thereon held council: who had all the air with evil mingled? or to the Jötun race Od's maid had given?

30. There alone was Thor with anger swollen. He seldom sits, when of the like he hears. Oaths are not held sacred; nor words, nor swearing, nor binding compacts reciprocally made.

31. She knows that Heimdall's horn is hidden under the heaven-bright holy tree. A river she sees flow, with foamy fall, from Valfather's pledge. Understand ye yet, or what?

32. East sat the crone, in Iârnvidir, and there reared up Fenrir's progeny: of all shall be one especially the moon's devourer, in a troll's semblance.

33. He is sated with the last breath of dying men; the god's seat he with red gore defiles: swart is the sunshine then for summers after; all weather turns to storm. Understand ye yet, or what?

34. There on a height sat, striking a harp, the giantess's watch, the joyous Egdir; by him crowed, in the bird-wood, the bright red cock, which Fialar hight.

35. Crowed o'er the Æsir Gullinkambi, which wakens heroes with the sire of hosts; but another crows beneath the earth, a soot-red cock, in the halls of Hel.

36. I saw of Baldr, the blood-stained god, Odin's son, the hidden fate. There stood grown up, high on the plain, slender and passing fair, the mistletoe.

37. From that shrub was made, as to me it seemed, a deadly, noxious dart. Hödr shot it forth; but Frigg bewailed, in Fensalir, Valhall's calamity. Understand ye yet, or what?

38. Bound she saw lying, under Hveralund, a monstrous form, to Loki like. There sits Sigyn, for her consort's sake, not right glad. Understand ye yet, or what?

39. Then the Vala knew the fatal bonds were twisting, most rigid, bonds from entrails made.

40. From the east a river falls, through venom dales, with mire and clods, Slîd is its name.

41. On the north there stood, on Nida-fells, a hall of gold, for Sindri's race; and another stood in Okôlnir, the Jötuns beer-hall which Brîmir hight.

42. She saw a hall standing, far from the sun, in Nâströnd; its doors are northward turned, venom-drops fall in through its apertures: entwined is that hall with serpents' backs.

43. She there saw wading the sluggish streams bloodthirsty men and perjurers, and him who the ear beguiles of another's wife. There Nidhögg sucks the corpses of the dead; the wolf tears men. Understand ye yet, or what?

44. Further forward I see, much can I say of Ragnarök and the gods' conflict.

45. Brothers shall fight, and slay each other; cousins shall kinship violate. The earth resounds, the giantesses flee; no man will another spare.

3

46. Hard is it in the world, great whoredom, an axe age, a sword age, shields shall be cloven, a wind age, a wolf age, ere the world sinks.

47. Mim's sons dance, but the central tree takes fire at the resounding Giallar-horn. Loud blows Heimdall, his horn is raised; Odin speaks with Mim's head.

48. Trembles Yggdrasil's ash yet standing; groans that aged tree, and the jötun is loosed. Loud bays Garm before the Gnupa-cave, his bonds he rends asunder; and the wolf runs.

49. Hrym steers from the east, the waters rise, the mundane snake is coiled in jötun-rage. The worm beats the water, and the eagle screams: the pale of beak tears carcases; Naglfar is loosed.

50. That ship fares from the east: come will Muspell's people o'er the sea, and Loki steers. The monster's kin goes all with the wolf; with them the brother is of Byleist on their course.

51. Surt from the south comes with flickering flame; shines from his sword the Val-gods' sun. The stony hills are dashed together, the giantesses totter; men tread the path of Hel, and heaven is cloven.

52. How is it with the Æsir? How with the Alfar? All Jötunheim resounds; the Æsir are in council. The dwarfs groan before their stony doors, the sages of the rocky walls. Understand ye yet, or what?

53. Then arises Hlîn's second grief, when Odin goes with the wolf to fight, and the bright slayer of Beli with Surt. Then will Frigg's beloved fall.

54. Then comes the great victor-sire's son, Vidar, to fight with the deadly beast. He with his hands will make his sword pierce to the heart of the giant's son: then avenges he his father.

55. Then comes the mighty son of Hlôdyn: (Odin's son goes with the monster to fight); Midgârd's Veor in his rage will slay the worm. Nine feet will go Fiörgyn's son, bowed by the serpent, who feared no foe. All men will their homes forsake.

56. The sun darkens, earth in ocean sinks, fall from heaven the bright stars, fire's breath assails the all-nourishing tree, towering fire plays against heaven itself.

57. She sees arise, a second time, earth from ocean, beauteously green, waterfalls descending; the eagle flying over, which in the fell captures fish.

58. The Æsir meet on Ida's plain, and of the mighty earth-encircler speak, and there to memory call their mighty deeds, and the supreme god's ancient lore.

59. There shall again the wondrous golden tables in the grass be found, which in days of old had possessed the ruler of the gods, and Fiölnir's race.

60. Unsown shall the fields bring forth, all evil be amended; Baldr shall come; Hödr and Baldr, the heavenly gods, Hropt's glorious dwellings shall inhabit. Understand ye yet, or what?

61. Then can Hoenir choose his lot, and the two brothers' sons inhabit the spacious Vindheim. Understand ye yet, or what?

62. She a hall standing than the sun brighter, with gold bedecked, in Gimill: there shall be righteous people dwell, and for evermore happiness enjoy.

64. Then comes the mighty one to the great judgment, the powerful from above, who rules o'er all. He shall dooms pronounce, and strifes allay, holy peace establish, which shall ever be.

65. There comes the dark dragon flying from beneath the glistening serpent, from Nida-fels. On his wings bears Nidhögg, flying o'er the plain, a corpse. Now she will descend.

THE LAY OF VAFTHRUDNIR.

Odin visits the Giant (Jötun) Vafthrûdnir, for the purpose of proving his knowledge. They propose questions relative to the Cosmogony of the Northern creed, on the conditions that the baffled party forfeit his head. The Jötun incurs the penalty.

Odin.

1. Counsel thou me now, Frigg! as I long to go Vafthrûdnir to visit; great desire, I say, I have, in ancient lore with that all-wise Jötun to contend.

Frigg.

2. At home to bide Hærfather I would counsel, in the gods' dwellings; because no Jötun is, I believe, so mighty as is Vafthrûdnir.

Odin.

3. Much have I journeyed, much experienced, mighty ones many proved; but this I fain would know, how in Vafthrûdnir's halls it is.

Frigg.

4. In safety mayest thou go, in safety return; in safety on thy journeyings be; may thy wit avail thee, when thou, father of men! shalt hold converse with the Jötun.

5. Then went Odin the lore to prove of that all-wise Jötun. To the hall he came which Im's father owned. Ygg went forthwith in.

Odin.

6. Hail to thee, Vafthrûdnir! to thy hall I am now come, thyself to see; for I fain would know, whether thou art a cunning and all-wise Jötun.

Vafthrûdnir.

7. What man is this, that in my habitation by word addresses me? Out thou goest not from our halls, if thou art not the wiser.

Odin.

8. Gagnrâd is my name, from my journey I am come thirsty to thy halls, needing hospitality,—for I long have journeyed—and kind reception from thee, Jötun!

Vafthrûdnir.

9. Why then, Gagnrâd! speakest thou from the floor? Take in the hall a seat; then shall be proved which knows most, the guest or the ancient talker.

Gagnrâd.

10. A poor man should, who to a rich man comes, speak usefully or hold his tongue: over-much talk brings him, I ween, no good, who visits an austere man.

Vafthrûdnir.

11. Tell me, Gagnrâd! since on the floor thou wilt prove thy proficiency, how the horse is called that draws each day forth over human kind?

Gagnrâd.

12. Skinfaxi he is named, that the bright day draws forth over human kind. Of coursers he is best accounted among the Reid-goths. Ever sheds light that horse's mane.

Vafthrûdnir.

13. Tell me now, Gagnrâd! since on the floor thou wilt prove thy proficiency, how that steed is called, which from the east draws night o'er the beneficent powers?

Gagnrâd.

14. Hrimfaxi he is called, that each night draws forth over the beneficent powers. He from his bit lets fall drops every morn, whence in the dales comes dew.

Vafthrûdnir.

15. Tell me, Gagnrâd! since on the floor thou wilt prove thy proficiency, how the stream is called, which earth divides between the Jötuns and the Gods?

Gagnrâd.

16. Ifing the stream is called which earth divides between the Jötuns and the Gods: open shall it run throughout all time. On that stream no ice shall be.

Vafthrûdnir.

17. Tell me, Gagnrâd! since on the floor thou wilt prove thy proficiency, how that plain is called, where in fight shall meet Surt and the gentle Gods?

Gagnrâd.

18. Vigrid the plain is called where in fight shall meet Surt and the gentle Gods; a hundred rasts it is on every side. That plain is to them decreed.

Vafthrûdnir.

19. Wise art thou, O guest! Approach the Jötuns bench, and sitting let us together talk; we will our heads in the hall pledge, guest! for wise utterance.

Gagnrâd.

20. Tell me first, if thy wit suffices, and thou, Vafthrûdnir! knowest, whence first came the earth, and the high heaven, thou, sagacious Jötun?

Vafthrûdnir.

21. From Ymir's flesh the earth was formed, and from his bones the hills, the heaven from the skull of that ice-cold giant, and from his blood the sea.

Gagnrâd.

22. Tell me secondly, if thy wit suffices, and thou, Vafthrûdnir! knowest, whence came the moon, which over mankind passes, and the sun likewise?

Vafthrûdnir.

23. Mundilfoeri hight he, who the moon's father is, and eke the sun's: round heaven journey each day they must, to count years for men.

Gagnrâd.

24. Tell me thirdly, since thou art called wise, and if thou, Vafthrûdnir! knowest, whence came the day, which over people passes, and night with waning moons?

Vafthrûdnir.

25. Delling hight he who the day's father is, but night was of Nörvi born; the new and waning moons the beneficent powers created, to count years for men.

Gagnrâd.

26. Tell me fourthly, since they pronounce thee sage, and if thou, Vafthrûdnir! knowest, whence winter came, and warm summer first among the wise gods?

Vafthrûdnir.

27. Vindsval hight he, who winter's father is, and Svâsud summer's; yearly they both shall ever journey, until the powers perish.

Gagnrâd.

28. Tell me fifthly, since they pronounce thee sage, and if thou, Vafthrûdnir! knowest, which of the Æsir earliest, or of Ymir's sons, in days of old existed?

Vafthrûdnir.

29. Countless winters, ere earth was formed, was Bergelmir born; Thrûdgelmir was his sire, his grandsire Aurgelmir.

Gagnrâd.

30. Tell me sixthly, since thou art called wise, and if thou, Vafthrûdnir! knowest, whence first came Aurgelmir, among the Jötun's sons, thou sagacious Jötun?

Vafthrûdnir.

31. From Elivâgar sprang venom drops, which grew till they became a Jötun; but sparks flew from the south-world: to the ice the fire gave life.

Gagnrâd.

33. Tell me seventhly, since thou are called wise, and if thou knowest, Vafthrûdnir! how he children begat, the bold Jötun, as he had no giantess's company?

Vafthrûdnir.

33. Under the armpit grew, 'tis said, of the Hrîmthurs, a girl and boy together; foot with foot begat, of that wise Jötun, a six-headed son.

Gagnrâd.

34. Tell me eighthly, since thou art called wise, and if thou knowest, Vafthrûdnir! what thou doest first remember, or earliest knowest? Thou art an all-wise Jötun.

Vafthrûdnir.

35. Countless winters, ere earth was formed, Bergelmir was born. That I first remember, when that wise Jötun in an ark was laid.

Gagnrâd.

36. Tell me ninthly, since thou art called wise, and if thou knowest, Vafthrûdnir! whence the wind comes, that over ocean passes, itself invisible to man?

Vafthrûdnir.

37. Hraesvelg he is called, who at the end of heaven sits, a Jötun in an eagle's plumage: from his wings comes, it is said, the wind, that over all men passes.

Gagnrâd.

38. Tell me tenthly, since thou all the origin of the gods knowest, Vafthrûdnir! whence Niörd came among the Æsir's sons? O'er fanes and offer-steads he rules by hundreds, yet was not among the Æsir born.

Vafthrûdnir.

39. In Vanaheim wise powers him created, and to the gods a hostage gave. At the world's dissolution, he will return to the wise Vanir.

Gagnrâd.

40. Tell me eleventhly, since all the condition of the gods thou knowest, Vafthrûdnir! what the Einheriar do in Haerfather's halls, until the powers perish?

Vafthrûdnir.

41. All the Einheriar in Odin's halls each day together fight; the fallen they choose, and from the conflict ride; beer with the Æsir drink, of Saehrimnir eat their fill, then sit in harmony together.

Gagnrâd.

42. Tell me twelfthly, as thou all the condition of the gods knowest, Vafthrûdnir! of the Jötuns' secrets, and of all the gods', say what truest is, thou all-knowing Jötun!

Vafthrûdnir.

43. Of the secrets of the Jötuns and of all the gods, I can truly tell; for I have over each world travelled; to nine worlds I came, to Niflhel beneath: here die men from Hel.

Gagnrâd.

44. Much have I journeyed, much experienced, mighty ones many proved. What mortals will live, when the great "Fimbul"-winter shall from men have passed?

Vafthrûdnir.

45. Lif and Lifthrasir; but they will be concealed in Hoddmimir's holt. The morning dews they will have for food. From, them shall men be born.

Gagnrâd.

46. Much have I journeyed, much experienced, mighty ones many proved. Whence will come the sun in that fair heaven, when Fenrir has this devoured?

Vafthrûdnir.

47. A daughter shall Alfrödull bear, ere Fenrir shall have swallowed her. The maid shall ride, when the powers die, on her mother's course.

Gagnrâd.

48. Much have I journeyed, etc. Who are the maidens that o'er the ocean travel, wise of spirit, journey?

Vafthrûdnir.

49. O'er people's dwellings three descend of Mögthrasir's maidens, the sole Hamingiur who are in the world, although with Jötuns nurtured.

Gagnrâd.

50. Much have I journeyed, etc. Which of the Æsir will rule o'er the gods' possession, when Surt's fire shall be quenched?

Vafthrûdnir.

51. Vidar and Vali will the gods' holy fanes inhabit, when Surt's fire shall be quenched. Môdi and Magni will Miöllnir possess, and warfare strive to end.

Gagnrâd.

52. Much have I journeyed, etc. What of Odin will the life's end be, when the powers perish?

Vafthrûdnir.

53. The wolf will the father of men devour; him Vidar will avenge: he his cold jaws will cleave, in conflict with the wolf.

Gagnrâd.

54. Much have I journeyed, etc. What said Odin in his son's ear, ere he on the pile was laid?

Vafthrûdnir.

55. That no one knoweth, what thou in days of old saidst in thy son's ear. With dying mouth my ancient saws I have said, and the gods' destruction. With Odin I have contended in wise utterances: of men thou ever art the wisest!

THE LAY OF GRIMNIR.

The subject is wholly mythological.

King Hraudung had two sons, one named Agnar, the other Geirröd. Agnar was ten, and Geirröd eight winters old. They both rowed out in a boat, with their hooks and lines, to catch small fish; but the wind drove them out to sea. In the darkness of the night they were wrecked on the shore, and went up into the country, where they found a cottager, with whom they stayed through the winter. The cottager's wife brought up Agnar, and the cottager, Geirröd, and gave him good advice. In the spring the man got them a ship; but when he and his wife accompanied them to the strand, the man talked apart with Geirröd. They had a fair wind, and reached their father's place. Geirröd was at the ship's prow: he sprang on shore, but pushed the ship out, saying, "Go where an evil spirit may get thee." The vessel was driven out to sea, but Geirröd went up to the town, where he was well received; but his father was dead. Geirröd was then taken for king, and became a famous man.

Odin and Frigg were sitting in Hlidskiâlf, looking over all the world. Odin said, "Seest thou Agnar, thy foster-son, where he is, getting children with a giantess in a cave? while Geirröd, my foster-son, is a king residing in his country." Frigg answered, "He is so inhospitable that he tortures his guests, if he thinks that too many come." Odin replied that that was the greatest falsehood; and they wagered thereupon. Frigg sent her waiting-maid Fulla to bid Geirröd be on his guard, lest the trollmann who was coming should do him harm, and also say that a token whereby he might be known was, that no dog, however fierce, would attack him. But that King Geirröd was not hospitable was mere idle talk. He, nevertheless, caused the man to be secured whom no dog would assail. He was clad in a blue cloak, and was named Grimnir, and would say no more concerning himself, although he was questioned. The king ordered him to be tortured to make him confess, and to be set between two fires; and there he sat for eight nights. King Geirröd had a son ten years old, whom he named Agnar, after his brother. Agnar went to Grimnir and gave him a full horn to drink from, saying that the king did wrong in causing him to be tortured, though innocent. Grimnir drank from it. The fire had then so approached him that his cloak was burnt; whereupon he said:—

1. Fire! thou art hot, and much too great; flame! let us separate. My garment is singed, although I lift it up, my cloak is scorched before it.

2. Eight nights have I sat between fires here, and to me no one food has offered, save only Agnar, the son of Geirröd, who alone shall rule over the land of Goths.

3. Be thou blessed, Agnar! as blessed as the god of men bids thee to be. For one draught thou never shalt get better recompense.

4. Holy is the land, which I see lying to Æsir and Alfar near; but in Thrûdheim Thor shall dwell until the powers perish.

5. Ydalir it is called, where Ullr has himself a dwelling made. Alfheim the gods to Frey gave in days of yore for a tooth-gift.

6. The third dwelling is, where the kind powers have with silver decked the hall; Valaskiâlf 'tis called, which for himself acquired the As in days of old.

7. Sökkvabekk the fourth is named o'er which the gelid waves resound; Odin and Saga there, joyful each day, from golden beakers quaff.

8. Gladsheim the fifth is named, there the golden-bright Valhall stands spacious, there Hropt selects each day those men who die by weapons.

9. Easily to be known is, by those who to Odin come, the mansion by its aspect. Its roof with spears is laid, its hall with shields is decked, with corslets are its benches strewed.

10. Easily to be known is, by those who to Odin come, the mansion by its aspect. A wolf hangs before the western door, over it an eagle hovers.

11. Thrymheim the sixth is named, where Thiassi dwelt that all-powerful Jötun; but Skadi now inhabits, the bright bride of gods, her father's ancient home.

12. Breidablik is the seventh, where Baldr has built for himself a hall, in that land, in which I know exists the fewest crimes.

13. Himinbiörg is the eighth, where Heimdall, it is said, rules o'er the holy fanes: there the gods' watchman, in his tranquil home, drinks joyful the good mead.

14. Fôlkvang is the ninth, there Freyia directs the sittings in the hall. She half the fallen chooses each day, but Odin th' other half.

15. Glitnir is the tenth; it is on gold sustained, and eke with silver decked. There Forseti dwells throughout all time, and every strife allays.

16. Nôatûn is the eleventh, there Niörd has himself a dwelling made, prince of men; guiltless of sin, he rules o'er the high-built fane.

17. O'ergrown with branches and high grass is Vidar's spacious Landvîdi: There will the son descend, from the steed's back, bold to avenge his father.

18. Andhrimnir makes, in Eldhrimnir, Sæhrimnir to boil, of meats the best; but few know how many Einheriar it feeds.

19. Geri and Freki the war-wont sates, the triumphant sire of hosts; but on wine only the famed in arms, Odin, ever lives.

20. Hugin and Munin fly each day over the spacious earth. I fear for Hugin, that he come not back, yet more anxious am I for Munin.

21. Thund roars; joyful in Thiodvitnir's water lives the fish; the rapid river seems too great for the battle-steed to ford.

22. Valgrind is the lattice called, in the plain that stands, holy before the holy gates: ancient is that lattice, but few only know how it is closed with lock.

23. Five hundred doors, and forty eke, I think, are in Valhall. Eight hundred Einheriar will at once from each door go when they issue with the wolf to fight.

24. Five hundred floors, and forty eke, I think, has Bilskirnir with its windings. Of all the roofed houses that I know, is my son's the greatest.

25. Heidrûn the goat is called, that stands o'er Odin's hall, and bites from Lærâd's branches. He a bowl shall fill with the bright mead; that drink shall never fail.

26. Eikthyrnir the hart is called, that stands o'er Odin's hall, and bites from Lærâd's branches; from his horns fall drops into Hvergelmir, whence all waters rise:—

27. Sid and Vid, Soekin and Eikin, Svöl and Gunnthrô, Fiörm and Fimbulthul, Rin and Rennandi, Gipul and Göpul, Gömul and Geirvimul: they round the gods' dwelling wind. Thyn and Vin, Thöll and Höll, Grâd and Gunnthorin.

28. Vina one is called, a second Vegsvin, a third Thiodnuma; Nyt and Nön and Hrön, Slid and Hrid, Sylg and Ylg, Vîd and Vân, Vönd and Strönd, Gioll and Leipt; these (two) fall near to men, but fall hence to Hel.

29. Körmt and Ormt, and the Kerlaugs twain: these Thor must wade each day, when he to council goes at Yggdrasil's ash; for the As-bridge is all on fire, the holy waters boil.

30. Glad and Gyllir, Gler and Skeidbrimir, Sillfrintopp and Sinir, Gisl and Falhôfnir, Gulltopp and Lettfeti; on these steeds the Æsir each day ride, when they to council go, at Yggdrasil's ash.

31. Three roots stand on three ways under Yggdrasil's ash: Hel under one abides, under the second the Hrimthursar, under the third mankind.

32. Ratatösk is the squirrel named, which, has to run in Yggdrasil's ash; he from above the eagle's words must carry, and beneath to Nidhögg repeat.

33. Harts there are also four, which from its summits, arch-necked, gnaw. Dâin and Dvalin, Duneyr and Durathrôr.

34. More serpents lie under Yggdrasil's ash, than any one would think of witless mortals: Gôin and Môin,—they are Grafvitnir's sons—Grâbak and Grafvöllud, Ofnir and Svafnir, will, I ween, the branches of that tree ever lacerate.

35. Yggdrasil's ash hardship suffers greater than men know of; a hart bites it above, and in its side it rots, Nidhögg beneath tears it.

36. Hrist and Mist the horn shall bear me Skeggöld and Skögul, Hlökk and Herfiotur, Hildi and Thrûdi, Göll and Geirölul, Randgríd and Râdgrîd, and Reginleif, these bear beer to the Einheriar.

37. Arvakr and Alsvid, theirs 'tis up hence fasting the sun to draw: under their shoulder the gentle powers, the Æsir, have concealed an iron-coolness.

38. Svalin the shield is called, which stands before the sun, the refulgent deity; rocks and ocean must, I ween, be burnt, fell it from its place.

39. Sköll the wolf is named, that the fair-faced goddess to the ocean chases; another Hati hight, he is Hrôdvitnir's son; he the bright maid of heaven shall precede.

40. Of Ymir's flesh was earth created, of his blood the sea, of his bones the hills, of his hair trees and plants, of his skull the heaven;

41. And of his brows the gentle powers formed Midgard for the sons of men; but of his brain the heavy clouds are all created.

42. Ullr's and all the gods' favour shall have, whoever first shall look to the fire; for open will the dwelling be, to the Æsir's sons, when the kettles are lifted off.

43. Ivaldi's sons went in days of old Skidbladnir to form, of ships the best, for the bright Frey, Niörd's benign son.

44. Yggdrasil's ash is of all trees most excellent, and of all ships, Skidbladnir, of the Æsir, Odin, and of horses, Sleipnir, Bifröst of bridges, and of skallds, Bragi, Hâbrôk of hawks, and of dogs, Garm,

45. Now I my face have raised to the gods' triumphant sons, at that will welcome help awake; from all the Æsir, that shall penetrate, to Oegir's bench, to Oegir's compotation.

46. I am called Grim, I am called Gangleri, Herian and Hiâlmberi, Thekk and Thridi, Thund and Ud, Helblindi and Har,

47. Sad and Svipall, and Sanngetall, Herteit and Hnikar Bileyg, Bâleyg, Bölverk, Fiölnir, Grîm and Grimnir, Glapsvid and Fiölsvid,

48. Sîdhött, Sîdskegg Sigfödr, Hnikud, Alfodr, Valfödr, Atrid and Farmatyr; by one name I never have been called, since among men I have gone.

49. Grimnir I am called at Geirröd's, and at Asmund's Jâlk and Kialar, when a sledge I drew; Thrôr at the public meetings, Vidur in battles, Oski and Omi, Jafnhâr and Biflindi, Gôndlir and Harbard with the gods.

50. Svidur and Svidrir I was at Sökkmimir's called, and beguiled that ancient Jötun, when of Midvitnir's renowned son I was the sole destroyer.

51. Drunken art thou, Geirröd, thou hast drunk too much, thou art greatly by mead beguiled. Much didst thou lose, when thou wast of my help bereft, of all the Einheriar's and Odin's favour.

52. Many things I told thee, but thou hast few remembered: thy friends mislead thee. My friend's sword lying I see, with blood all dripping.

53. The fallen by the sword Ygg shall now have; thy life is now run out: Wroth with thee are the Dîsir: Odin thou now shalt see: draw near to me if thou canst.

54. Odin I now am named, Ygg I was called before, before that, Thund, Vakr and Skilfing, Vâfudr and Hrôptatyr, with the gods, Gaut and Jâlk, Ofnir and Svafnir, all which I believe to be names of me alone.

King Geirröd was sitting with his sword lying across his knees, half drawn from the scabbard, but on finding that it was Odin, he rose for the purpose of removing him from the fires, when the sword slipt from his hand with the hilt downwards; and the king having stumbled, the sword pierced him through and killed him. Odin then vanished, and Agnar was king for a long time after.

THE LAY OF VEGTAM, OR BALDR'S DREAMS.

1. Together were the Æsir all in council, and the Asyniur all in conference, and they consulted, the mighty gods, why Baldr had oppressive dreams.

2.

6. Uprose Odin lord of men and on Sleipnir he the saddle laid; rode thence down to Niflhel. A dog he met, from Hel coming.

7. It was blood-stained on its breast, on its slaughter-craving throat, and nether jaw. It bayed and widely gaped at the sire of magic song:—long it howled.

8. Forth rode Odin—the ground rattled—till to Hel's lofty house he came. Then rode Ygg to the eastern gate, where he knew there was a Vala's grave.

9. To the prophetess, he began a magic song to chant, towards the north looked, potent runes applied, a spell pronounced, an answer demanded, until compelled she rose, and with deathlike voice she said:

Vala.

10. "What man is this, to me unknown, who has for me increased an irksome course? I have with snow been decked, by rain beaten, and with dew moistened: long have I been dead."

Vegtam.

11. "Vegtam is my name, I am Valtam's son. Tell thou me of Hel: from, earth I call on thee. For whom are those benches strewed o'er with rings, those costly couches o'erlaid with gold?"

Vala.

12. "Here stands mead, for Baldr brewed, over the bright potion a shield is laid; but the Æsir race are in despair. By compulsion I have spoken. I will now be silent."

Vegtam.

13. "Be not silent, Vala! I will question thee, until I know all. I will yet know who will Baldr's slayer be, and Odin's son of life bereave."

Vala.

14. "Hödr will hither his glorious brother send, he of Baldr will the slayer be, and Odin's son of life bereave. By compulsion I have spoken; I will now be silent."

Vegtam.

15. "Be not silent, Vala! I will question thee, until I know all. I will yet know who on Hödr vengeance will inflict, or Baldr's slayer raise on the pile."

Vala.

16. "Rind a son shall bear, in the western halls: he shall slay Odin's son, when one night old. He a hand will not wash, nor his head comb, ere he to the pile has borne Baldr's adversary. By compulsion I have spoken; I will now be silent."

Vegtam.

17. "Be not silent, Vala! I will question thee, until I know all. I will yet know who the maidens are, that weep at will, and heavenward cast their neck-veils? Tell me but that: till then thou sleepest not."

Vala.

18. "Not Vegtam art thou, as I before believed; rather art thou Odin, lord of men!"

Odin.

19. "Thou art no Vala, nor wise woman, rather art thou the mother of three Thursar."

Vala.

20. "Home ride thou, Odin! and exult. Thus shall never more man again visit me, until Loki free from his bonds escapes, and Ragnarök all-destroying comes."

THE HIGH ONE'S LAY.

1. All door-ways, before going forward, should be looked to; for difficult it is to know where foes may sit within a dwelling.

2. Givers, hail! A guest is come in: where shall he sit? In much haste is he, who on the ways has to try his luck.

3. Fire is needful to him who is come in, and whose knees are frozen; food and raiment a man requires, wheo'er the fell has travelled.

4. Water to him is needful who for refection comes, a towel and hospitable invitation, a good reception; if he can get it, discourse and answer.

5. Wit is needful to him who travels far: at home all is easy. A laughing-stock is he who nothing knows, and with the instructed sits.

6. Of his understanding no one should be proud, but rather in conduct cautious. When the prudent and taciturn come to a dwelling, harm seldom befalls the cautious; for a firmer friend no man ever gets than great sagacity.

7. A wary guest, who to refection comes, keeps a cautious silence, with his ears listens, and with his eyes observes: so explores every prudent man.

8. He is happy, who for himself obtains fame and kind words: less sure is that which a man must have in another's breast.

9. He is happy, who in himself possesses fame and wit while living; for bad counsels have oft been received from another's breast.

10. A better burthen no man bears on the way than much good sense; that is thought better than riches in a strange place; such is the recourse of the indigent.

11. A worse provision on the way he cannot carry than too much beer-bibbing; so good is not, as it is said, beer for the sons of men.

12. A worse provision no man can take from table than too much beer-bibbing: for the more he drinks the less control he has of his own mind.

13. Oblivion's heron 'tis called that over potations hovers; he steals the minds of men. With this bird's pinions I was fettered in Gunnlods dwelling.

14. Drunk I was, I was over-drunk, at that cunning Fialar's. It's the best drunkenness, when every one after it regains his reason.

15. Taciturn and prudent, and in war daring, should a king's children be; joyous and liberal every one should be until his hour of death.

16. A cowardly man thinks he will ever live, if warfare he avoids; but old age will give him no peace, though spears may spare him.

17. A fool gapes when to a house he comes, to himself mutters or is silent; but all at once, if he gets drink, then is the man's mind displayed.

18. He alone knows who wanders wide, and has much experienced, by what disposition each man is ruled, who common sense possesses.

19. Let a man hold the cup, yet of the mead drink moderately, speak sensibly or be silent. As of a fault no man will admonish thee, if thou goest betimes to sleep.

20. A greedy man, if he be not moderate, eats to his mortal sorrow. Oftentimes his belly draws laughter on a silly man, who among the prudent comes.

21. Cattle know when to go home, and then from grazing cease; but a foolish man never knows his stomach's measure.

22. A miserable man, and ill-conditioned, sneers at every thing: one thing he knows not, which he ought to know, that he is not free from faults.

23. A foolish man is all night awake, pondering over everything; he then grows tired; and when morning comes, all is lament as before.

24. A foolish man thinks all who on him smile to be his friends; he feels it not, although they speak ill of him, when he sits among the clever.

25. A foolish man thinks all who speak him fair to be his friends; but he will find, if into court he comes, that he has few advocates.

26. A foolish man thinks he knows everything if placed in unexpected difficulty; but he knows not what to answer, if to the test he is put.

27. A foolish man, who among people comes, had best be silent; for no one knows that he knows nothing, unless he talks too much. He who previously knew nothing will still know nothing, talk he ever so much.

28. He thinks himself wise, who can ask questions and converse also; conceal his ignorance no one can, because it circulates among men.

29. He utters too many futile words who is never silent; a garrulous tongue, if it be not checked, sings often to its own harm.

30. For a gazing-stock no man shall have another, although he come a stranger to his house. Many a one thinks himself wise, if he is not questioned, and can sit in a dry habit.

31. Clever thinks himself the guest who jeers a guest, if he takes to flight. Knows it not certainly he who prates at meat, whether he babbles among foes.

32. Many men are mutually well-disposed, yet at table will torment each other. That strife will ever be; guest will guest irritate.

33. Early meals a man should often take, unless to a friend's house he goes; else he will sit and mope, will seem half-famished, and can of few things inquire.

34. Long is and indirect the way to a bad friend's, though by the road he dwell; but to a good friend's the paths lie direct, though he be far away.

35. A guest should depart, not always stay in one place. The welcome becomes unwelcome, if he too long continues in another's house.

36. One's own house is best, small though it be; at home is every one his own master. Though he but two goats possess, and a straw-thatched cot, even that is better than begging.

37. One's own house is best, small though it be, at home is every one his own master. Bleeding at heart is he, who has to ask for food at every meal-tide.

38. Leaving in the field his arms, let no man go a foot's length forward; for it is hard to know when on the way a man may need his weapon.

39. I have never found a man so bountiful, or so hospitable that he refused a present; or of his property so liberal that he scorned a recompense.

40. Of the property which he has gained no man should suffer need; for the hated oft is spared what for the dear was destined. Much goes worse than is expected.

41. With arms and vestments friends should each other gladden, those which are in themselves most sightly. Givers and requiters are longest friends, if all goes well.

42. To his friend a man should be a friend, and gifts with gifts requite. Laughter with laughter men should receive, but leasing with lying.

43. To his friend a man should be a friend; to him and to his friend; but of his foe no man shall the friend's friend be.

44. Know, if thou hast a friend whom thou fully trustest, and from whom thou woulds't good derive, thou shouldst blend thy mind with his, and gifts exchange, and often go to see him.

45. If thou hast another, whom thou little trustest, yet wouldst good from him derive, thou shouldst speak him fair, but think craftily, and leasing pay with lying.

46. But of him yet further, whom thou little trustest, and thou suspectest his affection; before him thou shouldst laugh, and contrary to thy thoughts speak: requital should the gift resemble.

47. I was once young, I was journeying alone, and lost my way; rich I thought myself, when I met another. Man is the joy of man.

48. Liberal and brave men live best, they seldom cherish sorrow; but a base-minded man dreads everything; the niggardly is uneasy even at gifts.

49. My garments in a field I gave away to two wooden men: heroes they seemed to be, when they got cloaks: exposed to insult is a naked man.

50. A tree withers that on a hill-top stands; protects it neither bark nor leaves: such is the man whom no one favours: why should he live long?

51. Hotter than fire love for five days burns between false friends; but is quenched when the sixth day comes, and-friendship is all impaired.

52. Something great is not to be given, praise is often for a trifle bought. With half a loaf and a tilted vessel I got myself a comrade.

53. Little are the sand-grains, little the wits, little the minds of men; for all men are not wise alike: men are everywhere by halves.

54. Moderately wise should each one be, but never over-wise: of those men the lives are fairest, who know much well.

55. Moderately wise should each one be, but never over-wise; for a wise man's heart is seldom glad, if he is all-wise who owns it.

56. Moderately wise should each one be, but never over-wise. His destiny let know no man beforehand; his mind will be freest from' care.

57. Brand burns from brand until it is burnt out; fire is from fire quickened. Man to' man becomes known by speech, but a fool by his bashful silence.

58. He should early rise, who another's property or life desires to have. Seldom a sluggish wolf gets prey, or a sleeping man victory.

59. Early should rise he who has few workers, and go his work to see to; greatly is he retarded who sleeps the morn away. Wealth half depends on energy.

60. Of dry planks and roof-shingles a man knows the measure; of the fire-wood that may suffice, both measure and time.

61. Washed and refected let a man ride to the Thing, although his garments be not too good; of his shoes and breeches let no one be ashamed, nor of his horse, although he have not a good one.

62. Inquire and impart should every man of sense, who will be accounted sage. Let one only know, a second may not; if three, all the world knows.

63. Gasps and gapes, when to the sea he comes, the eagle over old ocean; so is a man, who among many comes, and has few advocates.

64. His power should every sagacious man use with discretion; for he will find, when among the bold he comes, that no one alone is doughtiest.

65. Circumspect and reserved every man should be, and wary in trusting friends. Of the words that a man says to another he often pays the penalty.

66. Much too early I came to many places, but too late to others: the beer was drunk, or not ready: the disliked seldom hits the moment.

67. Here and there I should have been invited, if I a meal had needed; or two hams had hung, at that true friend's, where of one I had eaten.

68. Fire is best among the sons of men, and the sight of the sun, if his health a man can have, with a life free from vice.

69. No man lacks everything, although his health be bad: one in his sons is happy, one in his kin, one in abundant wealth, one in his good works.

70. It is better to live, even to live miserably; a living man can always get a cow. I saw fire consume the rich man's property, and death stood without his door.

71. The halt can ride on horseback, the one-handed drive cattle; the deaf fight and be useful: to be blind is better than to be burnt no one gets good from a corpse.

72. A son is better, even if born late, after his father's departure. Gravestones seldom stand by the wayside unless raised by a kinsman to a kinsman.

73. Two are adversaries: the tongue is the bane of the head: under every cloak I expect a hand. * * *

74. At night is joyful he who is sure of travelling entertainment.   Variable is an autumn night. Many are the weather's changes in five days, but more in a month.

75. He knows not who knows nothing, that many a one apes another. One man is rich, another poor: let him not be thought blameworthy.

76. Cattle die, kindred die, we ourselves also die; but the fair fame never dies of him who has earned it.

77. Cattle die, kindred die, we ourselves also die; but I know one thing that never dies,—judgment on each one dead.

78. Full storehouses I saw at Dives' sons': now bear they the beggar's staff. Such are riches; as is the twinkling of an eye: of friends they are most fickle.

79. A foolish man, if he acquires wealth or woman's love, pride grows within him, but wisdom never: he goes on more and more arrogant.

80. Then 'tis made manifest, if of runes thou questionest him, those to the high ones known, which the great powers invented, and the great talker painted, that he had best hold silence.

81. At eve the day is to be praised, a woman after she is burnt, a sword after it is proved, a maid after she is married, ice after it has passed away, beer after it is drunk.

82. In the wind one should hew wood, in a breeze row out to sea, in the dark talk with a lass: many are the eyes of day. In a ship voyages are to be made, but a shield is for protection, a sword for striking, but a damsel for a kiss.

83. By the fire one should drink beer, on the ice slide; buy a horse that is lean, a sword that is rusty; feed a horse at home, but a dog at the farm.

84. In a maiden's words no one should place faith, nor in what a woman says; for on a turning wheel have their hearts been formed, and guile in their breasts been laid;

85. In a creaking bow, a burning flame, a yawning wolf, a chattering crow, a grunting swine, a rootless tree, a waxing wave, a boiling kettle,

86. A flying dart, a falling billow, a one night's ice, a coiled serpent, a woman's bed-talk, or a broken sword, a bear's play, or a royal child,

87. A sick calf, a self-willed thrall, a flattering prophetess, a corpse newly slain, ;

88. An early sown field let no one trust, nor prematurely in a son: weather rules the field, and wit the son, each of which is doubtful;

89. A brother's murderer, though on the high road met, a half-burnt house, an over-swift horse, (a horse is useless, if a leg be broken), no man is so confiding as to trust any of these.

90. Such is the love of women, who falsehood meditate, as if one drove not rough-shod, on slippery ice, a spirited two-years old and unbroken horse; or as in a raging storm a helmless ship is beaten; or as if the halt were set to catch a reindeer in the thawing fell.

91. Openly I now speak, because I both sexes know: unstable are men's minds towards women; 'tis then we speak most fair when we most falsely think: that deceives even the cautious.

92. Fair shall speak, and money offer, who would obtain a woman's love. Praise the form of a fair damsel; he gets who courts her.

93. At love should no one ever wonder in another: a beauteous countenance oft captivates the wise, which captivates not the foolish.

94. Let no one wonder at another's folly, it is the lot of many. All-powerful desire makes of the sons of men fools even of the wise.

95. The mind only knows what lies near the heart, that alone is conscious of our affections. No disease is worse to a sensible man than not to be content with himself.

96. That I experienced, when in the reeds I sat, awaiting my delight. Body and soul to me was that discreet maiden: nevertheless I possess her not.

97. Billing's lass on her couch I found, sun-bright, sleeping. A prince's joy to me seemed naught, if not with that form to live.

98. "Yet nearer eve must thou, Odin, come, if thou wilt talk the maiden over; all will be disastrous, unless we alone are privy to such misdeed."

99. I returned, thinking to love, at her wise desire. I thought I should obtain her whole heart and love.

100. When next I came the bold warriors were all awake, with lights burning, and bearing torches: thus was the way to pleasure closed.

101. But at the approach of morn, when again I came, the household all was sleeping; the good damsel's dog alone I found tied to the bed.

102. Many a fair maiden, when rightly known, towards men is fickle: that I experienced, when that discreet maiden I strove to seduce: contumely of every kind that wily girl heaped upon me; nor of that damsel gained I aught.

103. At home let a man be cheerful, and towards a guest liberal; of wise conduct he should be, of good memory and ready speech; if much knowledge he desires, he must often talk on good.

104. Fimbulfambi he is called who' little has to say: such is the nature of the simple.

105. The old Jotun I sought; now I am come back: little got I there by silence; in many words I spoke to my advantage in Suttung's halls.

106. Gunnlod gave me, on her golden seat, a draught of the precious mead; a bad recompense I afterwards made her, for her whole soul, her fervent love.

107. Rati's mouth I caused to make a space, and to gnaw the rock; over and under me were the Jotun's ways: thus I my head did peril.

108. Of a well-assumed form I made good use: few things fail the wise; for Odhrærir is now come up to men's earthly dwellings.

109. 'Tis to me doubtful that I could have come from the Jotun's courts, had not Gunnlod aided me, that good damsel, over whom I laid my arm.

110. On the day following came the Hrimthursar, to learn something of the High One, in the High One's hall: after Bolverk they inquired, whether he with the gods were come, or Suttung had destroyed him?

111. Odin, I believe, a ring-oath gave. Who in his faith will trust? Suttung defrauded, of his drink bereft, and Gunnlod made to weep!

112. Time 'tis to discourse from the preacher's chair. By the well of Urd I silent sat, I saw and meditated, I listened to men's words.

113. Of runes I heard discourse, and of things divine, nor of graving them were they silent, nor of sage counsels, at the High One's hall. In the High One's hall. I thus heard say:

114. I counsel thee, Loddfafnir, to take advice: thou wilt profit if thou takest it. Rise not at night, unless to explore, or art compelled to go out.

115. I counsel thee, Loddfafnir, to take advice, thou wilt profit if thou takest it. In an enchantress's embrace thou mayest not sleep, so that in her arms she clasp thee.

116. She will be the cause that thou carest not for Thing or prince's words; food thou wilt shun and human joys; sorrowful wilt thou go to sleep.

117. I counsel thee, etc. Another's wife entice thou never to secret converse.

118. I counsel thee, etc. By fell or firth if thou have to travel, provide thee well with food.

119. I counsel thee, etc. A bad man let thou never know thy misfortunes; for from a bad man thou never wilt obtain a return for thy good will.

120. I saw mortally wound a man a wicked woman's words; a false tongue caused his death, and most unrighteously.

121. I counsel thee, etc. If thou knowest thou hast a friend, whom thou well canst trust, go oft to visit him; for with brushwood over-grown, and with high grass, is the way that no one treads.

122. I counsel thee, etc. A good man attract to thee in pleasant converse; and salutary speech learn while thou livest.

123. I counsel thee, etc. With thy friend be thou never first to quarrel. Care gnaws the heart, if thou to no one canst thy whole mind disclose.

124. I counsel thee, etc. Words thou never shouldst exchange with a witless fool;

125. For from an ill-conditioned man thou wilt never get a return for good; but a good man will bring thee favour by his praise.

126. There is a mingling of affection, where one can tell another all his mind. Everything is better than being with the deceitful. He is not another's friend who ever says as he says.

127. I counsel thee, etc. Even in three words quarrel not with a worse man: often the better yields, when the worse strikes.

128. I counsel thee, etc. Be not a shoemaker, nor a shaftmaker, unless for thyself it be; for a shoe if ill made, or a shaft if crooked, will call down evil on thee.

129. I counsel thee, etc. Wherever of injury thou knowest, regard that injury as thy own; and give to thy foes no peace.

130. I counsel thee, etc. Rejoiced at evil be thou never; but let good give thee pleasure.

131. I counsel thee, etc. In a battle look not up, (like swine the sons of men then become) that men may not fascinate thee.

132. If thou wilt induce a good woman to pleasant converse, thou must promise fair, and hold to it: no one turns from good if it can be got.

133. I enjoin thee to be wary, but not over wary; at drinking be thou most wary, and with another's wife; and thirdly, that thieves delude thee not.

134. With insult or derision treat thou never a guest or wayfarer. They often little know, who sit within, of what race they are who come.

135. Vices and virtues the sons of mortals bear in their breasts mingled; no one is so good that no failing attends him, nor so bad as to be good for nothing.

136. At a hoary speaker laugh thou never; often is good that which the aged utter, oft from a shriveled hide discreet words issue; from those whose skin is pendent and decked with scars, and who go tottering among the vile.

137. I counsel thee, etc. Rail not at a guest, nor from thy gate thrust him; treat well the indigent; they will speak well of thee.

138. Strong is the bar that must be raised to admit all. Do thou give a penny, or they will call down on thee every ill in thy limbs.

139. I counsel thee, etc. Wherever thou beer drinkest, invoke to thee the power of earth; for earth is good against drink, fire for distempers, the oak for constipation, a corn-ear for sorcery, a hall for domestic strife. In bitter hates invoke the moon; the biter for bite-injuries is good; but runes against calamity; fluid let earth absorb.

140. I know that I hung, on a wind-rocked tree, nine whole nights, with a spear wounded, and to Odin offered, myself to myself; on that tree, of which no one knows from what root it springs.

141. Bread no one gave me, nor a horn of drink, downward I peered, to runes applied myself, wailing learnt them, then fell down thence.

142. Potent songs nine from the famed son I learned of Bolthorn, Bestla's sire, and a draught obtained of the precious mead, drawn from Odhrærir.

143. Then I began to bear fruit, and to know many things, to grow and well thrive: word by word I sought out words, fact by fact I sought out facts.

144. Runes thou wilt find, and explained characters, very large characters, very potent characters, which the great speaker depicted, and the high powers formed, and the powers' prince graved:

145. Odin among the Æsir, but among the Alfar, Dain, and Dvalin for the dwarfs, Asvid for the Jotuns: some I myself graved.

146. Knowest thou how to grave them? knowest thou how to expound them? knowest thou how to depict them? knowest thou how to prove them? knowest thou how to pray? knowest thou how to offer? knowest thou how to send? knowest thou how to consume?

147. 'Tis better not to pray than too much offer; a gift ever looks to a return. 'Tis better not to send than too much consume. So Thund graved before the origin of men, where he ascended, to whence he afterwards came.

148. Those songs I know which the king's wife knows not nor son of man. Help the first is called, for that will help thee against strifes and cares.

149. For the second I know, what the sons of men require, who will as leeches live. * * * *

150. For the third I know, if I have great need to restrain my foes, the weapons' edge I deaden: of my adversaries nor arms nor wiles harm aught.

151. For the fourth I know, if men place bonds on my limbs, I so sing that I can walk; the fetter starts from my feet, and the manacle from my hands.

152. For the fifth I know, if I see a shot from a hostile hand, a shaft flying amid the host, so swift it cannot fly that I cannot arrest it, if only I get sight of it.

153. For the sixth I know, if one wounds me with a green tree's roots; also if a man declares hatred to me, harm shall consume them sooner than me.

154. For the seventh I know, if a lofty house I see blaze o'er its inmates, so furiously it shall not burn that I cannot save it. That song I can sing.

155. For the eighth I know, what to all is useful to learn: where hatred grows among the sons of men—that I can quickly assuage.

156. For the ninth I know, if I stand in need my bark on the water to save, I can the wind on the waves allay, and the sea lull.

157. For the tenth I know, if I see troll-wives sporting in air, I can so operate that they will forsake their own forms, and their own minds.

158. For the eleventh I know, if I have to lead my ancient friends to battle, under their shields I sing, and with power they go safe to the fight, safe from the fight; safe on every side they go.

159. For the twelfth I know, if on a tree I see a corpse swinging from a halter, I can so grave and in runes depict, that the man shall walk, and with me converse.

160. For the thirteenth I know, if on a young man I sprinkle water, he shall not fall, though he into battle come: that man shall not sink before swords.

161. For the fourteenth I know, if in the society of men I have to enumerate the gods, Æsir and Alfar, I know the distinctions of all. This few unskilled can do.

162. For the fifteenth I know what the dwarf Thiodreyrir sang before Delling's doors. Strength he sang to the Æsir, and to the Alfar prosperity, wisdom to Hroptatyr.

163. For the sixteenth I know, if a modest maiden's favour and affection I desire to possess, the soul I change of the white-armed damsel, and wholly turn her mind.

164. For the seventeenth I know, that that young maiden will reluctantly avoid me. These songs, Loddfafnir! thou wilt long have lacked; yet it may be good if thou understandest them, profitable if thou learnest them.

165. For the eighteenth I know that which I never teach to maid or wife of man, (all is better what one only knows. This is the closing of the songs) save her alone who clasps me in her arms, or is my sister.

166. Now are sung the High-one's songs, in the High-one's hall, to the sons of men all-useful, but useless to the Jotuns' sons. Hail to him who has sung them! Hail to him who knows them! May he profit who has learnt them! Hail to those who have listened to them!

THE LAY OF HYMIR.

1. Once the celestial gods had been taking fish, and were in compotation, ere they the truth discovered. Rods they shook, and blood inspected, when they found at Oegir's a lack of kettles.

2. Sat the rock-dweller glad as a child, much like the son of Miskorblindi. In his eyes looked Ygg's son steadfastly. "Thou to the Æir shalt oft a compotation give."

3. Caused trouble to the Jotun th' unwelcome-worded As: he forthwith meditated vengeance on the gods. Sif's husband he besought a kettle him to bring, "in which I beer for all of you may brew."

4. The illustrious gods found that impossible, nor could the exalted powers it accomplish, till from true-heartedness, Ty to Hlorridi much friendly counsel gave.

5. "There dwells eastward of Elivagar the all-wise Hymir, at heaven's end. My sire, fierce of mood, a kettle owns, a capacious cauldron, a rast in depth."

Thor.

6. "Knowest thou whether we can get the liquor-boiler?"

Ty.

"Yes, friend! if we stratagem' employ." Rapidly they drove forward that day from Asgard, till to the giant's home they came.

7. Thor stalled his goats, splendid of horn, then turned him to the hall that Hymir owned. The son his granddam found to him most loathful; heads she had nine hundred.

8. But another came all-golden forth, fair-browed, bearing the beer-cup to her son:

9. "Ye Jotuns' kindred! I will you both, ye daring pair, under the kettles place. My husband is oftentimes niggard towards guests, to ill-humour prone."

10. But the monster, the fierce-souled Hymir, late returned home from the chase. He the hall entered, the icebergs resounded, as the churl approached; the thicket on his cheeks was frozen.

11. "Hail to thee, Hymir! be of good cheer: now thy son is come to thy hall, whom we expected from his long journey; him accompanies our famed adversary, the friend of man, who Veor hight.

12. See where they sit under the hall's gable, as if to shun thee: the pillar stands before them." In shivers flew the pillar at the Jotun's glance; the beam was first broken in two.

13. Eight kettles fell, but only one of them, a hard-hammered cauldron, whole from the column. The two came forth, but the old Jotun with eyes surveyed his adversary.

14. Augured to him his mind no good, when he saw the giantess's sorrow on the floor coming. Then were three oxen taken, and the Jotun bade them forthwith be boiled.

15. Each one they made by the head shorter, and to the fire afterwards bore them. Sif's consort ate, ere to sleep he went, completely, he alone, two of Hymir's beeves.

16. Seemed to the hoary friend of Hrungnir Hlorridi's refection full well large: "We three to-morrow night shall be compelled on what we catch to live."

17. Veor said he would on the sea row, if the bold Jotun him would with baits supply: "To the herd betake thee, (if thou in thy courage trustest, crusher of the rock-dwellers!) for baits to seek.

18. I expect that thou wilt bait from an ox easily obtain." The guest in haste to the forest went, where stood an all-black ox before him.

19. The Thursar's bane wrung from an ox the high fastness of his two horns. "To me thy work seems worse by far, ruler of keels! than if thou hadst sat quiet."

20. The lord of goats the apes' kinsman besought the horse of plank farther out to move; but the Jotun declared his slight desire farther to row.

21. The mighty Hymir drew, he alone, two whales up with his hook; but at the stern abaft Veor cunningly made him a line.

22. Fixed on the hook the shield of men, the serpent's slayer, the ox's head. Gaped at the bait the foe of gods, the encircler beneath of every land.

23. Drew up boldly the mighty Thor the worm with venom glistening, up to the side; with his hammer struck, on his foul head's summit, like a rock towering, the wolf's own brother.

24. The icebergs resounded, the caverns howled, the old earth shrank together: at length the fish back into ocean sank.

25. The Jotun was little glad, as they rowed back, so that the powerful Hymir nothing spake, but the oar moved in another course.

26. "Wilt thou do half the work with me, either the whales home to the dwelling bear, or the boat fast bind?"

27. Hlorridi went, grasped the prow, quickly, with its hold-water, lifted the water-steed, together with its oars and scoop; bore to the dwelling the Jotun's ocean-swine, the curved vessel, through the wooded hills.

28. But the Jotun yet ever frowned, to strife accustomed, with Thor disputed, said that no one was strong, however vigorously he might row, unless he his cup could break.

29. But Hlorridi, when to his hands it came, forthwith brake an upright stone in twain; sitting dashed the cup through the pillars: yet they brought it whole to Hymir back.

30. Until the beauteous woman gave important, friendly counsel, which she only knew: "Strike at the head of Hymir, the Jotun with food oppressed, that is harder than any cup."

31. Rose then on his knee the stern lord of goats, clad in all his godlike power. Unhurt remained the old man's helm-block, but the round wine-bearer was in shivers broken.

32. "Much good, I know, has departed from me, now that my cup I see hurled from my knees." Thus the old man spake: "I can never say again, beer thou art too hot.

33. "Now 'tis to be tried if ye can carry the beer-vessel out of our dwelling." Ty twice assayed to move the vessel, yet at each time stood the kettle fast.

34. Then Modi's father by the brim grasped it, and trod through the dwelling's floor. Sif's consort lifted the kettle on his head, while about his heels its rings jingled.

35. They had far journeyed before Odin's son cast one look backward: he from the caverns saw, with Hymir from the east, a troop of many-headed monsters coming.

36. From his shoulders he lifted the kettle down; Miollnir hurled forth towards the savage crew, and slew all the mountain-giants, who with Hymir had him pursued.

37. Long they had not journeyed when of Hlorridi's goats one lay down half-dead before the car. It from the pole had sprung across the trace; but the false Loki was of this the cause.

38. Now ye have heard,—for what fabulist can more fully tell—what indemnity he from the giant got: he paid for it with his children both.

39. In his strength exulting he to the gods' council came, and had the kettle, which Hymir had possessed, out of which every god shall beer with Oegir drink at every harvest-tide.

THE LAY OF THRYM, OR THE HAMMER RECOVERED.

1. Wroth was Vingthor, when he awoke, and his hammer missed; his beard he shook, his forehead struck, the son of earth felt all around him;

2. And first of all these words he uttered: "Hear now, Loki! what I now say, which no one knows anywhere on earth, nor in heaven above; the As's hammer is stolen!"

3. They went to the fair Freyia's dwelling, and he these words first of all said: "Wilt thou me, Freyia, thy feather-garment lend, that perchance my hammer I may find?"

Freyia.

4. "That I would give thee, although of gold it were, and trust it to thee, though it were of silver."

5. Flew then Loki—the plumage rattled—until he came beyond the Æsir's dwellings, and came within the Jotun's land.

6. On a mound sat Thrym, the Thursar's lord, for his greyhounds plaiting gold bands and his horses' manes smoothing.

7. "How goes it with the Æsir? How goes it with the Alfar? Why art thou come alone to Jotunheim?"

Loki.

8. "Ill it goes with the Æsir, Ill it goes with the Alfar. Hast thou Hlorridi's hammer hidden?"

Thrym.

9. "I have Hlorridi's hammer hidden eight rasts beneath the earth; it shall no man get again, unless he bring me Freyia to wife."

10. Flew then Loki—the plumage rattled—until he came beyond the Jotun's dwellings, and came within the Æsir's courts; there he met Thor, in the middle court, who these words first of all uttered.

11. "Hast thou had success as well as labour? Tell me from the air the long tidings. Oft of him who sits are the tales defective, and he who lies down utters falsehood."

Loki.

12. "I have had labour and success: Thrym has thy hammer, the Thursar's lord. It shall no man get again, unless he bring him Freyia to wife."

13. They went the fair Freyia to find; and he those words first of all said: "Bind thee, Freyia, in bridal raiment, we two must drive to Jotunheim."

14. Wroth then was Freyia, and with anger chafed, all the Æsir's hall beneath her trembled: in shivers flew the famed Brisinga necklace. "Know me to be of women lewdest, if with thee I drive to Jotunheim."

15. Straightway went the Æsir all to council, and the Asyniur all to hold converse; and deliberated the mighty gods, how they Hlorridi's hammer might get back.

16. Then said Heimdall, of Æsir brightest—he well foresaw, like other Vanir—"Let us clothe Thor with bridal raiment, let him have the famed Brisinga necklace.

17. "Let by his side keys jingle, and woman's weeds fall round his knees, but on his breast place precious stones, and a neat coif set on his head."

18. Then said Thor, the mighty As: "Me the Æsir will call womanish, if I let myself be clad in bridal raiment."

19. Then spake Loki, Laufey's son: "Do thou, Thor! refrain from suchlike words: forthwith the Jotuns will Asgard inhabit, unless thy hammer thou gettest back."

20. Then they clad Thor in bridal raiment, and with the noble Brisinga necklace, let by his side keys jingle, and woman's weeds fall round his knees; and on his breast placed precious stones, and a neat coif set on his head.

21. Then said Loki, Laufey's son: "I will with thee as a servant go: we two will drive to Jotunheim."

22. Straightway were the goats homeward driven, hurried to the traces; they had fast to run. The rocks were shivered, the earth was in a blaze; Odin's son drove to Jotunheim.

23. Then said Thrym, the Thursar's lord: "Rise up, Jotuns! and the benches deck, now they bring me Freyia to wife, Niord's daughter, from Noatun.

24. "Hither to our court let bring gold-horned cows, all-black oxen, for the Jotuns' joy. Treasures I have many, necklaces many, Freyia alone seemed to me wanting."

25. In the evening they early came, and for the Jotuns beer was brought forth. Thor alone an ox devoured, salmons eight, and all the sweetmeats women should have. Sif's consort drank three salds of mead.

26. Then said Thrym, the Thursar's prince: "Where hast thou seen brides eat more voraciously? I never saw brides feed more amply, nor a maiden drink more mead."

27. Sat the all-crafty serving-maid close by, who words fitting found against the Jotun's speech: "Freyia has nothing eaten for eight nights, so eager was she for Jotunheim."

28. Under her veil he stooped desirous to salute her, but sprang back along the hall. "Why are so piercing Freyia's looks? Methinks that fire burns from her eyes."

29. Sat the all-crafty serving-maid close by, who words fitting found against the Jotun's speech: "Freyia for eight nights has not slept, so eager was she for Jotunheim."

30. In came the Jotun's luckless sister, for a bride-gift she dared to ask: "Give me from thy hands the ruddy rings, if thou wouldst gain my love, my love and favour all."

31. Then said Thrym, the Thursar's lord: "Bring the hammer in, the bride to consecrate; lay Miollnir on the maiden's knee; unite us each with other by the hand of Vor."

32. Laughed Hlorridi's soul in his breast, when the fierce-hearted his hammer recognized. He first slew Thrym, the Thursar's lord, and the Jotun's race all crushed;

33. He slew the Jotun's aged sister, her who a bride-gift had demanded; she a blow got instead of skillings, a hammer's stroke for many rings. So got Odin's son his hammer back.

THE LAY OF THE DWARF ALVIS.

Alvis.

1. The benches they are decking, now shall the bride with me bend her way home. That beyond my strength I have hurried will to every one appear: at home naught shall disturb my quiet.

Vingthor.

2. What man is this? Why about the nose art thou so pale? Hast thou last night with corpses lain? To me thou seemst to bear resemblance to the Thursar. Thou art not born to carry off a bride.

Alvis.

3. Alvis I am named, beneath the earth I dwell, under the rock I own a place. The lord of chariots I am come to visit. A promise once confirmed let no one break. *Vingthor.*

4. I will break it; for o'er the maid I have, as father, greatest power. I was from home when the promise was given thee. Among the gods I the sole giver am.

Alvis.

5. What man is this, who lays claim to power over that fair, bright maiden? For far-reaching shafts few will know thee. Who has decked thee with bracelets?

Vingthor.

6. Vingthor I am named, wide I have wandered; I am Sidgrani's son: with my dissent thou shalt not that young maiden have, nor that union obtain.

Alvis.

7. Thy consent I fain would have, and that union obtain. Rather would I possess than be without that snow-white maiden.

Vingthor.

8. The maiden's love shall not, wise guest! be unto thee denied, if thou of every world canst tell all I desire to know.

Alvis.

9. Vingthor! thou canst try, as thou art desirous the knowledge of the dwarf to prove. All the nine worlds I have travelled over, and every being known.

Vingthor.

10. Tell me, Alvis!—for all men's concerns I presume thee, dwarf, to know—how the earth is called, which lies before the sons of men, in every world.

Alvis.

11. Jord among men 'tis called, but with the Æsir fold; the Vanir call it vega, the Jotuns igroen, the Alfar groandi, the powers supreme aur.

Vingthor.

12. Tell me, Alvis, etc. how the heaven is called, which is perceptible in every world.

Alvis.

13. Himinn 'tis called by men; but hlyrnir with the gods; vindofni the Vanir call it, uppheimr the Jotuns, the Alfar fagraræfr, the dwarfs driupansal.

Vingthor.

14. Tell me, Alvis! etc., how the moon is called, which men see in every world.

Alvis.

15. Mani 'tis called by men, but mylinn with the gods, hverfanda hvel in Hel they call it, skyndi the Jotuns, but the dwarfs skin; the Alfar name it artali.

Vingthor.

16. Tell me, Alvis! etc., how the sun is called, which men's sons see in every world.

Alvis.

17. Sol among men 'tis called, but with the gods sunna, the dwarfs call it Dvalinn's leika, the Jotuns eyglo, the Alfar fagrahvel, the Æsir's sons alskir.

Vingthor.

18. Tell me, Alvis, etc., how the clouds are called, which with showers are mingled in every world.

Alvis.

19. Sky they are called by men, but skurvan by the gods; the Vanir call them vindflot, the Jotuns urvan, the Alfar vedrmegin; in Hel they are called hialm hulids.

Vingthor.

20. Tell me, Alvis! etc., how the wind is called, which widely passes over every world.

Alvis.

21. Windr 'tis called by men, but vavudr by the gods, the wide-ruling powers call it gneggiud, the Jotuns oepir, the Alfar dynfari, in Hel they call it hvidudr.

Vingthor.

22. Tell me, Alvis! etc., how the calm is called, which has to rest in every world.

Alvis.

23. Logn 'tis called by men, but lægi by the gods, the Vanir call it vindslot, the Jotuns ofhly, the Alfar dagsevi, the Dwarfs call it dags vera.

Vingthor.

24. Tell me, Alvis! etc., what the sea is called, which men row over in every world.

Alvis.

25. Sær 'tis called by men, but silægia with the gods; the vanir call it vagr, the Jotuns alheimr, the Alfar lagastafr, the Dwarfs call it diupan mar.

Vingthor.

26. Tell me, Alvis! etc., how the fire is called, which burns before men's sons in every world.

Alvis.

27. Eldr 'tis called by men, but by the Æsir funi; the Vanir call it vagr, the Jotuns frekr, but the Dwarfs forbrennir; in Hel they call it hrodudr.

Vingthor.

28. Tell me, Alvis! etc., how the forest is called, which grows for the sons of men in every world.

Alvis.

29. Vidr 'tis called by men, but vallarfax by the gods, Hel's inmates call it hlidthangr, the Jotuns eldi, the Alfar fagrlimi; the Vanir call it vondr.

Vingthor.

30. Tell me, Alvis! etc., how the night is called, that Norvi's daughter hight, in every world.

Alvis.

31. Nott it is called by men, but by the gods niol; the wide-ruling powers call it grima, the Jotuns olios, the Alfar svefngaman; the Dwarfs call it draumniorunn.

Vingthor.

32. Tell me, Alvis! etc., how the seed is called, which the sons of men sow in every world.

Alvis.

33. Bygg it is called by men, but by the gods barr, the Vanir call it vaxtr, the Jotuns æti, the Alfar lagastafr; in Hel 'tis hnipinn called.

Vingthor.

34. Tell me, Alvis! etc., how the beer is called, which the sons of men drink in every world.

Alvis.

35. Ol it is called by men, but by the Æsir biorr, the Vanir call it veig, hreina logr the Jotuns, but in Hel 'tis called miodr: Suttung's sons call it sumbl.

Vingthor.

36. In one breast I have never found more ancient lore. By great wiles thou hast, I tell thee, been deluded. Thou art above ground, dwarf! at dawn; already in the hall the sun is shining!

44

THE LAY OF HARBARD.

Thor journeying from the eastern parts came to a strait or sound, on the other side of which was a ferryman with his boat. Thor cried out:—

1. Who is the knave of knaves, that by the sound stands yonder?

Harbard.

2. Who is the churl of churls, that cries across the water?

Thor.

3. Ferry me across the sound, to-morrow I'll regale thee. I have a basket on my back: there is no better food: at my ease I ate, before I quitted home, herrings and oats, with which I yet feel sated.

Harbard.

4. Thou art in haste to praise thy meal: thou surely hast no foreknowledge; for sad will be thy home: thy mother, I believe, is dead.

Thor.

5. Thou sayest now what seems to every one most unwelcome to know—that my mother is dead.

Harbard.

6. Thou dost not look like one who owns three coun try dwellings, bare-legged thou standest, and like a beggar clothed; thou hast not even breeches.

Thor.

7. Steer hitherward thy boat; I will direct thee where to land. But who owns this skiff, which by the strand thou holdest?

Harbard.

8. Hildolf fie is named who bade me hold it, a man in council wise, who dwells in Radso sound. Robbers he bade me not to ferry, or horse-stealers, but good men only, and those whom I well knew. Tell me then thy name, if thou wilt cross the sound.

Thor.

9. I my name will tell, (although I am an outlaw) and all my kin: I am Odin's son, Meili's brother, and Magni's sire, the gods' mighty leader: With Thor thou here mayest speak. I will now ask how thou art called.

Harbard.

10. I am Harbard called; seldom I my name conceal.

Thor.

11. Why shouldst thou thy name conceal, unless thou crime hast perpetrated?

Harbard.

12. Yet, though I may crime have perpetrated, I will nathless guard my life against such as thou art; unless I death-doomed am.

Thor.

13. It seems to me a foul annoyance to wade across the strait to thee, and wet my garments: but I will pay thee, mannikin! for thy sharp speeches, if o'er the sound I come.

Harbard.

14. Here will I stand, and here await thee. Thou wilt have found no stouter one since Hrungnir's death.

Thor.

15. Thou now remindest me how I with Hrungnir fought, that stout-hearted Jotun, whose head was all of stone; yet I made him fall, and sink before me. What meanwhile didst thou, Harbard?

Harbard.

16. I was with Fiolvari five winters through, in the isle which Algron hight. There we could fight, and slaughter make, many perils prove, indulge in love.

Thor.

17. How did your women prove towards you?

Harbard.

18. Sprightly women we had, had they but been meek; shrewd ones we had, had they but been kind. Of sand a rope they twisted, and from the deep valley dug the earth: to them all I alone was superior in cunning. I rested with the sisters seven, and their love and pleasures shared. What meanwhile didst thou, Thor?

Thor.

19. I slew Thiassi, that stout-hearted Jotun: up I cast the eyes of Allvaldi's son into the heaven serene: they are signs the greatest of my deeds. What meanwhile didst thou, Harbard?

Harbard.

20. Great seductive arts I used against the riders of the night, when from their husbands I enticed them. A mighty Jotun I believed Hlebard to be: a magic wand he gave me, but from his wits I charmed him.

Thor.

21. With evil mind then thou didst good gifts requitè *Harbard.*

22. One tree gets that which, is from another scraped: each one in such case is for self. What meanwhile didst thou, Thor?

Thor.

23. In the east I was, and slew the Jotun brides, crafty in evil, as they to the mountain went. Great would have been the Jotun race, had they all lived; and not a man left in Midgard. What meanwhile didst thou, Harbard?

Harbard.

24. I was in Valland, and followed warfare; princes I excited, but never reconciled. Odin has all the jarls that in conflict fall; but Thor the race of thralls.

Thor.

25. Unequally thou wouldst divide the folk among the Æsir, if thou but hadst the power.

Harbard.

36. Thor has strength over-much, but courage none; from cowardice and fear, thou wast crammed into a glove, and hardly thoughtest thou wast Thor. Thou durst not then, through thy terror, either sneeze or cough, lest Fialar it might hear.

Thor.

27. Harbard, thou wretch! I would strike thee dead, could I but stretch my arm across the sound.

Harbard.

28. Why wouldst thou stretch thy arm across the sound, when there is altogether no offence? But what didst thou, Thor?

Thor.

39. In the east I was, and a river I defended, when the sons of Svarang me assailed, and with stones pelted me, though in their success they little joyed: they were the first to sue for peace. What meanwhile didst thou, Harbard?

Harbard.

30. I was in the east, and with a certain lass held converse; with that fair I dallied, and long meetings had. I that gold-bright one delighted; the game amused her.

Thor.

31. Then you had kind damsels there?

Harbard.

32. Of thy aid I had need, Thor! in retaining that maiden lily-fair.

Thor.

33. I would have given it thee, if I had had the opportunity.

Harbard.

34. I would have trusted thee, my confidence if thou hadst not betrayed it.

Thor.

35. I am not such a heel-chafer as an old leather shoe in spring.

Harbard.

36. What meanwhile didst thou, Thor?

Thor.

37. The Berserkers' brides I on Læsso cudgeled; they the worst had perpetrated, the whole people, had seduced.

Harbard.

38. Dastardly didst thou act, Thor! when thou didst cudgel women.

Thor.

39. She-wolves they were, and scarcely women. They crushed my ship, which with props I had secured, with iron clubs threatened me, and drove away Thialfi. What meanwhile didst thou, Harbard?

Harbard.

40. I in the army was, which was hither sent, war-banners to raise, lances to redden.

Thor.

41. Of that thou now wilt speak, as thou wentest forth us hard terms to offer.

Harbard.

42. That shall be indemnified by a hand-ring, such as arbitrators give, who wish to reconcile us.

Thor.

43. Where didst thou learn words than which I never heard more irritating?

Harbard.

44. From men I learned them, from ancient men, whose home is in the woods.

Thor.

45. Thou givest certainly a good name to grave-mounds, when thou callest them, homes in the woods.

Harbard.

46. So speak I of such a subject.

Thor.

47. Thy shrewd words will bring thee evil, if I resolve the sound to ford. Louder than a wolf thou wilt howl, I trow, if of my hammer thou gettest a touch.

Harbard.

48. Sif has a gallant at home; thou wilt anxious be to find him: thou shalt that arduous work perform; it will beseem thee better.

Thor.

49. Thou utterest what comes upmost, so that to me it be most annoying, thou dastardly varlet! I believe thou art lying.

Harbard.

50. I believe I am telling truth. Thou art travelling slowly; thou wouldst have long since arrived, hadst thou assumed another form.

Thor.

51. Harbard! thou wretch! rather is it thou who hast detained me.

Harbard.

52. I never thought that a ferryman could the course of Asa-Thor retard.

Thor.

53. One advice I now will give thee: row hither with thy boat; let us cease from threats; approach the sire of Magni.

Harbard.

54. Go farther from the sound, the passage is refused thee.

Thor.

55. Show me then the way, if thou wilt not ferry me across the water.

Harbard.

56. That's too little to refuse. 'Tis far to go; 'tis to the stock an hour, and to the stone another; then keep the left hand way, until thou reachest Verland; there will Fiorgyn find her son Thor, and point out to him his kinsmen's ways to Odin's land.

Thor.

57. Can I get there to-day?

Harbard.

58. With pain and toil thou mayest get there, while the sun is up, which, I believe, is now nigh.

Thor.

59. Our talk shall now be short, as thou answerest with scoffing only. For refusing to ferry me I will reward thee, if another time we meet.

Harbard.

60. Just go to where all the powers of evil may have thee.

THE JOURNEY OR LAY OF SKIRNIR.

Frey, son of Niord; had one day seated himself in Hlidskialf, and was looking over all regions, when turning his eyes to Jotunheim, he there saw a beautiful girl, as she was passing from her father's dwelling to her bower. Thereupon he became greatly troubled in mind. Frey's attendant was named Skirnir; him Niord desired to speak with Frey; when Skadi said:—

1. Rise up now, Skirnir! go and request our son to speak; and inquire with whom he so sage may be offended.

Skirnir.

2. Harsh words I have from your son to fear, if I go to speak with him, and to inquire with whom he so sage may be offended.

Skirnir.

3. Tell me now, Frey, prince of gods! for I desire to know, why alone thou sittest in the spacious hall the livelong day?

Frey.

4. Why shall I tell thee, thou young man, my mind's great trouble? for the Alfs' illuminator shines every day, yet not for my pleasure.

Skirnir.

5. Thy care cannot, I think, be so great, that to me thou canst not tell it; for in early days we were young together: well might we trust each other.

Frey.

6. In Gymir's courts I saw walking a maid for whom I long. Her arms gave forth light wherewith shone all air and water.

7. Is more desirable to me that maid than to any youth in early days; yet will no one, Æsir or Alfar, that we together live.

Skirnir.

8. Give me but thy steed, which can bear me through the dusk, flickering flame, and that sword, which brandishes itself against the Jotuns' race.

Frey.

9. I will give thee my steed, which can bear thee through the dusk, flickering flame, and that sword, which will itself brandish, if he is bold who raises it.

Skirnir Speaks to the Horse.

10. Dark it is without, 'tis time, I say, for us to go across the misty fells, over the Thursar's land: we shall both return, or the all-potent Jotun will seize us both. Skirnir rides to Jotunheim, to Gymir's mansion, where fierce dogs were chained at the gate of the enclosure that was round Gymir's hall. He rides on to where a cowherd was sitting on a mound, and says to him:

11. Tell me, cowherd! as on the mound thou sittest, and watchest all the ways, how I to the speech may come, of the young maiden, for Gymir's dogs?

Cowherd.

12. Either thou art death-doomed, or thou art a departed one. Speech wilt thou ever lack with the good maid of Gymir.

Skirnir.

13. Better choices than to whine there are for him who is prepared to die: for one day was my age decreed, and my whole life determined.

Gerd.

14. What is that sound of sounds, which I now sounding hear within our dwelling? The earth is shaken, and with it all the house of Gymir trembles.

A serving-maid.

15. A man is here without, dismounted from his horse's back: he lets his steed browse on the grass.

Gerd.

16. Bid him enter into our hall, and drink of the bright mead; although I fear it is my brother's slayer who waits without.

17. Who is this of the Alfar's, or of the Æsir's sons, or of the wise Vanir's? Why art thou come alone, through the hostile fire, our halls to visit?

Skirnir.

18. I am not of the Alfar's, nor of the Æsir's sons, nor of the wise Vanir's; yet I am come alone, through the hostile fire, your halls to visit.

19. Apples all-golden I have here eleven: these I will give thee, Gerd, thy love to gain, that thou mayest say that Frey to thee lives dearest.

Gerd.

20. The apples eleven I never will accept for any mortal's pleasure; nor will I and Frey, while our lives last, live both together.

Skirnir.

21. The ring too I will give thee, which was burnt with the young son of Odin. Eight of equal weight will from it drop, every ninth night.

Gerd.

22. The ring I will not accept, burnt though it may have been with the young son of Odin. I have no lack of gold in Gymir's courts; for my father's wealth I share.

Skirnir.

23. Seest thou this sword, young maiden! thin, glittering-bright, which I have here in hand? I thy head will sever from thy neck, if thou speakst not favourably to me.

Gerd.

24. Suffer compulsion will I never, to please any man; yet this I foresee, if thou and Gymir meet, ye will eagerly engage in fight.

Skirnir.

25. Seest thou this sword, young maiden! thin, glittering-bright, which I have here in hand? Beneath its edge shall the old Jotun fall: thy sire is death-doomed.

26. With a taming-wand I smite thee, and I will tame thee, maiden! to my will. Thou shalt go thither, where the sons of men shall never more behold thee.

27. On an eagle's mount thou shalt early sit, looking and turned towards Hel. Food shall to thee more loathsome be than is to any one the glistening serpent among men.

28. As a prodigy thou shalt be, when thou goest forth; Hrimnir shall at thee gaze, all beings at thee stare; more wide-known thou shalt become than the watch among the gods, if thou from thy gratings gape.

29. Solitude and disgust, bonds and impatience, shall thy tears with grief augment. Set thee down, and I will tell thee of a whelming flood of care, and a double grief.

30. Terrors shall bow thee down the livelong day, in the Jotuns' courts. To the Hrimthursar's halls, thou shalt each day crawl exhausted, joyless crawl; wail for pastime shalt thou have, and tears and misery.

31. With a three-headed Thurs thou shalt be ever bound, or be without a mate. Thy mind shall tear thee from morn to morn: as the thistle thou shalt be which has thrust itself on the house-top.

32. To the wold I have been, and to the humid grove, a magic wand to get. A magic wand I got.

33. Wroth with thee is Odin, wroth with thee is the Æsir's prince; Frey shall loathe thee, even ere thou, wicked maid! shalt have felt the gods' dire vengeance.

34. Hear ye, Jotuns! hear ye, Hrimthursar! sons of Suttung! also ye, iEsir's friends! how I forbid, how I prohibit man's joy unto the damsel, man's converse to the damsel.

35. Hrimgrimnir the Thurs is named, that shall possess thee, in the grating of the dead beneath; there shall wretched thralls, from the tree's roots, goats' water give thee. Other drink shalt thou, maiden! never get, either for thy pleasure, or for my pleasure.

36. Thurs I cut for thee, and three letters mere: ergi, and oedi, and othola. So will I cut them out, as I have cut them, in, if there need shall be.

Gerd.

37. Hail rather to thee, youth! and accept an icy cup, filled with old mead; although I thought not that I ever should love one of Vanir race.

Skirnir.

38. All my errand will I know, ere I hence ride home. When wilt thou converse hold with the powerful son of Niord?

Gerd.

39. Barri the grove is named, which we both know, the grove of tranquil paths. Nine nights hence, there to Niord's son Gerd will grant delight.

Skimir then rode home. Frey was standing without, and spoke to him, asking tidings:

40. Tell me, Skirnir! ere thou thy steed unsaddlest, and a foot hence thou goest, what thou hast accomplished in Jotunheim, for my pleasure or thine?

Skirnir.

41. Barri the grove is named, which we both know, the grove of tranquil paths. Nine nights hence, there to Niord's son Gerd will grant delight.

Frey.

42. Long is one night, yet longer two will be; how shall I three endure. Often a month to me less has seemed than half a night of longing.

THE LAY OF RIG.

In ancient Sagas it is related that one of the Æsir named Heimdall, being on a journey to a certain sea-shore, came to a village, where he called himself Rig. In accordance with this Saga is the following:

1. In ancient days, they say, along the green ways went the powerful and upright sagacious As, the strong and active Rig, his onward course pursuing.

2. Forward he went on the mid-way, and to a dwelling came. The door stood ajar, he went in, fire was on the floor. The man and wife sat there, hoary-haired, by the hearth, Ai and Edda, in old guise clad.

3. Rig would counsel give to them both, and himself seated in the middle seat, having on either side the domestic pair.

4. Then Edda from the ashes took a loaf, heavy and thick, and with bran mixed; more besides she laid on the middle of the board; there in a bowl was broth on the table set, there was a calf boiled, of cates most excellent.

5. Then rose he up, prepared to sleep: Rig would counsel give to them both; laid him down in the middle of the bed; the domestic pair lay one on either side.

6. There he continued three nights together, then departed on the mid-way. Nine months then passed way.

7. Edda a child brought forth: they with water sprinkled its swarthy skin, and named it Thræl.

8. It grew up, and well it throve; of its hands the skin was shriveled, the knuckles knotty, * * * and the fingers thick; a hideous countenance it had, a curved back, and protruding heels.

9. He then began his strength to prove, bast to bind, make of it loads; then faggots carried home, the livelong day.

10. Then to the dwelling came a woman walking, scarred were her foot-soles, her arms sunburnt, her nose compressed, her name was Thy.

11. In the middle seat herself she placed; by her sat the house's son. They spoke and whispered, prepared a bed, Thræl and Thy, and days of care.

12. Children they begat, and lived content: Their names, I think, were Hreimr and Fiosnir, Klur and Kleggi, Kefsir, Fulnir, Drumb, Digraldi, Drott and Hosvir, Lut and Leggialdi. Fences they erected, fields manured, tended swine, kept goats, dug turf.

13. The daughters were Drumba and Kumba, Okkvinkalfa, and Arinnefia, Ysia and Ambatt, Eikintiasna, Totrughypia, and Tronubeina, whence are sprung the race of thralls.

14. Rig then went on, in a direct course, and came to a house; the door stood ajar: he went in; fire was on the floor, man and wife sat there engaged at work.

15. The man was planing wood for a weaver's beam; his beard was trimmed, a lock was on his forehead, his shirt close; his chest stood on the floor.

16. His wife sat by, plied her rock, with outstretched arms, prepared for clothing. A hood was on her head, a loose sark over her breast, a kerchief round her neck, studs on her shoulders. Afi and Amma owned the house.

17. Rig would counsel give to them both; rose from the table, prepared to sleep; laid him down in the middle of the bed, the domestic pair lay one on either side.

18. There he continued three nights together. Nine months then passed away. Amma a child brought forth, they with water sprinkled it, and called it Karl. The mother in linen swathed the ruddy redhead: its eyes twinkled.

19. It grew up, and well throve; learned to tame oxen, make a plough, houses build, and barns construct, make carts, and the plough drive.

20. Then they home conveyed a lass with pendent keys, and goatskin kirtle; married her to Karl. Snor was her name, under a veil she sat. The couple dwelt together, rings exchanged, spread couches, and a household formed.

21. Children they begat, and lived content. Hal and Dreng, these were named, Held, Thegn, Smith, Breidr-bondi, Bundinskegg, Bui and Boddi, Brattskegg and Segg.

22. But were thus called, by other names: Snot, Brud, Svanni, Svarri, Sprakki, Fliod, Sprund, and Vif, Feima, Ristil; whence are sprung the races of churls.

23. Rig then went thence, in a direct course, and came to a hall: the entrance looked southward, the door was half closed, a ring was on the door-post.

24. He went in; the floor was strewed, a couple sat facing each other, Fadir and Modir, with fingers playing.

25. The husband sat, and twisted string, bent his bow, and arrow-shafts prepared; but the housewife looked on her arms, smoothed her veil, and her sleeves fastened;

26. Her head-gear adjusted. A clasp was on her breast; ample her robe, her sark was blue; brighter was her brow, her breast fairer, her neck whiter than driven snow.

27. Rig would counsel give to them both, and himself seated on the middle seat, having on either side the domestic pair.

28. Then took Modir a figured cloth of white linen, and the table decked. She then took thin cakes of snow-white wheat, and on the table laid.

29. She set forth salvers full, adorned with silver, on the table game and pork, and roasted birds. In a can was wine; the cups were ornamented. They drank and talked; the day was fast departing, Rig would counsel give to them both.

30. Rig then rose, the bed prepared; there he then remained three nights together, then departed on the mid-way. Nine months after that passed away.

31. Modir then brought forth a boy: in silk they wrapped him, with water sprinkled him, and named him Jarl. Light was his hair, bright his cheeks, his eyes piercing as a young serpent's.

32. There at home Jarl grew up, learned the shield to shake, to fix the string, the bow to bend, arrows to shaft, javelins to hurl, spears to brandish, horses to ride, dogs to let slip, swords to draw, swimming to practise.

33. Thither from the forest came Rig walking, Rig walking: runes he taught him, his own name gave him, and his own son declared him, whom he bade possess his alodial fields, his alodial fields, his ancient dwellings.

34. Jarl then rode thence, through a murky way, over humid fells, till to a hall he came. His spear he brandished, his shield he shook, made his horse curvet, and his falchion drew, strife began to raise, the field to redden, carnage to make; and conquer lands.

35. Then he ruled alone over eight vills, riches distributed, gave to all treasures and precious things; lank-sided horses, rings he dispersed, and collars cut in pieces.

36. The nobles drove through humid ways, came to a hall, where Hersir dwelt; there they found a slender maiden, fair and elegant, Erna her name.

37. They demanded her, and conveyed her home, to Jarl espoused her; she under the linen went. They together lived, and well throve, had offspring, and old age enjoyed.

38. Bur was their eldest, Barn the second, Jod and Adal, Arfi, Mog, Nid and Nidjung. They learned games; Son and Svein swam and at tables played. One was named Kund, Kon was youngest.

39. There grew up Jarl's progeny; horses they broke, curved shields, cut arrows, brandished spears.

40. But the young Kon understood runes, æfin-runes, and aldr-runes; he moreover knew men to preserve, edges to deaden, the sea to calm.

41. He knew the voice of birds, how fires to mitigate, assuage and quench; sorrows to allay. He of eight men had the strength and energy.

42. He with Rig Jarl in runes contended, artifices practised, and superior proved; then acquired Rig to be called, and skilled in runes.

43. The young Kon rode through swamps and forests, hurled forth darts, and tamed birds.

44. Then sang the crow, sitting lonely on a bough! "Why wilt thou, young Kon: tame the birds? rather shouldst thou, young Kon! on horses ride * * * and armies overcome.

45. Nor Dan nor Danp halls more costly had, nobler paternal seats, than ye had. They well knew how the keel to ride, the edge to prove, wounds to inflict. *The rest is wanting.*

OEGIR'S COMPOTATION, OR LOKI'S ALTERCATION.

Oegir, who is also named Gymir, had brewed beer for the Æsir, after he had got the great kettle, as has been already related. To the entertainment came Odin and his wife Frigg. Thor did not come, being in the East, but his wife Sif was there, also Bragi and his wife Idun, and Ty, who was one-handed, Fenrisulf having bitten off his hand while being bound. Besides these there were Niord and his wife Skadi, Frey and Freyia, and Odin's son Vidar. Loki too was there, and Frey's attendants, Byggvir and Beyla. Many other Æsir and Alfar were also present.

Oegir had two servants, Fimafeng and Eldir. Bright gold was there used instead of fire-light. The beer served itself to the guests. The place was a great sanctuary. The guests greatly praised the excellence of Oegir's servants. This Loki could not hear with patience, and so slew Fimafeng; whereupon the Æsir shook their shields, exclaimed against Loki, chased him into the forest, and then returned to drink. Loki came again, and found Eldir standing without, whom he thus addressed:

1. Tell me, Eldir! ere thou thy foot settest one step forward, on what converse the sons of the triumphant gods at their potation?

Eldir.

2. Of their arms converse, and of their martial fame, the sons of the triumphant gods. Of the Æsir and the Alfar that are here within not one has a friendly word for thee.

Loki.

3. I will go into Oegir's halls, to see the compotation. Strife and hate to the Æsir's sons I bear, and will mix their mead with bale.

Eldir.

4. Knowest thou not that if thou goest into Oegir's halls to see the compotation, but contumely and clamour pourest forth on the kindly powers, they will wipe it all off on thee?

Loki.

5. Knowest thou not, Eldir, that if we two with bitter words contend, I shall be rich in answers, if thou sayest too much?

Loki then went into the hall, but when those present saw who was come in, they all sat silent.

Loki.

6. I Lopt am come thirsty into this hall, from a long journey, to beseech the Æsir one draught to give me of the bright mead.

7. Why gods! are ye so silent, so reserved, that ye cannot speak? A seat and place choose for me at your board, or bid me hie me hence.

Bragi.

8. A seat and place will the Æsir never choose for thee at their board; for well the Æsir know for whom they ought to hold a joyous compotation.

Loki.

9. Odin! dost thou remember when we in early days blended our blood together? When to taste beer thou didst constantly refuse, unless to both 'twas offered?

Odin.

10. Rise up, Vidar! and let the wolf's sire sit at our compotation; that Loki may not utter words of contumely in Oegir's hall.

Vidar then rising, presented Loki with drink, who before drinking thus addressed the Æsir:

11. Hail, Æsir! Hail, Asyniur! And ye, all-holy gods! all, save that one As, who sits within there, Bragi, on yonder bench.

Bragi.

12. A horse and falchion I from my stores will give thee, and also with a ring reward thee, if thou the Æsir wilt not requite with malice. Provoke not the gods against thee.

Loki.

13. Of horse and rings wilt thou ever, Bragi! be in want. Of the Æsir and the Alfar, that are here present, in conflict thou art the most backward, and in the play of darts most timid.

Bragi.

14. I know that were I without, as I am now within, the hall of Oegir, I thy head would bear in my hand, and so for lying punish thee.

Loki.

15. Valiant on thy seat art thou, Bragi! but so thou shouldst not be, Bragi, the bench's pride! Go and fight, if thou art angry; a brave man sits not considering.

Idun.

16. I pray thee, Bragi! let avail the bond of children, and of all adopted sons, and to Loki speak not in reproachful words, in Oegir's hall.

Loki.

17. Be silent, Idun! of all women I declare thee most fond of men, since thou thy arms, carefully washed, didst twine round thy brother's murderer.

Idun.

18. Loki I address not with opprobrious words, in Oegir's hall. Bragi I soothe, by beer excited. I desire not that angry ye fight.

Gefion.

19. Why will ye, Æsir twain, here within, strive with reproachful words? Lopt perceives not that he is deluded, and is urged on by fate.

Loki.

20. Be silent, Gefion! I will now just mention, how that fair youth thy mind corrupted, who thee a necklace gave, and around whom thou thy limbs didst twine?

Odin.

21. Thou art raving, Loki! and hast lost thy wits, in calling Gefion's anger on thee; for all men's destinies, I ween, she knows as thoroughly as I do.

Loki.

22. Be silent, Odin! Thou never couldst allot conflicts between men: oft hast thou given to those to whom thou oughtest not—victory to cowards.

Odin.

23. Knowest thou that I gave to those I ought not—victory to cowards? Thou wast eight winters on the earth below, a milch cow and a woman, and didst there bear children. Now that, methinks, betokens a base nature.

Loki.

24. But, it is said, thou wentest with tottering steps in Samso, and knocked at houses as a Vala. In likeness of a fortune teller, thou wentest among people. Now that, methinks, betokens a base nature.

Frigg.

25. Your doings ye should never publish among men, what ye, Æsir twain, did in days of yore. Ever forgotten be men's former deeds!

Loki.

26. Be thou silent, Frigg! Thou art Fiorgyn's daughter, and ever hast been fond of men, since Ve and Vili, it is said, thou, Vidrir's wife, didst both to thy bosom take.

Frigg.

27. Know thou that if I had, in Oegir's halls, a son like Baldr, out thou shouldst not go from the Æsir's sons: thou should'st have been fiercely assailed.

Loki.

28. But wilt thou, Frigg! that of my wickedness I more recount? I am the cause that thou seest not Baldr riding to the halls.

Freyia.

29. Mad art thou, Loki! in recounting thy foul misdeeds. Frigg, I believe, knows all that happens, although she says it not.

Loki.

30. Be thou silent, Freyia! I know thee full well; thou art not free from vices: of the Æsir and the Alfar, that are herein, each has been thy paramour.

Freyia.

31. False is thy tongue. Henceforth it will, I think, prate no good to thee. Wroth with thee are the Æsir, and the Asyniur. Sad shalt thou home depart.

Loki.

32. Be silent, Freyia! Thou art a sorceress, and with much evil blended; since against thy brother thou the gentle powers excited. And then, Freyia! what didst thou do?

Niord.

33. It is no great wonder, if silk-clad dames get themselves husbands, lovers; but 'tis a wonder that a wretched As, that has borne children, should herein enter.

Loki.

34. Be silent, Niord! Thou wast sent eastward hence, a hostage from the gods. Hymir's daughters had thee for an utensil, and flowed into thy mouth. *Niord.*

35. 'Tis to me a solace, as I a long way hence was sent, a hostage from the gods, that I had a son, whom no one hates, and accounted is a chief among the Æsir.

Loki.

36. Cease now, Niord! in bounds contain thyself; I will no longer keep it secret: it was with thy sister thou hadst such a son; hardly worse than thyself.

Ty.

37. Frey is best of all the exalted gods in the Æsir's courts: no maid he makes to weep, no wife of man, and from bonds looses all.

Loki.

38. Be silent, Ty! Thou couldst never settle a strife 'twixt two; of thy right hand also I must mention make, which Fenrir from thee tore.

Ty.

39. I of a hand am wanting, but thou of honest fame; sad is the lack of either. Nor is the wolf at ease: he in bonds must bide, until the gods' destruction.

Loki.

40. Be silent, Ty; to thy wife it happened to have a son by me. Nor rag nor penny ever hadst thou, poor wretch! for this injury.

Frey.

41. I the wolf see lying at the river's mouth, until the powers are swept away. So shalt thou be bound, if thou art not silent, thou framer of evil.

Loki.

42. With gold thou boughtest Gymir's daughter, and so gavest away thy sword: but when Muspell's sons through the dark forest ride, thou, unhappy, wilt not have wherewith to fight.

Byggvir.

43. Know that were I of noble race, like Ingun's Frey, and had so fair a dwelling, than marrow softer I would bray that ill-boding crow, and crush him limb by limb.

Loki.

44. What little thing is that I see wagging its tail, and snapping eagerly? At the ears of Frey thou shouldst ever be, and clatter under mills.

Byggvir.

45. Byggvir I am named, and am thought alert, by all gods and men; therefore am I joyful here, that all the sons of Hropt drink beer together.

Loki.

46. Be silent, Byggvir! Thou couldst never dole out food to men, when, lying in thy truckle bed, thou wast not to be found, while men were fighting.

Heimdall.

47. Loki, thou art drunk, and hast lost thy wits. Why dost thou not leave off, Loki? But drunkenness so rules every man, that he knows not of his garrulity.

Loki.

48. Be silent, Heimdall! For thee in early days was that hateful life decreed: with a wet back thou must ever be, and keep watch as guardian of the gods.

Skadi.

49. Thou art merry, Loki! Not long wilt thou frisk with an unbound tail; for thee, on a rock's point, with the entrails of thy ice-cold son, the gods will bind.

Loki.

50. Know, if on a rock's point, with the entrails of my ice-cold son, the gods will bind me, that first and foremost I was at the slaying, when we assailed Thiassi.

Skadi.

51. Know, if first and foremost thou wast at the slaying, when ye assailed Thiassi, that from my dwellings and fields shall to thee ever cold counsels come.

Loki.

52. Milder wast thou of speech to Laufey's son, when to thy bed thou didst invite me. Such matters must be mentioned, if we accurately must recount our vices.

Then came Sif forth, and poured out mead for Loki in an icy cup, saying:

53. Hail to thee, Loki! and this cool cup receive, full of old mead: at least me alone, among the blameless Æsir race, leave stainless.

He took the horn, drank, and said:

54. So alone shouldst thou be, hadst thou strict and prudent been towards thy mate; but one I know, and, I think, know him well, a favoured rival of Hlorridi, and that is the wily Loki.

Beyla.

55. The fells all tremble: I think Hlorridi is from home journeying. He will bid be quiet him who here insults all gods and men.

Loki.

56. Be silent, Beyla! Thou art Byggvir's wife, and with much evil mingled: never came a greater monster among the Æsir's sons. Thou art a dirty strumpet.

Thor then came in and said:

57. Silence, thou impure being! My mighty hammer, Miollnir, shall stop thy prating. I will thy head from thy neck strike; then will thy life be ended.

Loki.

58. Now the son of earth is hither come. Why dost thou chafe so, Thor? Thou wilt not dare do so, when with the wolf thou hast to fight, and he the all-powerful father swallows whole.

Thor.

59. Silence, thou impure being! My mighty hammer, Miollnir, shall stop thy prating. Up I will hurl thee to the east region, and none shall see thee after.

Loki.

60. Of thy eastern travels thou shouldest never to people speak, since in a glove-thumb thou, Einheri! wast doubled up, and hardly thoughtest thou wast Thor.

Thor.

61. Silence, thou impure being! My mighty hammer, Miollnir, shall stop thy prating: with this right hand I, Hrungnir's bane, will smite thee, so that thy every bone be broken.

Loki.

62. 'Tis my intention a long life to live, though with thy hammer thou dost threaten me. Skrymir's thongs seemed to thee hard, when at the food thou couldst not get, when, in full health, of hunger dying.

Thor.

63. Silence, thou impure being! My mighty hammer, Miollnir, shall stop thy prating. Hrungnir's bane shall cast thee down to Hel, beneath the gratings of the dead.

Loki.

64. I have said before the Æsir, I have said before the Æsir's sons, that which my mind suggested: but for thee alone will I go out; because I know that thou wilt fight.

65. Oegir! thou hast brewed beer; but thou never shalt henceforth a compotation hold. All thy possessions, which are herein, flame shall play over, and on thy back shall burn thee.

After this Loki, in the likeness of a salmon, cast himself into the waterfall of Franangr, where the Æsir caught him, and bound him with the entrails of his son Nari; but his other son, Narfi, was changed into a wolf. Skadi took a venomous serpent, and fastened it up over Loki's face. The venom trickled down from it. Sigyn, Loki's wife, sat by, and held a basin under the venom; and when the basin was full, carried the venom out. Meanwhile the venom dropped on Loki, who shrank from it so violently that the whole earth trembled. This causes what are now called earthquakes.

THE LAY OF FIOLSVITH.

1. From the outward wall he saw one ascending to the seat of the giant race.

Fiolsvith.

Along the humid ways haste thee back hence, here, wretch! is no place for thee.

2. What monster is it before the fore-court standing, and hovering round the perilous flame? Whom dost thou seek? Of what art thou in quest? Or what, friendless being! desirest thou to know?

Wanderer.

3. What monster is that, before the fore-court standing, who to the wayfarer offers not hospitality? Void of honest fame, prattler! hast thou lived: but hence hie thee home.

Fiolsvith.

4. Fiolsvith is my name; wise I am of mind, though of food not prodigal. Within these courts thou shalt never come: so now, wretch! take thyself off.

Wanderer.

5. From the eye's delight few are disposed to hurry, where there is something pleasant to be seen. These walls, methinks, shine around golden halls. Here I could live contented with my lot.

Fiolsvith.

6. Tell me, youth; of whom thou art born, or of what race hast sprung.

Wanderer.

7. Vindkald I am called, Varkald was my father named, his sire was Fiolkald.

8. Tell me, Fiolsvith! that which I will ask thee, and I desire to know: who here holds sway, and has power over these lands and costly halls?

Fiolsvith.

9. Menglod is her name, her mother her begat with Svaf, Thorin's son. She here holds sway, and has power over these lands and costly halls.

Vindkald.

10. Tell me, Fiolsvith! etc., what the grate is called, than which among the gods mortals never saw a greater artifice?

Fiolsvith.

11. Thrymgioll it is called, and Solblindi's three sons constructed it: a fetter fastens, every wayfarer, who lifts it from its opening.

Vindkald.

12. Tell me, Fiolsvith! etc., what that structure is called, than which among the gods mortals never saw a greater artifice?

Fiolsvith.

13. Gastropnir it is called, and I constructed it of Leirbrimir's limbs. I have so supported it, that it will ever stand while the world lasts.

Vindkald.

14. Tell me, Fiolsvith! etc., what those dogs are called, that chase away the giantesses, and safety to the fields restore?

Fiolsvith.

15. Gifr the one is called, the other Geri, if thou that wouldst know. Eleven watches they will keep, until the powers perish.

Vindkald.

16. Tell me, Fiolsvith! etc., whether any man can enter while those fierce assailants sleep?

Fiolsvith.

17. Alternate sleep was strictly to them enjoined, since to the watch they were appointed. One sleeps by night, by day the other, so that no wight can enter if he comes.

Vindkald.

18. Tell me, Fiolsvith! etc., whether there is any food that men can get, such that they can run in while they eat?

Fiolsvith.

19. Two repasts lie in Vidofnir's wings, if thou that wouldst know: that is alone such food as men can give them and run in while they eat.

Vindkald.

20. Tell me, Fiolsvith! etc., what that tree is called that with its branches spreads itself over every land?

Fiolsvith.

21. Mimameidir it is called; but few men know from what roots it springs: it by that will fall which fewest know. Nor fire nor iron will harm it.

Vindkald.

22. Tell me, Fiolsvith! etc., to what the virtue is of that famed tree applied, which nor fire nor iron will harm?

Fiolsvith.

23. Its fruit shall on the fire be laid, for labouring women; out then will pass what would in remain: so is it a creator of mankind.

Vindkald.

24. Tell me, Fioisvith! etc., what the cock is called that sits in that lofty tree, and all-glittering is with gold?

Fiolsvith.

25. Vidofnir he is called; in the clear air he stands, in the boughs of Mima's tree: afflictions only brings, together indissoluble, the swart bird at his lonely meal.

Vindkald.

26. Tell me, Fiolsvith! etc., whether there be any weapon, before which Vidofnir may fall to Hel's abode?

Fiolsvith.

27. Hævatein the twig is named, and Lopt plucked it, down by the gate of Death. In an iron chest it lies with Sinmoera, and is with nine strong locks secured.

Vindkald.

28. Tell me, Fiolsvith! etc., whether he will alive return, who seeks after, and will take, that rod?

Fiolsvith.

29. He will return who seeks after, and will take, the rod, if he bears that which few possess to the dame of the glassy clay.

Vindkald.

30. Tell me, Fiolsvith! etc., whether there is any treasure, that mortals can obtain, at which the pale giantess will rejoice?

Fiolsvith.

31. The bright sickle that lies in Vidofnir's wings, thou in a bag shalt bear, and to Sinmoera give, before she will think fit to lend an arm for conflict.

Vindkald.

32. Tell me, Fiolsvith! etc., what this hall is called, which is girt round with a curious flickering flame?

Fiolsvith.

33. Hyr it is called, and it will long tremble as on a lance's point. This sumptuous house shall, for ages hence, be but from hearsay known.

Vindkald.

34. Tell me, Fiolsvith! etc., which of the Æsir's sons has that constructed, which within the court I saw?

Fiolsvith.

35. Uni and Iri, Bari and Ori, Var and Vegdrasil, Dorri and Uri, Delling and Atvard, Lidskialf, Loki.

Vindkald.

36. Tell me, Fiolsvith! etc., what that mount is called, on which I see a splendid maiden stand?

Fiolsvith.

37. Hyfiaberg 'tis called, and long has it a solace been to the bowed-down and sorrowful: each woman becomes healthy, although a year's disease she have, if she can but ascend it.

Vindkald.

38. Tell me, Fiolsvith! etc., how those maids are called, who sit at Menglod's knees in harmony together?

Fiolsvith.

39. Hlif the first is called, the second is Hlifthursa, the third Thiodvarta, Biort and Blid, Blidr, Frid, Eir and Orboda.

Vindkald.

40. Tell me, Fiolsvith! etc., whether they protect those who offer to them, if it should, be needful?

Fiolsvith.

41. Every summer in which men offer to them, at the holy place, no pestilence so great shall come to the sons of men, but they will free each from peril.

Vindkald.

42. Tell me, Fiolsvith! etc., whether there is any man that may in Menglod's soft arms sleep?

Fiolsvith.

43. There is no man who may in Menglod's soft arms sleep, save only Svipdag; to him the sun-bright maid is for wife betrothed.

Vindkald.

44. Set the doors open! Let the gate stand wide; here thou mayest Svipdag see; but yet go learn if Menglod will accept my love.

Fiolsvith.

45. Hear, Menglod! A man is hither come: go and behold the stranger; the dogs rejoice; the house has itself opened. I think it must be Svipdag.

Menglod.

46. Fierce ravens shall, on the high gallows, tear out thy eyes, if thou art lying, that hither from afar is come the youth unto my halls.

47. Whence art thou come? Whence hast thou journeyed? How do thy kindred call thee? Of thy race and name I must have a token, if I was betrothed to thee.

Svipdag.

48. Svipdag I am named, Solbiart was my father named; thence the winds on the cold ways drove me. Urd's decree may no one gainsay, however lightly uttered.

Menglod.

49. Welcome thou art: my will I have obtained; greeting a kiss shall follow. A sight unlooked-for gladdens most persons, when one the other loves.

50. Long have I sat on my loved hill, day and night expecting thee. Now that is come to pass which I have hoped, that thou, dear youth, again to my halls art come.

Svipdag.

51. Longing I have undergone for thy love; and thou, for my affection. Now it is certain, that we shall pass our lives together.

THE LAY OF HYNDLA.

Freyia rides with her favourite Ottar to Hyndla, a Vala, for the purpose of obtaining information respecting Ottar's genealogy, such information being required by him in a legal dispute with Angantyr. Having obtained this, Freyia further requests Hyndla to give Ottar a potion (minnisol) that will enable him to remember all that has been told him. This she refuses, but is forced to comply by Freyia having encircled her cave with flames. She gives him the potion, but accompanied by a malediction, which is by Freyia turned to a blessing.

Freyia.

1. Wake, maid of maids! Wake, my friend! Hyndla! Sister! who in the cavern dwellest. Now there is dark of darks; we will both to Valhall ride, and to the holy fane.

2. Let us Heriafather pray into our minds to enter, he gives and grants gold to the deserving. He gave to Hermod a helm and corslet, and from him Sigmund a sword received.

3. Victory to his sons he gives, but to some riches; eloquence to the great, and to men, wit; fair wind he gives to traders, but poesy to skallds; valour he gives to many a warrior.

4. She to Thor will offer, she to him will pray, that to thee he may be well disposed; although he bears ill will to Jotun females.

5. Now of thy wolves take one from out the stall; let him run with runic rein. *Hyndla.*

6. Sluggish is thy hog the god's way to tread:

Freyia.

7. I will my noble palfrey saddle.

Hyndla.

8. False are thou, Freyia! who temptest me: by thy eyes thou showest it, so fixed upon us; while thou thy man hast on the dead-road, the young Ottar, Innstein's son.

9. Dull art thou, Hyndla! methinks thou dreamest, since thou sayest that my man is on the dead-road with me; there where my hog sparkles with its golden bristles, hight Hildisvini, which for me made the two skilful dwarfs, Dain and Nabbi. From the saddle we will talk: let us sit, and of princely families discourse, of those chieftains who from the gods descend. They have contested for the dead's gold, Ottar the young and Angantyr.

10. A duty 'tis to act so that the young prince his paternal heritage may have, after his kindred.

11. An offer-stead to me he raised, with stones constructed; now is that stone as glass become. With the blood of oxen he newly sprinkled it. Ottar ever trusted in the Asyniur.

12. Now let us reckon up the ancient families, and the races of exalted men. Who are the Skioldungs? Who are the Skilfings? Who the Odlings? Who the Ylfings? Who the hold-born? Who the hers-born? The choicest race of men under heaven?

Hyndla.

13. Thou, Ottar! art of Innstein born, but Innstein was from Alf the Old, Alf was from Ulf, Ulf from Sæfari, but Sæfari from Svan the Red.

14. Thy father had a mother, for her necklaces famed, she, I think, was named Hledis the priestess; Frodi her father was, and her mother Friant: all that stock is reckoned among chieftains.

15. Ali was of old of men the strongest, Halfdan before him, the highest of the Skioldungs; (Famed were the wars by those chieftains led) his deeds seemed to soar to the skirts of heaven.

16. By Eimund aided, chief of men, he Sigtrygg slew with the cold steel. He Almveig had to wife, first of women. They begat and had eighteen sons.

17. From them the Skioldungs, from them the Skilfings, from them the Odlings, from them the Ynglings, from them the hold-born, from them the hers-born, the choicest race of men under heaven. All that race is thine, Ottar Heimski!

18. Hildegun her mother was, of Svafa born and a sea-king. All that race is thine, Ottar Heimski! Carest thou this to know? Wishest thou a longer narrative?

19. Dag wedded Thora, mother of warriors: of that race were born the noble champions, Fradmar, Gyrd, and the Frekis both, Am, Josur, Mar, Alf the Old. Carest thou this to know? Wishest thou a longer narrative?

20. Ketil their friend was named, heir of Klyp; he was maternal grandsire of thy mother. Then was Frodi yet before Kari, but the eldest born was Alf.

21. Nanna was next, Nokkvi's daughter; her son was thy father's kinsman, ancient is that kinship. I knew both Brodd and Horfi. All that race is thine, Ottar Heimski!

22. Isolf, Asolf, Olmod's sons and Skurhild's Skekkil's daughter; thou shalt yet count chieftains many. All that race is thine, Ottar Heimski!

23. Gunnar, Balk, Grim, Ardskafi, Jarnskiold, Thorir, Ulf, Ginandi, Bui and Brami, Barri and Reifnir, Tind and Hyrfing, the two Haddingis. All that race is thine, Ottar Heimski!

24. To toil and tumult were the sons of Arngrim born, and of Eyfura: ferocious berserkir, calamity of every kind, by land and sea, like fire they carried. All that race is thine, Ottar Heimski!

25. I knew both Brodd and Horfi, they were in the court of Hrolf the Old; all descended from Jormunrek, son-in-law of Sigurd. (Listen to my story) the dread of nations, him who Fafnir slew.

26. He was a king, from Volsung sprung, and Hiordis from Hrodung; but Eylimi from the Odlings. All that race is thine, Ottar Heimski!

27. Gunnar and Hogni, sons of Giuki; and Gudrun likewise, their sister. Guttorm; was not of Giuki's race, although he brother was of them both. All that race is thine, Ottar Heimski!

28. Harald Hildetonn, born of Hrærekir Slongvanbaugi; he was a son of Aud, Aud the rich was Ivar's daughter; but Radbard was Randver's father. They were heroes to the gods devoted. All that race is thine, Ottar Heimski!

29. There were eleven Æsir reckoned, when Baldr on the pile was laid; him Vali showed himself worthy to avenge, his own brother: he the slayer slew. All that race is thine, Ottar Heimski!

30. Baldr's father was son of Bur: Frey to wife had Gerd, she was Gymir's daughter, from Jotuns sprung and Aurboda; Thiassi also was their relation, that haughty Jotun; Skadi was his daughter.

31. We tell thee much, and remember more: I admonish thee thus much to know. Wishest thou yet a longer narrative?

32. Haki was not the worst of Hvedna's sons, and Hiorvard was Hvedna's father; Heid and Hrossthiof were of Hrimnir's race.

33. All the Valas are from Vidolf; all the soothsayers from Vilmeidr, all the sorcerers from Svarthofdi; all the Jotuns come from Ymir.

34. We tell thee much, and more remember, I admonish thee thus much to know. Wishest thou yet a longer narrative?

35. There was one born, in times of old, with wondrous might endowed, of origin divine: nine Jotun maids gave birth to the gracious god, at the world's margin.

36. Gialp gave him birth, Greip gave him birth, Eistla gave him birth, and Angeia; Ulfrun gave him birth, and Eyrgiafa, Imd and Atla, and Jarnsaxa.

37. The boy was nourished with the strength of earth, with the ice-cold sea, and with Son's blood. We tell thee much, and more remember. I admonish thee thus much to know. Wishest thou a yet longer narrative?

38. Loki begat the wolf with Angrboda, but Sleipnir he begat with Svadilfari: one monster seemed of all most deadly, which from Byleist's brother sprang.

39. Loki, scorched up in his heart's affections, had found a half-burnt woman's heart. Loki became guileful from that wicked woman; thence in the world are all giantesses come.

40. Ocean towers with storms to heaven itself, flows o'er the land; the air is rent: thence come snows and rapid winds; then it is decreed that the rain should cease.

41. There was one born greater than all, the boy was nourished with the strength of earth; he was declared a ruler, mightiest and richest, allied by kinship to all princes.

42. Then shall another come, yet mightier, although I dare not his name declare. Few may see further forth than when Odin meets the wolf.

Freyia.

43. Bear thou the memory-cup to my guest, so that he may all the words repeat of this, discourse, on the third morn, when he and Angantyr reckon up races.

Hyndla.

44. Go thou quickly hence, I long to sleep; more of my wondrous power thou gettest not from me. Thou runnest, my hot friend, out at nights, as among he-goats the she-goat goes.

45. Thou hast run thyself mad, ever longing; many a one has stolen under thy girdle. Thou runnest, my hot friend, out at nights, as among he-goats, the she-goat goes.

Freyia.

46. Fire I strike over thee, dweller of the wood! so that thou goest not ever away from hence.

Hyndla.

47. Fire I see burning, and the earth blazing; many will have their lives to save. Bear thou the cup to Ottar's hand, the mead with venom mingled, in an evil hour!

Freyia.

48. Thy malediction shall be powerless; although thou, Jotun-maid! dost evil threaten. He shall drink delicious draughts. All the gods I pray to favour Ottar.

THE INCANTATION OF GROA.

Son.

1. Wake up, Groa! wake up, good woman! at the gates of death I wake thee! if thou rememberest, that thou thy son badest to thy grave-mound to come.

Mother.

2. What now troubles my only son? With what affliction art thou burthened, that thou thy mother callest, who to dust is come, and from human homes departed?

Son.

3. A hateful game thou, crafty woman, didst set before me, whom my has father in his bosom cherished, when thou badest me go no one knows whither, Menglod to meet.

Mother.

4. Long is the journey, long are the ways, long are men's desires. If it so fall out, that thou thy will obtainest, the event must then be as it may.

Son.

5. Sing to me songs which are good. Mother! protect thy son. Dead on my way I fear to be. I seem too young in years.

Mother.

6. I will sing to thee first one that is thought most useful, which Rind sang to Ran; that from thy shoulders thou shouldst cast what to thee seems irksome: let thyself thyself direct.

7. A second I will sing to thee, as thou hast to wander joyless on thy ways. May Urd's protection hold thee on every side, where thou seest turpitude.

8. A third I will sing to thee. If the mighty rivers to thy life's peril fall, Horn and Rud, may they flow down to Hel, and for thee ever be diminished.

9. A fourth I will sing to thee. If foes assail thee ready on the dangerous road, their hearts shall fail them, and to thee be power, and their minds to peace be turned.

10. A fifth I will sing to thee. If bonds be cast on thy limbs, friendly spells I will let on thy joints be sung, and the lock from thy arms shall start, .

11. A sixth I will sing to thee. If on the sea thou comest, more stormy than men have known it, air and water shall in a bag attend thee, and a tranquil course afford thee.

12. A seventh I will sing to thee. If on a mountain high frost should assail thee, deadly cold shall not thy carcase injure, nor draw thy body to thy limbs.

13. An eighth I will sing to thee. If night overtake thee, when out on the misty way, that the dead Christian woman no power may have to do thee harm.

14. A ninth I will sing to thee. If with a far-famed spear-armed Jotun thou words exchangest, of words and wit to thy mindful heart abundance shall be given.

15. Go now ever where calamity may be, and no harm shall obstruct thy wishes. On a stone fast in the earth I have stood within the door, while songs I sang to thee.

16. My son! bear hence thy mother's words, and in thy breast let them dwell; for happiness abundant shalt thou have in life, while of my words thou art mindful.

THE SONG OF THE SUN.

This singular poem, the authorship of which is, in some manuscripts, assigned to Sæmund himself, may be termed a Voice from the Dead, given under the form of a dream, in which a deceased father is supposed to address his son from another world. The first 7 strophes seem hardly connected with the following ones, which, as far as the 32nd consist chiefly in aphorisms with examples, some closely resembling those in the Havamal. In the remaining portion is given the recital of the last illness of the supposed speaker, his death, and the scenes his soul passed through on the way to its final home.

The composition exhibits a strange mixture of Christianity and Heathenism, whence it would seem that the poet's own religion was in a transition state. Of the allusions to Heathenism it is, however, to be observed that they are chiefly to persons and actions of which there is no trace in the Odinic mythology, as known to us, and are possibly the fruits of the poet's own imagination. The title of the poem is no doubt derived from the allusion to the Sun at the beginning of strophes 39-45.

For an elaborate and learned commentary, with an interlinear version of "the Song of the Sun," the reader may consult "Les Chants de Sol," by Professor Bergmann, Strasbourg & Paris, 1858.

1. Of life and property a fierce freebooter despoiled mankind; over the ways beset by him might no one living pass.

2. Alone he ate most frequently, no one invited he to his repast; until weary, and with failing strength, a wandering guest came from the way.

3. In need of drink that way-worn man, and hungry feigned to be: with trembling heart he seemed to trust him who had been so evil-minded.

4. Meat and drink to the weary one he gave, all with upright heart; on God he thought, the traveller's wants supplied; for he felt he was an evil-doer.

5. Up stood the guest, he evil meditated, he had not been kindly treated; his sin within him swelled, he while sleeping murdered his wary cautious host.

6. The God of heaven he prayed for help, when being struck he woke; but he was doomed the sins of him on himself to take, whom sackless he had slain.

7. Holy angels came from heaven above, and took to them his soul: in a life of purity it shall ever live with the almighty God.

8. Riches and health no one may command, though all go smoothly with him. To many that befalls which they least expect. No one may command his tranquillity.

9. Unnar and Sævaldi never imagined that happiness would fall from them, yet naked they became, and of all bereft, and, like wolves, ran to the forest.

10. The force of pleasure has many a one bewailed. Cares are often caused by women; pernicious they become, although the mighty God them pure created.

11. United were Svafud and Skarthedin, neither might without the other be, until to frenzy they were driven for a woman: she was destined for their perdition.

12. On account of that fair maid, neither of them cared for games or joyous days; no other thing could they in memory bear than that bright form.

13. Sad to them were the gloomy nights, no sweet sleep might they enjoy: but from that anguish rose hate intense between the faithful friends.

14. Hostile deeds are in most places fiercely avenged. To the holm they went, for that fair woman, and each one found his death.

15. Arrogance should no one entertain: I indeed have seen that those who follow her, for the most part, turn from God.

16. Rich were both, Radey and Vebogi, and thought only of their well-being; now they sit and turn their sores to various hearths.

17. They in themselves confided, and thought themselves alone to be above all people; but their lot Almighty God was pleased otherwise to appoint.

18. A life of luxury they led, in many ways, and had gold for sport. Now they are requited, so that they must walk between frost and fire.

19. To thy enemies trust thou never, although they speak thee fair: promise them good: 'tis good to have another's injury as a warning.

20. So it befell Sorli the upright, when he placed himself in Vigolf's power; he confidently trusted him, his brother's murderer, but he proved false.

21. Peace to them he granted, with heart sincere; they in return promised him gold, feigned themselves friends, while they together drank; but then came forth their guile.

22. Then afterwards, on the second day, when they in Rygiardal rode, they with swords wounded him who sackless was, and let his life go forth.

23. His corpse they dragged (on a lonely way, and cut up piecemeal) into a well, and would it hide; but the holy Lord beheld from heaven.

24. His soul summoned home the true God into his joy to come; but the evil doers will, I wean, late be from torments called.

25. Do thou pray the Disir of the Lord's words to be kind to thee in spirit: for a week after, all shall then go happily, according to thy will.

26. For a deed of ire that thou hast perpetrated, never atone with evil: the weeping thou shalt soothe with benefits: that is salutary to the soul.

27. On God a man shall for good things call, on him who has mankind created. Greatly sinful is every man who late finds the Father.

28. To be solicited, we opine, is with all earnestness for that which is lacking: of all things may be destitute he who for nothing asks: few heed the wants of the silent.

29. Late I came, though called betimes, to the supreme Judge's door; thitherward I yearn; for it was promised me, he who craves it shall of the feast partake.

30. Sins are the cause that sorrowing we depart from this world: no one stands in dread, if he does no evil: good it is to be blameless.

31. Like unto wolves all those seem who have a faithless mind: so he will prove who has to go through ways strewed with gleeds.

32. Friendly counsels, and wisely composed, seven I have imparted to thee: consider thou them well, and forget them never: they are all useful to learn.

33. Of that I will speak, how happy I was in the world, and secondly, how the sons of men reluctantly become corpses.

34. Pleasure and pride deceive the sons of men who after money crave; shining riches at last become a sorrow: many have riches driven to madness.

35. Steeped in joys I seemed to men; for little did I see before me: our worldly sojourn has the Lord created in delights abounding.

36. Bowed down I sat, long I tottered, of life was most desirous; but He prevailed who was all-powerful: onward are the ways of the doomed.

37. The cords of Hel were tightly bound round my sides; I would rend them, but they were strong. 'Tis easy free to go.

38. I alone knew, how on all sides my pains increased. The maids of Hel each eve with horror bade me to their home.

39. The sun I saw, true star of day, sink in its roaring home; but Hel's grated doors on the other side I heard heavily creaking.

40. The sun I saw with blood-red beams beset: (fast was I then from this world declining) mightier she appeared, in many ways, than she was before.

41. The sun I saw, and it seemed to me as if I saw a glorious god: I bowed before her, for the last time, in the world of men.

42. The sun I saw: she beamed forth so that I seemed nothing to know; but Gioll's streams roared from the other side mingled much with blood.

43. The sun I saw, with quivering eyes, appalled and shrinking; for my heart in great measure was dissolved in languor.

44. The sun I saw seldom sadder; I had then almost from the world declined: my tongue was as wood become, and all was cold without me.

45. The sun I saw never after, since that gloomy day; for the mountain-waters closed over me, and I went called from torments.

46. The star of hope, when I was born, fled from my breast away; high it flew, settled nowhere, so that it might find rest.

47. Longer than all was that one night, when stiff on my straw I lay; then becomes manifest the divine word: "Man is the same as earth."

48. The Creator God can it estimate and know, (He who made heaven and earth) how forsaken many go hence, although from kindred parted.

49. Of his works each has the reward: happy is he who does good. Of my wealth bereft, to me was destined a bed strewed with sand.

50. Bodily desires men oftentimes seduce, of them has many a one too much: water of baths was of all things to me most loathsome.

51. In the Norns' seat nine days I sat, thence I was mounted on a horse: there the giantess's sun shone grimly through the dripping clouds of heaven.

52. Without and within, I seemed to traverse all the seven nether worlds: up and down, I sought an easier way, where I might have the readiest paths.

53. Of that is to be told, which I first saw, when I to the worlds of torment came:—scorched birds, which were souls, flew numerous as flies.

54. From the west I saw Von's dragons fly, and Glæval's paths obscure: their wings they shook; wide around me seemed the earth and heaven to burst.

55. The sun's hart I saw from the south coming, he was by two together led: his feet stood on the earth, but his horns reached up to heaven.

56. From the north riding I saw the sons of Nidi, they were seven in all: from full horns, the pure mead they drank from the heaven-god's well.

57. The wind was silent, the waters stopped their course; then I heard a doleful sound: for their husbands false-faced women ground earth for food.

58. Gory stones those dark women turned sorrowfully; bleeding hearts hung out of their breasts, faint with much affliction.

59. Many a man I saw wounded go on those gleed-strewed paths; their faces seemed to me all reddened with reeking blood.

60. Many men I saw to earth gone down, who holy service might not have; heathen stars stood above their heads, painted with deadly characters.

61. I saw those men who much envy harbour at another's fortune; bloody runes were on their breasts graved painfully.

62. I there saw men many not joyful; they were all wandering wild: this he earns, who by this world's vices is infatuated.

63. I saw those men who had in various ways acquired other's property: in shoals they went to Castle-covetous, and burthens bore of lead.

64. I saw those men who many had of life and property bereft: through the breasts of those men passed strong venomous serpents.

65. I saw those men who the holy days would not observe: their hands were on hot stones firmly nailed.

66. I saw those men who from pride valued themselves too highly; their garments ludicrously were in fire enveloped.

67. I saw those men who had many false words of others uttered: Hel's ravens from their heads their eyes miserably tore.

68. All the horrors thou wilt not get to know which Hel's inmates suffer. Pleasant sins end in painful penalties: pains ever follow pleasure.

69. I saw those men who had much given for God's laws; pure lights were above their heads brightly burning.

70. I saw those men who from exalted mind helped the poor to aid: angels, read holy books above their heads.

71. I saw those men who with much fasting had their bodies wasted: God's angels bowed before them: that is the highest joy.

72. I saw those men who had put food into their mothers' mouth: their couches were on the rays of heaven pleasantly placed.

73. Holy virgins had cleanly washed the souls from sin of those men, who for a long time had themselves tormented.

74. Lofty cars I saw towards heaven going; they were on the way to God: men guided them who had been murdered wholly without crime.

75. Almighty Father! greatest Son! holy Spirit of heaven! Thee I pray, who hast us all created; free us all from miseries.

76. Biugvor and lyistvor sit at Herdir's doors, on resounding seat; iron gore falls from their nostrils, which kindles hate among men.

77. Odin's wife rows in earth's ship, eager after pleasures; her sails are reefed late, which on the ropes of desire are hung.

78. Son! I thy father and Solkatla's sons have alone obtained for thee that horn of hart, which from the grave-mound bore the wise Vigdvalin.

79. Here are runes which have engraven Niord's daughters nine, Radvor the eldest, and the youngest Kreppvor, and their seven sisters.

80. How much violence have they perpetrated Svaf and Svaflogi! bloodshed they have excited, and wounds have sucked, after an evil custom.

81. This lay, which I have taught thee, thou shalt before the living sing, the Sun-Song, which will appear in many parts no fiction.

82. Here we part, but again shall meet on the day of men's rejoicing. Oh Lord! unto the dead grant peace, and to the living comfort.

83. Wondrous lore has in dream to thee been sung, but thou hast seen the truth: no man has been so wise created that has before heard the Sun-song.

THE LAY OF VOLUND.

There was a king in Sweden named Nidud: he had two sons and a daughter, whose name was Bodvild. There were three brothers, sons of a king of the Finns, one was called Slagfid, the second Egil, the third Volund. They went on snow-shoes and hunted wild-beasts. They came to Ulfdal, and there made themselves a house, where there is a water called Ulfsiar. Early one morning they found on the border of the lake three females sitting and spinning flax. Near them lay their swan-plumages: they were Valkyriur. Two of them, Hladgud-Svanhvit and Hervor-Alvit, were daughters of King Hlodver; the third was Olrun, a daughter of Kiar of Valland. They took them home with them to their dwelling. Egil had Olrun, Slagfid Svanhvit, and Volund Alvit. They lived there seven years, when they flew away seeking conflicts, and did not return. Egil then went on snow-shoes in search of Olrun, and Slagfid in search of Svanhvit, but Volund remained in Ulfdal. He was a most skilful man, as we learn from old traditions. King Nidud ordered him to be seized, so as it is here related.

1. Maids flew from the south, through the murky wood, Alvit the young, fate to fulfil. On the lake's margin they sat to repose, the southern damsels; precious flax they spun.

2. One of them, of maidens fairest, to his comely breast Egil clasped. Svanhvit was the second, she a swan's plumage bore; but the third, their sister, the white neck clasped of Volund.

3. There they stayed seven winters through; but all the eighth were with longing seized; and in the ninth fate parted them. The maidens yearned for the murky wood, the young Alvit, fate to fulfil.

4. Prom the chase came the ardent hunters, Slagfid and Egil, found their house deserted, went out and in, and looked around. Egil went east after Olrun, and Slagfid west after Svanhvit;

5. But Volund alone remained in Ulfdal. He the red gold set with the hard gem, well fastened all the rings on linden bast, and so awaited his bright consort, if to him she would return.

6. It was told to Nidud, the Niarars' lord, that Volund alone remained in Ulfdal. In the night went men, in studded corslets, their shields glistened in the waning moon.

7. From their saddles they alighted at the house's gable, thence went in through the house. On the bast they saw the rings all drawn, seven hundred, which the warrior owned.

8. And they took them off, and they put them on, all save one, which they bore away. Came then from the chase the ardent hunter, Volund, gliding on the long way.

9. To the fire he went, bear's flesh to roast. Soon blazed the brushwood, and the arid fir, the wind-dried wood, before Volund.

10. On the bearskin sat, his rings counted, the Alfar's companion: one was missing. He thought that Hlodver's daughter had it, the young Alvit, and that she was returned.

11. So long he sat until he slept; and he awoke of joy bereft: on his hands he felt heavy constraints, and round his feet fetters clasped.

12. "Who are the men that on the rings' possessor have laid bonds? and me have bound?"

13. Then cried Nidud, the Niarars' lord: "Whence gottest thou, Volund! Alfars' chief! our gold, in Ulfdal?"

14. "No gold was here in Grani's path, far I thought our land from the hills of Rhine. I mind me that we more treasures possessed, when, a whole family, we were at home.

15. Hladgud and Hervor were of Hlodver born; known was Olrun, Kiar's daughter, she entered into the house, stood on the floor, her voice moderated: Now is he not mirthful, who from the forest comes."

King Nidud gave to his daughter Bodvild the ring which had been taken from the bast in Volund's house; but he himself bore the sword that had belonged to Volund. The queen said:

16. His teeth he shows, when the sword he sees, and Bodvild's ring he recognizes: threatening are his eyes as a glistening serpent's: let be severed his sinews' strength; and set him then in Sævarstad.

This was done; he was hamstrung, and then set on a certain small island near the shore, called Sævarstad. He there forged for the king all kinds of jewellery work. No one was allowed to go to him, except the king. Volund said:

17. "The sword shines in Nidud's belt, which I whetted as I could most skilfully, and tempered, as seemed to me most cunningly. That bright blade forever is taken from me: never shall I see it borne into Volund's smithy.

18. Now Bodvild wears my consort's red-gold rings: for this I have no indemnity." He sat and never slept, and his hammer plied; but much more speedy vengeance devised on Nidud.

19. The two young sons of Nidud ran in at the door to look, in Sævarstad. To the chest they came, for the keys asked; manifest was their grudge, when therein they looked.

20. Many necklaces were there, which to those youths appeared of the red gold to be, and treasures. "Come ye two alone, to-morrow come; that gold shall be given to you.

21. Tell it not to the maidens, nor to the household folk, nor to any one, that ye have been with me." Early called one the other, brother, brother: "Let us go see the rings."

22. To the chest they came, for the keys asked; mani fest was their grudge, when therein they looked. Of those children he the heads cut off, and under the prison's mixen laid their bodies.

23. But their skulls beneath the hair he in silver set, and to Nidud gave; and of their eyes precious stones he formed, which to Nidud's wily wife he sent.

24. But of the teeth of the two breast-ornaments he made, and to Bodvild sent. Then did Bodvild praise the ring: to Volund brought it, when she had broken it: "I dare to no tell it, save alone to thee."

Volund.

25. "I will so repair the fractured gold, that to thy father it shall fairer seem, and to thy mother much more beautiful, and to thyself, in the same degree."

26. He then brought her beer, that he might succeed the better, as on her seat she fell asleep. "Now have I my wrongs avenged, all save one in the wood perpetrated."

27. "I wish," said Volund, "that on my feet I were, of the use of which Nidud's men have deprived me." Laughing Volund rose in air: Bodvild weeping from the isle departed. She mourned her lover's absence, and for her father's wrath.

28. Stood without Nidud's wily wife; then she went in through the hall; but he on the enclosure sat down to rest. "Art thou awake Niarars' lord!"

29. "Ever am I awake, joyless I lie to rest, when I call to mind my children's death: my head is chilled, cold are to me thy counsels. Now with Volund I desire to speak."

30. "Tell me, Volund, Alfars' chief! of my brave boys what is become?"

31. "Oaths shalt thou first to me swear, by board of ship, by rim of shield, by shoulder of steed, by edge of sword, that thou wilt not slay the wife of Volund, nor of my bride cause the death; although a wife I have whom ye know, or offspring within thy court.

32. To the smithy go, which thou hast made, there wilt thou the bellows find with blood besprinkled. The heads I severed of thy boys, and under the prison's mixen laid their bodies.

33. But their skulls beneath the hair I in silver set, and to Nidud gave; and of their eyes precious stones I formed, which to Nidud's wily wife I sent.

34. Of the teeth of the two, breast-ornaments I made, and to Bodvild sent. Now Bodvild goes big with child, the only daughter of you both."

35. "Word didst thou never speak that more afflicted me, or for which I would more severely punish thee. There is no man so tall that he from thy horse can take thee, or so skilful that he can shoot thee down, thence where thou floatest up in the sky."

36. Laughing Volund rose in air, but Nidud sad remained sitting.

37. "Rise up Thakrad, my best of thralls! bid Bodvild, my fair-browed daughter, in bright attire come, with her sire to speak.

38. Is it, Bodvild! true what has been told to me, that thou and Volund in the isle together sat?"

39. "True it is, Nidud! what has been told to thee, that Volund and I in the isle together sat, in an unlucky hour: would it had never been! I could not against him strive, I might not against him prevail."

THE LAY OF HELGI HIORVARD'S SON.

There was a king named Hiorvard, who had four wives, one of whom was named Alfhild, their son was named Hedin; the second was named Særeid, their son was Humlung; the third was named Sinriod, their son was Hymling. King Hiorvard made a vow that he would have to wife the most beautiful woman he knew of, and was told that King Svafnir had a daughter of incomparable beauty, named Sigrlinn. He had a jarl named Idmund, whose son Atli was sent to demand the hand of Sigrlinn for the king. He stayed throughout the winter with King Svafnir. There was a jarl there named Franmar, who was the foster-father of Sigrlinn, and had a daughter named Alof. This jarl advised that the maiden should be refused, and Atli returned home. One day when the jarl's son Atli was standing in a grove, there was a bird sitting in the boughs above him, which had heard that his men called the wives which King Hiorvard had the most beautiful. The bird talked, and Atli listened to what it said. The bird said:

1. Hast thou seen Sigrlinn, Svafnir's daughter, of maidens fairest, in her pleasant home? though fair the wives of Hiorvard seem to men in Glasis-lund.

Atli.

2. With Atli, Idmund's son, sagacious bird! wilt thou further speak?

Bird.

I will if the prince will offer to me, and I may choose what I will from the king's court.

Atli.

3. Choose not Hiorvard nor his sons, nor the fair daughters of that prince, nor the wives which the king has. Let us together bargain; that is the part of friends.

Bird.

4. A fane I will chose, offer steads many, gold-horned cows from the chief's land, if Sigrlinn sleep in his arms, and unconstrained with that prince shall live.

This took place before Atli's journey; but after his return, when the king asked his tidings, he said:

5. Labour we have had, but errand none performed; our horses failed us in the vast fell; we had afterwards a swampy lake to ford; then was denied us Svafnir's daughter with rings adorned, whom we would obtain.

The king commanded them to go a second time, and also went himself. But when they had ascended a fell, and saw in Svavaland the country on fire, and a great reek from the horses of cavalry, the king rode down the fell into the country, and took up his night-quarters by a river. Atli kept watch, and crossed the river, and came to a house, on which sat a great bird to guard it, but was asleep. Atli shot the bird dead with an arrow. In the house he found the king's daughter Sigrlinn, and Alof daughter of Franmar, and brought them both away with him. The jarl Franmar had taken the form of an eagle, and protected them from a hostile army by sorcery. There was a king named Hrodmar, a wooer of Sigrlinn: he had slain the king of Svavaland, and ravaged and burnt the country. Hiorvard obtained Sigrlinn, and Atli Alof. Hiorvard and Sigrlinn had a son tall and comely: he was taciturn and had no fixed name. As he was sitting on a mound he saw nine Valkyriur, one of whom was of most noble aspect. She said:

6. Late wilt thou, Helgi! rings possess, a potent warrior, or Rodulsvellir,—so at morn the eagle sang—if thou art ever silent; although thou, prince! a fierce mood mayest show.

Helgi.

7. What wilt thou let accompany the name of Helgi, maid of aspect bright! since that thou art pleased to give me? Think well over what thou art saying. I will not accept it, unless I have thee also.

Valkyria.

8. Swords I know lying in Sigarsholm, fewer by four than five times ten: one of them is of all the best, of shields the bale, with gold adorned.

9. A ring is on the hilt, courage in the midst, in the point terror for his use who owns it: along the edge a blood-stained serpent lies, and on the guard the serpent casts its tail.

There was a king named Eylimi; Svava was his daughter; she was a Valkyria and rode through air and water. It was she who gave Helgi that name, and afterwards often protected him in battle. Helgi said:

10. Hiorvard! thou art not a king of wholesome counsel, leader of people! renowned though thou mayest be. Thou hast let fire devour the homes of princes, though harm to thee they none have done.

11. But Hrodmar shall of the rings dispose, which our relations have possessed. That chief recks little of his life; he thinks only to obtain the heritage of the dead.

Hiorvard answers, that he will supply Helgi with an army, if he will avenge his mother's father. Helgi thereupon seeks the sword that Svava had indicated to him. Afterwards he and Atli went and slew Hrodmar, and performed many deeds of valour. He killed the Jotun Hati, as he sat on a crag. Helgi and Atli lay with their ships in Hatafiord. Atli kept watch in the first part of the night. Hrimgerd, Hati's daughter, said:

12. Who are the chieftains in Hatafiord? With shields are your ships bedecked; boldly ye bear yourselves, few things ye fear, I ween: tell me how your king is named.

Atli.

13. Helgi is his name; but thou nowhere canst to the chief do harm; iron forts are around the prince's fleet; giantesses may not assail us.

Hrimgerd.

14. How art thou named? most powerful champion! How do men call thee? Thy king confides in thee, since in the ship's fair prow he grants thee place.

Atli.

15. Atli I am named, fierce I shall prove to thee; towards giantesses I am most hostile. The humid prow I have oft occupied, and the night-riders slain.

16. How art thou called? corpse-greedy gigantess! hag! name thy father. Nine rasts shouldst thou be underground, and a forest grow on thy breast.

Hrimgerd.

17. Hrimgerd I am called, Hati was my father called, whom I knew the mightiest Jotun. He many women had from their dwellings taken, until him Helgi slew.

Atli.

18. Thou wast, hag! before the prince's ships, and layest before them in the fiord's mouth. The chieftain's warriors thou wouldst to Ran consign, had a bar not crossed thee.

Hrimgerd.

19. Now, Atli! thou art wrong, methinks thou art dreaming; thy brows thou lettest over thy eyelids fall. My mother lay before the prince's ships; I Hlodvard's sons drowned in the ocean.

20. Thou wouldst neigh, Atli! if thou wert not a gelding. See! Hrimgerd cocks her tail. Thy heart, methinks, Atli! is in thy hinder part, although thy voice is clear.

Atli.

21. I think I shall the stronger prove, if thou desirest to try; and I can step from the port to land. Thou shalt be soundly cudgeled, if I heartily begin, and let thy tail fall, Hrimgerd!

Hrimgerd.

22. Just come on shore, Atli! if in thy strength thou trustest, and let us meet in Varinsvik. A rib-roasting thou shalt get, brave boy! if in my claws thou comest.

Atli.

23. I will not come before the men awake, and o'er the king hold watch. It would not surprise me, if from beneath our ship some hag arose.

Hrimgerd.

24. Keep watch, Atli! and to Hrimgerd pay the blood-fine for Hati's death. If one night she may sleep with the prince, she for the slain will be indemnified.

Helgi.

25. Lodin is named he who shall thee possess, thou to mankind art loathsome. In Tholley dwells that Thurs, that dog-wise Jotun, of all rock-dwellers the worst: he is a fitting man for thee.

Hrimgerd.

26. Helgi would rather have her who last night guarded the port and men, the gold-bright maiden. She methought had strength, she stept from port to land, and so secured your fleet. She was alone the cause that I could not the king's men slay.

Helgi.

27. Hear now, Hrimgerd! If I may indemnify thee, say fully to the king: was it one being only, that saved the prince's ships, or went many together?

Hrimgerd.

28. Three troops of maidens; though one maid foremost rode, bright, with helmed head. Their horses shook themselves, and from their manes there sprang dew into the deep dales, hail on the lofty trees, whence comes fruitfulness to man. To me all that I saw was hateful.

Atli.

29. Look eastward now, Hrimgerd! whether Helgi has not stricken thee with death-bearing words. By land and water the king's fleet is safe, and the chief's men also.

30. It is now day, Hrimgerd! and Atli has thee detained to thy loss of life. A ludicrous haven-mark 'twill, indeed, be, where thou a stone-image standest.

King Helgi was a renowned warrior. He came to King Eylimi and demanded his daughter Svava. Helgi and Svava were united, and loved each other ardently. Svava remained at home with her father, but Helgi was engaged in warfare. Svava was a Valkyria as before. Hedin was at home with his father, King Hiorvard in Norway. Returning home alone from the forest on a Yule-eve, Hedin met a troll-wife riding on a wolf, with serpents for reins, who offered to attend him, but he declined her offer; whereupon she said: "Thou shalt pay for this at the Bragi-cup." In the evening solemn vows were made, and the son-hog was led forth, on which the guests laid their hands, and then made solemn vows at the Bragi-cup. Hedin bound himself by a vow to possess Svava, the beloved of his brother Helgi; but repented it so bitterly that he left home and wandered through wild paths to the southern lands, and there found his brother Helgi. Helgi said:

31. Welcome art thou, Hedin! What new tidings canst thou give from Norway? Why art thou, prince! from the land driven, and alone art come to find us?

Hedin.

32. Of a much greater crime I am guilty. I have chosen a royal daughter, thy bride, at the Bragi-cup.

Helgi.

33. Accuse not thyself; true will prove words at drinking uttered by us both. Me a chieftain has to the strand summoned; within three nights I must be there. 'Tis to me doubtful whether I return; then may well such befall, if it so must be.

Hedin.

34. Thou saidst, Helgi! that Hedin well deserved of thee, and great gifts: It would beseem thee better thy sword to redden, than to grant peace to thy foes.

Helgi so spoke, for he had a foreboding that his death was at hand, and that his fylgiur (attendant spirit) had accosted Hedin, when he saw the woman riding on a wolf. There was a king named Alf, a son of Hrodmar, who had appointed a place of combat with Helgi in Sigar's plain within three days. Then said Helgi:

35. On a wolf rode, at evening twilight, a woman who him offered to attend. She well knew, that the son of Sigrlinn would be slain, on Sigar's plain.

There' was a great conflict, in which Helgi got his death-wound.

36. Helgi sent Sigar riding, after Eylimi's only daughter: he bade her quickly be in readiness, if she would find the king alive.

Sigar.

37. Helgi has me hither sent, with thee, Svava! thyself to speak. Thee, said the king, he fain would see, ere the noble-born breathes forth his last.

Svava.

38. What has befallen Helgi, Hiorvard's son? I am sorely by afflictions stricken. Has the sea him deluded, or the sword wounded? On that man I will harm inflict.

Sigar.

39. This morning fell, at Frekastein, the king who beneath the sun was of all the best. Alf has complete victory, though this time it should not have been!

Helgi.

40. Hail to thee, Svava! Thy love thou must divide: this in this world, methinks, is our last meeting. They say the chieftain's wounds are bleeding. The sword came too near my heart.

41. I pray thee, Svava!—weep not, my wife!—if thou wilt my voice obey, that for Hedin thou a couch prepare, and the young prince in thy arms clasp.

Svava.

42. I had said, in our pleasant home, when for me Helgi rings selected, that I would not gladly, after my king's departure, an unknown prince clasp in my arms.

Hedin.

43. Kiss me, Svava! I will not return, Rogheim to behold, nor Rodulsfioll, before I have avenged Hiorvard's son, who was of kings under the sun the best.

Helgi and Svava were, it is said, born again.

THE FIRST LAY OF HELGI HUNDINGCIDE.

1. It was in times of yore, when the eagles screamed, holy waters fell from the heavenly hills; then to Helgi, the great of soul, Borghild gave birth in Bralund.

2. In the mansion it was night: the Norns came, who should the prince's life determine. They him decreed a prince most famed to be, and of leaders accounted best.

3. With all their might they span the fatal threads, when that burghs should overthrow in Bralund. They stretched out the golden cord, and beneath the middle of the moon's mansion fixed it.

4. East and west they hid the ends, where the prince had lands between; towards the north Neri's sister cast a chain, which she bade last for ever.

5. One thing disquieted the Ylfing's offspring, and the woman who had the child brought forth. Sitting on a lofty tree, on prey intent, a raven to a raven said: "I know something.

6. Stands cased in mail Sigmund's son, one day old: now is our day come. His eyes are piercing as a warrior's; the wolf's friend is he: we shall rejoice!"

7. He to the folk appeared a noble chief to be; among men 'twas said that happy times were come; went the king himself from the din of war, noble garlic to bring to the young prince;

8. Gave him the name of Helgi, and Hringstadir, Solfioll, Snæfioll, and Sigarsvellir, Hringstad, Hatun, and Himinvangar, a sword ornate, to Sinfiotli's brother.

9. Then grew up, in his friends' bosom, the high-born youth, in joyous splendour. He paid and gave gold for deserts; nor spared the chief the blood-stained sword.

10. A short time only the leader let warfare cease. When the prince was fifteen winters old, he caused the fierce Hunding to fall, who long had ruled over lands and people.

11. The sons of Hunding afterwards demanded from Sigmund's son treasure and rings; because they had on the prince to avenge their great loss of wealth, and their father's death.

12. The prince would neither the blood-fine pay, nor for the slain indemnity would give. They might expect, he said, a terrific storm of grey arrows, and Odin's ire.

13. The warriors went to the trysting place of swords, which they had appointed at Logafioll. Broken was Frodi's peace between the foes: Vidrir's hounds went about the isle slaughter-greedy.

14. The leader sat under the Arastein, after he had slain Alf and Eyiolf, Hiorvard and Havard, sons of Hunding: he had destroyed all Geirmimir's race.

15. Then gleamed a ray from Logafioll, and from that ray lightnings issued; then appeared, in the field of air, a helmed band of Valkyriur: their corslets were with blood besprinkled, and from their spears shone beams of light.

16. Forthwith inquired the chieftain bold, from the wolf-congress of the southern Disir, whether they would, with the warriors, that night go home?—then was a clash of arms!

17. One from her horse, Hogni's daughter, stilled the crash of shields, and to the leader said: "We have, I ween, other objects than with princely warriors to drink beer.

18. My father has his daughter promised to the fierce son of Granmar; but I have, Helgi! declared Hodbrodd, the proud prince, like to a cat's son.

19. That chief will come in a few days, unless thou him call to a hostile meeting; or the maiden take from the prince."

Helgi.

20. Fear thou not Isung's slayer; there shall be first a clash of foes, unless I am dead.

21. Thence sent messengers the potent prince through air and over water, succours to demand, and abundance of ocean's gleam to men to offer, and to their sons.

22. "Bid them speedily to the ships to go, and those from Brandey to hold them ready." There the king abode, until thither came warriors in hundreds from Hedinsey.

23. From the strands also, and from Stafnsnes, a naval force went out, with gold adorned. Helgi then of Hiorleif asked: "Hast thou mustered the valiant people?"

24. But the young king the other answered: "Slowly" said he "are counted from Tronuey the long-beaked ships, under the seafarers, which sail without in the Oresund,—

25. Twelve hundred faithful men; though in Hatun there is more than half of the king's host—We are to war inured."

26. Then the steersman threw the ship's tents aside, that the princes' people might awake, and the noble chiefs the dawn might see; and the warriors hauled the sails up to the mast in Varinsfiord.

27. There was a dash of oars, and clash of iron, shield against shield resounded: the vikings rowed; roaring went, under the chieftains the royal fleet far from the land.

28. So might be heard, when together came the tempest's sister and the long keels, as when rock and surge on each other break.

29. Higher still bade Helgi the deep sail be hauled. No port gave shelter to the crews; when Oegir's terrific daughter the chieftains' vessels would o'erwhelm,

30. But from above Sigrun intrepid, saved them and their fleet also; from the hand of Ran powerfully was wrested the royal ship at Gnipalund.

31. At eve they halted in Unavagar; the splendid ships might into port have floated, but the crews, from Svarinshaug, in hostile mood, espied the host.

32. Then demanded the god-born Gudmund: "Who is the chieftain that commands the fleet, and that formidable force brings to our land?"

33. Sinfiotli said, slinging up on the yard a red-hued shield with golden rim;—He at the strait kept watch, and able was to answer, and with nobles words exchange—

34. "Tell it at eve, when you feed your pigs, and your dogs lead to their food, that the Ylfings from the east are come, ready to fight at Gnipalund.

35. Hodbrodd will Helgi find in the fleet's midst, a king hard to make flee, who has oft the eagles sated, while thou wast at the mills, kissing the thrall-wenches.

Gudmund.

36. Little dost thou remember of ancient saws, when of the noble thou falsehoods utterest. Thou hast been eating wolves' dainties, and of thy brother wast the slayer; wounds hast thou often sucked with cold mouth; every where loathed, thou hast crawled in caverns.

Sinfiotli.

37. Thou wast a Valacrone in Varinsey, cunning as a fox, a spreader of lies. Thou saidst thou no man wouldst ever marry, no corsleted warrior, save Sinfiotli.

38. A mischievous crone wast thou, a giantess, a Valkyria, insolent, monstrous, in Alfather's hall. All the Einheriar fought with each other, deceitful woman! for thy sake. Nine wolves we begat in Sagunes; I alone was father of them all.

Gudmund.

39. Father thou wast not of Fenriswolves, older than all, as far as I remember; since by Gnipalund, the Thurs-maidens thee emasculated upon Thorsnes.

40. Thou wast Siggeir's stepson, at home under the benches layest, accustomed to the wolf's howl out in the forests: calamity of every kind came over thee, when thou didst lacerate thy brother's breast. Notorious thou mad'st thyself by thy atrocious works.

Sinfiotli.

41. Thou wast Grani's bride at Bravollr, hadst a golden bit, ready for the course. Many a time have I ridden thee tired, hungry and saddled, through the fells, thou hag!

Gudmund.

42. A graceless lad thou wast thought to be, when Gulnir's goats thou didst milk. Another time thou wast a giantess's daughter, a tattered wretch. Wilt thou a longer chat?

Sinfiotli.

43. I rather would at Frekastein the ravens cram with thy carcase, than thy dogs lead to their meat, or thy hogs feed. May the fiend deal with thee!

Helgi.

44. "Much more seemly, Sinfiotli! would it be for you both in battle to engage, and the eagles gladden, than with useless words to contend, however princes may foster hate.

45. Not good to me appear Granmar's sons, yet 'tis right that princes should speak the truth: they have shown, at Moinsheimar, that they have courage to draw the sword."—

46. Rapidly they their horses made to run, Svipud and Svegiud, to Solheimar, over dewy dales, dark mountain-sides; trembled the sea of mist, where the men went.

47. The king they met at the burgh's gate, to the prince announced the hostile advent. Without stood Hodbrodd with helmet decked: he the speed noticed of his kinsmen. "Why have ye Hniflungs such wrathful countenances?"

48. "Hither to the shore are come rapid keels, towering masts, and long yards, shields many, and smooth-shaven oars, a king's noble host, joyous Ylfings.

49. Fifteen bands are come to land; but there are out at sea, before Gnipalund, seven thousand blue-black ocean-beasts with gold adorned; there is by far their greatest multitude. Now will Helgi not delay the conflict."

Hodbrodd.

50. "Let a bridled steed to the chief assembly run, but Sporvitnir to Sparinsheid; Melnir and Mylnir to Myrkvid; let no man stay behind of those who swords can brandish.

51. Summon to you Hogni, and the sons of Hring, Atli and Yngvi, Alf the old; they will gladly engage in conflict. We will let the Volsungs find resistance."

52. It was a whirlwind, when together came the fallow blades at Frekastein: ever was Helgi Hundingsbani foremost in the host, where men together fought: ardent for battle, disdaining flight; the chieftain had a valiant heart.

53. Then came a maid from heaven, helmed, from above—the clash of arms increased—for the king's protection. Then said Sigrun—well skilled to fly to the host of heroes from Hugin's grove—

54. "Unscathed shalt thou, prince! possess thy people, pillar of Yngvi's race! and life enjoy; thou hast laid low the slow of flight, the chief who caused the dread warrior's death. And thee, O king! well beseem both red-gold rings and a powerful maid: unscathed shalt thou, prince! both enjoy, Hogni's daughter, and Hringstadir, victory and lands: then is conflict ended."

THE SECOND LAY OF HELGI HUNDINGCIDE.

King Sigmund, son of Volsung, had to wife Borghild of Bralund. They named their son Helgi, after Helgi Hiorvard's son. Helgi was fostered by Hagal. There was a powerful king named Hunding, after whom the land was called Hundland. He was a great warrior, and had many sons, who were engaged in warfare. There was enmity, both open and concealed, between King Hunding and King Sigmund, and they slew each other's kinsmen. King Sigmund and his kindred were called Volsungs, and Ylfings. Helgi went forth and secretly explored the court of King Hunding. Heming, Hunding's son, was at home. On departing Helgi met a herdsman, and said:

1. "Say thou to Heming, that Helgi bears in mind who the mailed warrior was, whom the men laid low, when the grey wolf ye had within, and King Hunding thought it was Hamal."

 Hamal was the son of Hagal. King Hunding sent men to Hagal in search of Helgi, and Helgi had no other way to save himself than by taking the clothes of a female slave and going to grind. They sought but did not find him. Then said Blind the Baleful:

2. Sharp are the eyes of Hagal's thrall-wench; of no churlish race is she who at the mill stands. The millstones are split, the receiver flies asunder. Now a hard fate has befallen the warrior, when a prince must barley grind: much more fitting to that hand is the falchion's hilt than a mill-handle.

Hagal answered and said:—

3. No wonder 'tis that the receiver rattles, when a royal damsel the handle turns. She hovered higher than the clouds, and, like the vikings, dared to fight, until Helgi made her captive. She is a sister of Sigar and Hogni; therefore has fierce eyes the Ylfing maid.

Helgi escaped and went on board a ship of war. He slew King Hunding, and was afterwards named Helgi Hundingsbani. He lay with his force in Brunavagar, and carried on "strand-hogg" and ate raw flesh. There was a king named Hogni, whose daughter was Sigrun: she was a Valkyria, and rode through the air and over the sea. She was Svava regenerated. Sigrun rode to Helgi, and said:—

4. What men cause a ship along the coasts to float? where do ye warriors a home possess? what await ye in Brunavagar? whither desire ye to explore a way?

 Helgi.

5. Hamal causes a ship along the coasts to float; we have home in Hlesey; a fair wind we await in Brunavagar; eastward we desire to explore a way.

Sigrun.

6. Where, O prince! hast thou wakened war, or fed the birds of conflict's sisters? Why is thy corslet sprinkled with blood? Why beneath the helm eat ye raw flesh?

Helgi.

99

7. It was the Ylfings' son's last achievement,—if thou desirest to know—west of the ocean, that I took bears in Bragalund, and the eagles' race with our weapons sated. Now, maiden! I have said what the reasons were, why at sea we little cooked meat ate.

Sigrun.

8. To a battle thou alludest. Before Helgi has King Hunding been doomed to fall. In conflict ye have engaged, when your kindred ye avenged, and stained with blood the falchion's edge.

Helgi.

9. Why dost thou suppose, sagacious maiden! that it was they, who their kin avenged? Many a warrior's bold sons there are, and hostile to our kindred.

Sigrun.

10. I was not far, leader of people! eager, at many a chieftain's end: yet crafty I account Sigmund's son, when in val-runes the slaughter he announces.

11. A while ago I saw thee commanding the warships, when thou hadst station on the bloody prow, and the cold sea waves were playing. Now, prince! thou wilt from me conceal it, but Hogni's daughter recognizes thee.

Granmar was the name of a powerful prince who dwelt at Svarinshaug. He had many sons: one was called Hodbrodd, the second Gudmund, the third Starkadr. Hodbrodd was at the assembly of kings, and there betrothed himself to Sigrun, the daughter of Hogni. But when she was informed of it, she rode with the Valkyriur through the air and over the sea in quest of Helgi. Helgi was at that time at Logafioll, warring against the sons of Hunding, where he slew Alf and Eyiolf, Hiorvard and Hervard. Being over-fatigued with the conflict, he was sitting under the Arastein, where Sigrun found him, and running to him, threw her arms around his neck, and, kissing him, told him her errand so as it related in the first Volsungakvida.

12. Sigrun sought the joyous prince, Helgi's hand she forthwith grasped, kissed and addressed the helm-decked king.

13. Then was the chieftain's mind to the lady turned. She declared that she had loved, with her whole heart, Sigmund's son, before she had seen him.

14. "To Hodbrodd I was in th' assembly betrothed, but I another prince would have: yet, chieftain! I foresee my kindred's wrath: I have my father's promise broken."

15. Hogni's daughter spoke not at variance with her heart: she said that Helgi's affection she must possess.

Helgi.

16. Care thou not for Hogni's wrath, nor for the evil mind of thy kin. Thou shalt, young maiden! live with me: of a good race thou art, as I perceive.

Helgi then collected a large fleet and proceeded to Frekastein, and at sea experienced a perilous storm. Lightnings came over them, and the flashes entered the ships. They saw that nine Valkyriur were riding in the air, and recognized Sigrun among them. The storm then abated and they reached land in safety. The sons of Granmar were sitting on a hill as the ships were sailing towards the land. Gudmund leapt on a horse, and rode to explore on the hill by the haven. The Volsungs then lowered their sails, and Gudmund spoke as is before written in the Helgakvida:—

"Who is the leader that commands the fleet, and an appalling host leads to our land?"

This said Gudmund, Granmar's son:

17. Who is the warrior that commands the ships, and lets his golden banner wave o'er his prow? No peace seems to me in that ship's front; it casts a warlike glow around the vikings.

Sinfiotli, Sigmund's son, answered:

18. Here may Hodbrodd Helgi learn to know, the hard of flight, in the fleet's midst: he the possession holds of thy race; he the fishes' heritage has to him subjected.

Gudmund.

19. Therefore ought we first, at Frekastein, to settle together, and decide our quarrels! Hodbrodd! 'tis time vengeance to take, if an inferior lot we long have borne.

Sinfiotli.

20. Rather shalt thou, Gudmund! tend goats, and steep mountain-tops shalt climb, have in thy hand a hazel staff, that will better please thee than judgments of the sword.

Gudmund rode home with intelligence of the hostile armament; whereupon the sons of Granmar collected a host, and many kings came thither. Among them were Hogni, the father of Sigrun, with his sons, Bragi and Dag. There was a great battle, and all the sons of Hogni, and all their chiefs were slain, except Dag, who obtained peace, and swore oaths to the Volsungs. Sigrun, going among the slain, found Hodbrodd at the point of death. She said:

23. Not will Sigrun of Sefafioll, King Hodbrodd! sink in thy arms: thy life is departed. Oft the axe's blade the head approaches of Granmar's sons.

She then met Helgi, and was overjoyed. He said:

24. Not to thee, all-wise maiden! are all things granted, though, I say, in somewhat are the Norns to blame. This morn have fallen at Frekastein Bragi and Hogni: I was their slayer.

25. But at Styrkleifar King Starkadr, and at Hlebiorg the son of Hrollaug. That prince I saw of all most fierce, whose trunk yet fought when the head was far.

26. On the earth lie the greater number of thy kinsmen, to corpses turned. Thou hast not fought the battle, yet 'twas decreed, that thou, potent maiden! shouldst cause the strife.

Sigrun then wept. Helgi said:

27. Sigrun! console thyself; a Hild thou hast been to us. Kings cannot conquer fate: gladly would I have them living who are departed, if I might clasp thee to my breast.

Helgi obtained Sigrun, and they had sons. Helgi lived not to be old. Dag, the son of Hogni, sacrificed to Odin, for vengeance for his father. Odin lent Dag his spear. Dag met with his relation Helgi in a place called Fioturlund, and pierced him through with his spear. Helgi fell there, but Dag rode to the mountains and told Sigrun what had taken place.

28. Loath am I, sister! sad news to tell thee; for unwillingly I have my sister caused to weep. This morning fell, in Fioturlund, the prince who was on earth the best, and on the necks of warriors stood.

Sigrun.

29. Thee shall the oaths all gnaw, which to Helgi thou didst swear, at the limpid Leiptr's water, and at the cold dank wave-washed rock.

30. May the ship not move forward, which under thee should move, although the wished-for wind behind thee blow. May the horse not run, which under thee should run, although from enemies thou hast to flee!

31. May the sword not bite which thou drawest, unless it sing round thy own head. Then would Helgi's death be on thee avenged, if a wolf thou wert, out in the woods, of all good bereft, and every joy, have no sustenance, unless on corpses thou shouldst spring.

Dag.

32. Sister! thou ravest, and hast lost thy wits, when on thy brother thou callest down such miseries. Odin alone is cause of all the evil; for between relatives he brought the runes of strife.

33. Thy brother offers thee rings of red gold, all Vandilsve and Vigdalir: have half the land, thy grief to compensate, woman ring-adorned! thou and thy sons.

Sigrun.

34. So happy I shall not sit at Sefafioll, neither at morn nor night, as to feel joy in life, if o'er the people plays not the prince's beam of light; if his war-steed runs not under the chieftain hither, to the gold bit accustomed; if in the king I cannot rejoice.

35. So had Helgi struck with fear all his foes and their kindred, as before the wolf the goats run frantic from the fell, of terror full.

36. So himself Helgi among warriors bore, as the towering ash is among thorns, or as the fawn, moistened with dew, that more proudly stalks than all the other beasts, and its horns glisten against the sky.

A mound was raised for Helgi; but when he came to Valhall, Odin offered him the rule over all jointly with himself. Helgi said:

37. Thou, Hunding! shalt for every man a foot-bath get, and fire kindle; shalt bind the dogs, to the horses look, to the swine give wash, ere to sleep thou goest.

A female slave passing at evening by Helgi's mound, saw him riding towards it with many men:

38. Is it a delusion which methinks I see, or the powers' dissolution, that ye, dead men, ride, and your horses with spurs urge on, or to warriors is a home journey granted?

Helgi.

39. 'Tis no delusion which thou thinkst to see, nor of mankind the end, although thou seest us, although our horses we with spurs urge on, nor to warriors is a home-journey granted.

The slave went home and said to Sigrun:

40. Sigrun! go forth from Sefafioll, if the people's chief thou desirest to meet. The mound is opened, Helgi is come, his wounds still bleed; the prince prayed thee that thou wouldst still the trickling blood.

Sigrun entered the mound to Helgi and said:

41. Now am I as glad, at our meeting, as the voracious hawks of Odin, when they of slaughter know; of warm prey, or, dewy-feathered, see the peep of day.

43. I will kiss my lifeless king, ere thou thy bloody corslet layest aside. Thy hair is, Helgi! tumid with sweat of death; my prince is all bathed in slaughter-dew; cold, clammy are the hands of Hogni's son. How shall I, prince! for this make thee amends?

Helgi.

43. Thou art alone the cause, Sigrun of Sefafioll! that Helgi is with sorrow's dew suffused. Thou weepest, gold-adorned! cruel tears, sun-bright daughter of the south! ere to sleep thou goest; each one falls bloody on the prince's breast, wet, cold, and piercing, with sorrow big.

44. We shall surely drink delicious draughts, though we have lost life and lands. No one shall a song of mourning sing, though on my breast he wounds behold. Now are women in the mound enclosed, daughters of kings, with us the dead.

Sigrun prepares a bed in the mound.

35. Here, Helgi! have I for thee a peaceful couch prepared, for the Ylfings' son. On thy breast I will, chieftain! repose, as in my hero's lifetime I was wont.

Helgi.

46. Nothing I now declare unlooked for, at Sefafioll, late or early, since in a corpse's arms thou sleepest, Hogni's fair daughter! in a mound, and thou art living, daughter of kings!

47. Time 'tis for me to ride on the reddening ways: let the pale horse tread the aerial path. I towards the west must go over Vindhialm's bridge, ere Salgofnir awakens heroes.

Helgi and his attendants rode their way, but Sigrun and hers proceeded to their habitation. The following evening Sigrun ordered her serving-maid to hold watch at the mound; but at nightfall, when Sigrun came thither, she said:

48. Now would he come, if he to come intended, Sigmund's son, from Odin's halls. I think the hope lessens of the king's coming, since on the ash's boughs the eagles sit, and all the folk to the dreams' tryst are hastening.

Serving-maid.

49. Be not so rash alone to go, daughter of heroes! to the house of draugs: more powerful are, in the night-season, all dead warriors, than in the light of day.

Sigrun's life was shortened by grief and mourning. It was a belief in ancient times that men were regenerated, but that is now regarded as an old crone's fancy. Helgi and Sigrun are said to have been regenerated. He was then called Helgi Haddingiaskadi, and she Kara Halfdan's daughter, as it is said in the songs of Kara; and she also was a Valkyria.

SINFIOTLI'S END.

Sigmund Volsung's son was a king in Frankland. Sinfiotli was the eldest of his sons, the second was Helgi, the third Hamund. Borghild, Sigmund's wife, had a brother named Gunnar; but Sinfiotli her stepson and Gunnar both courted one woman, on which account Sinfiotli slew Gunnar. When he came home, Borghild bade him go away, but Sigmund offered the blood-fine, which it was incumbent on her to accept. At the funeral feast Borghild presented the beer: she took a large horn full of poison, and offered it to Sinfiotli; who, when he looked into the horn, and saw that there was poison in it, said to Sigmund: "the drink ferments!" Sigmund took the horn and drank up the contents. It is said that Sigmund was so strong that no poison could hurt him, either outwardly or inwardly; but that all his sons could endure poison outwardly. Borghild bore another horn to Sinfiotli, and prayed him to drink, when all took place as before. Yet a third time she offered him the horn, using reproachful words on his refusing to drink. He said as before to Sigmund, but the latter answered: "Let it pass through thy lips, my son." Sinfiotli drank and instantly died. Sigmund bore him a long way in his arms, and came to a long and narrow firth, where there was a little vessel and one man in it. He offered Sigmund to convey him over the firth; but when Sigmund had borne the corpse into the vessel, the boat was full-laden. The man then said that Sigmund should go before through the firth. He then pushed off his boat and instantly departed.

King Sigmund sojourned long in Denmark, in Borghild's kingdom, after having espoused her. He then went south to Frankland, to the kingdom he there possessed. There he married Hiordis, the daughter of Eylimi. Sigurd was their son. King Sigmund fell in a battle with the sons of Hunding. Hiordis was afterwards married to Alf, son of King Hialprek, with whom Sigurd grew up in childhood. Sigmund and his sons exceeded all other men in strength, and stature, and courage, and all accomplishments, though Sigurd was foremost of all; and in old traditions he is mentioned as excelling all men, and as the most renowned of warlike kings.

THE FIRST LAY OF SIGURD FAFNICIDE, OR GRIPIR'S PROPHECY.

Gripir was the name of the son of Eylimi, the brother of Hiordis. He ruled over lands, and was of all men wisest and prescient of the future. Sigurd rode alone, and came to Gripir's dwelling. Sigurd was of a distinguished figure. He found a man to address outside the hall, whose name was Geitir. Sigurd applied to him, and asked:

1. Who here inhabits, in these towers? what nation's king do people name him?

Geitir.

Gripir is named the chief of men, he who rules a firm realm and people.

Sigurd.

2. Is the wise king of the land at home? Will the chief with me come and converse? With him needs speech an unknown man: I desire speedily Gripir to see.

Geitir.

3. The glad king will of Geitir ask, who the man is that demands speech of Gripir.

Sigurd.

Sigurd I am named, born of Sigmund, and Hiordis is the chieftain's mother.

4. Then went Geitir, Gripir to inform: "Here is a man without, a stranger, come; of aspect he is most distinguished. He desires, king! with thee to speak."

5. Goes from the hall the lord of men, and the stranger prince kindly greets: "Welcome, Sigurd! better had it been earlier: but do thou, Geitir! take charge of Grani."

6. They began to talk, and much to tell, when the sagacious men together met. "Tell me, if thou knowest, my mother's brother! how will Sigurd's life fall out?"

Gripir.

7. Thou wilt foremost be of men beneath the sun, exalted high above every king; liberal of gold, but of flight sparing, of aspect comely, and wise of words.

Sigurd.

8. Say thou, sage king! more than I ask, thou wise one, to Sigurd, if thou thinkst to see it: what will first happen for my advancement, when from thy dwelling I shall have departed?

Gripir.

9. First wilt thou, prince! avenge thy father, and for the wrongs of Eylimi wilt retaliate; thou wilt the cruel sons of Hunding boldly lay low; thou wilt have victory

Sigurd.

10. Say, noble king! kinsman mine! with all forethought, as we hold friendly converse; seest thou of Sigurd those bold achievements, that will highest soar under heaven's regions?"

Gripir.

11. Thou alone wilt slay that glistening serpent, which greedy lies on Gnitaheid; thou shalt of both the slayer be, Regin and Fafnir. Gripir tells truly.

Sigurd.

12. Riches will abound, if I so bring conflict among men, as thou for certain sayest. Apply thy mind, and at length say what will yet my life befall.

Gripir.

13. Thou wilt find Fafnir's lair, and thence wilt take splendid riches, with gold wilt load Grani's back. Thou wilt to Giuki ride, the war-famed prince.

Sigurd.

14. Yet must thou, prince! in friendly speech, foresighted king! more relate. I shall be Giuki's guest, and I shall thence depart: what will next my life befall?

Gripir.

15. A king's daughter will on a mountain sleep, fair, in corslet cased, after Helgi's death. Thou wilt strike with a keen sword, wilt the corslet sever with Fafnir's bane.

Sigurd.

16. The corslet is ript open, the maid begins to speak. When awakened from her sleep, on what will she chiefly with Sigurd converse hold, which to the prince's benefit may tend?

Gripir.

17. She to thee, powerful one! runes will teach, all those which men ought to know; and in every man's tongue to speak, and medicines for healing. May good await thee, king!

Sigurd.

18. Now that is past, the knowledge is acquired, and I am ready thence away to ride. Apply thy mind, and at length say what more will my life befall.

Gripir.

19. Thou wilt find Heimir's dwellings, and the glad guest wilt be of that great king. Vanished is, Sigurd! that which I foresaw; no further mayest thou Gripir question.

Sigurd.

20. Now bring me grief the words thou speakest; for thou foreseest, king! much further; thou knowest of too great calamity to Sigurd; therefore thou, Gripir! wilt not utter it.

Gripir.

21. Of thy life the early portion lay before me clearest to contemplate. I am not truly accounted sage, nor of the future prescient: that which I knew is gone.

Sigurd.

22. No man I know on the earth's surface, who greater prescience has than thou, Gripir! Thou mayest not conceal it, unhappy though it be, or if ill betide my life.

Gripir.

23. Not with vices will thy life be sullied; let that, noble prince! in thy mind be borne; for while mankind exists, thy name, director of the spear-storm! will be supreme.

Sigurd.

24. The worst seems to me, that Sigurd is compelled from the king to part in such uncertainty. Show me the way—all is decreed before—great chieftain! if thou wilt, my mother's brother!

Gripir.

25. To Sigurd I will now openly tell, since the chieftain me thereto compels: thou wilt surely find that I lie not. A certain day is for thy death decreed.

Sigurd.

26. I would not importune the mighty prince, but rather Gripir's good counsel have. Now I fain would know, though grateful it may not be, what prospect Sigurd has lying before him.

Gripir.

27. There is with Heimir a maiden fair of form, she is by men Brynhild named, daughter of Budli; but the dear king Heimir nurtures the hard-souled damsel.

Sigurd.

28. What is it to me, although the maiden be of aspect fair? nurtured with Heimir? That thou, Gripir! must fully declare; for thou foreseest my whole destiny.

Gripir.

29. She will thee bereave of almost every joy, the fair-faced foster-child of Heimir. Thou wilt not sleep, nor of affairs discourse, nor men regard; only this maiden thou wilt see.

Sigurd.

30. What remedy for Sigurd will be applied; tell me that, Gripir! if it seem good to thee. Shall I obtain the damsel? with dowry purchase the lovely royal daughter?

Gripir.

31. Ye will each swear unnumbered oaths, solemnly binding, but few will keep. Hast thou been Giuki's guest one night, thou wilt have forgotten the fair ward of Heimir.

Sigurd.

32. How is that, Gripir! explain it to me: seest thou such fickleness in the king's mind, that with that maiden I shall my engagement break, whom with my whole heart I thought to love?

Gripir.

33. Prince! thou wilt be snared in another's wiles, thou wilt pay the penalty of Grimhild's craft; the bright-haired maiden, her daughter, she to thee will offer. This snare for the king she lays.

Sigurd.

34. Shall I then with Gunnar form relationship, and with Gudrun join in wedlock? Well wived then the king would be, if the pangs of perjury caused me no pain.

Gripir.

35. Thee will Grimhild wholly beguile; she will implore thee Brynhild to demand for the hand of Gunnar, king of Goths: the journey thou wilt forthwith promise to the king's mother.

Sigurd.

36. Evils are at hand, I can that perceive; Sigurd's wits will have wholly perished, if I shall demand for another's hand, a noble maiden whom I well love.

Gripir.

37. All of you will swear mutual oaths, Gunnar, and Hogni, and thou the third; and ye will forms exchange, when on the way ye are, Gunnar and thou: Gripir lies not.

Sigurd.

38. To what end is that? why shall we exchange forms and manners, when on the way we are? Another fraud will surely follow this, altogether horrible. But say on, Gripir!

Gripir.

39. Thou wilt have Gunnar's semblance, and his manners, thy own eloquence, and great sagacity: there thou wilt betroth the high-minded ward of Heimir: no one can that prevent.

Sigurd.

40. To me that seems worst, that among men I shall be a false traitor called, if such take place. I would not deception practise on a royal maid the most excellent I know.

Gripir.

41. Thou wilt repose, leader of hosts! pure with the maiden, as she thy mother were; therefore exalted, lord of men! while the world endures thy name will be.

42. The nuptials will of both be solemnized, of Sigurd and of Gunnar, in Giuki's halls; then will ye forms exchange, when ye home return; yet to himself will have each his own senses.

Sigurd.

43. Will then Gunnar, chief among men, the noble woman wed? Tell me that, Gripir! although three nights by me the chieftain's bride glad of heart has slept? The like has no example.

44. How for happiness shall hereafter be this affinity? Tell me that, Gripir! Will the alliance for Gunnar's solace henceforth prove, or even for mine?

Gripir.

45. Thou wilt the oaths remember, and must silence keep, and let Gudrun enjoy a happy union. Brynhild nathless will herself think an ill-married woman. She will wiles devise to avenge herself.

Sigurd.

46. What atonement will that woman take, for the frauds we shall have practised on her? From me the maiden has oaths sworn, but never kept, and but little joy.

Gripir.

47. She to Gunnar will plainly declare, that thou didst not well the oaths observe, when the noble king, Giuki's heir, with his whole soul, in thee confided.

Sigurd.

48. What will then follow? let me know that. Will that tale appear as true, or that the noble woman falsely accuses me, and herself also. Tell me that, Gripir!

Gripir.

49. From spite towards thee, and from o'erwhelmmg grief, the powerful dame will not most wisely act. To the noble woman do thou no further harm, though thou the royal bride with guiles hast circumvented.

Sigurd.

50. Will the prudent Gunnar, Guthorm, and Hogni, at her instigation, then proceed? Will Giuki's sons on their relative redden their swords? Tell me further, Gripir!

Gripir.

51. Then will Gudrun be furious at heart, when her brothers shall on thy death resolve. In nothing then will that wise woman take delight. Such is Grimhild's work.

52. In this thou shalt find comfort, leader of hosts! This fortune is allotted to the hero's life: a more renowned man on earth shall never be, under the sun's abode, than thou wilt be accounted.

Sigurd.

53. Now part we, now farewell! Fate may not be withstood. Now hast thou, Gripir! done as I prayed thee: thou wouldst have fain a happier end foretold me of my life's days, hadst thou been able.

THE SECOND LAY OF SIGURD FAFNICIDE.

Sigurd went to Hialprek's stud and chose himself a horse, which was afterwards named Grani. Regin, Hreidmar's son, was then come to Hialprek; he was the most skilful of men, and a dwarf in stature; he was wise, cruel, and versed in magic. Regin undertook the rearing and instruction of Sigurd, and bore him great affection. He informed Sigurd of his parentage, and how it befell that Odin, and Hoenir, and Loki came to Andvarafors (the waterfall of Andvari). In the fall there was an abundance of fish. There was a dwarf named Andvari, who had long lived in the fall in the likeness of a pike, and in which he supplied himself with food. "Our brother," continued Regin, "was named Otr, who often went into the fall in the likeness of an otter. He had caught a salmon, and was sitting on the bank of the river with his eyes shut eating it, when Loki killed him with a stone. The Æsir thought themselves very lucky, and stripped off the otter's skin. That same evening they sought entertainment with Hreidmar, and showed their prize. Thereupon we laid hands on them, and imposed on them, as the redemption of their lives, that they should fill the otter's skin with gold, and cover it over with red gold. They thereupon sent Loki to procure gold. He went to Ran, and obtained her net, and thence proceeded to Andvarafors, and cast the net before a pike, which leapt into the net. Whereupon Loki said:

1. What fish is this, that in the river swims, and cannot from harm itself protect? Redeem thy life from Hel, and find me the water's flame. *The Pike.*

2. Andvari I am named, Oin was my father named; many a cataract have I passed. A luckless Norn in times of old decreed, that in the water I should wade.

Loki.

3. Tell me, Andvari! if thou wilt enjoy life in the halls of men, what retribution get the sons of mortals, if with foul words they assail each other.

Andvari.

4. Cruel retribution get the sons of mortals, who in Vadgelmir wade: for the false words they have against others uttered, the punishments too long endure.

Loki viewed all the gold that Andvari owned; but when he had produced the gold, he retained a single ring, which Loki also took from him. The dwarf went into his stone and said:

5. That gold which the dwarf possessed, shall to two brothers be cause of death, and to eight princes, of dissension. From my wealth no one shall good derive.

The Æsir produced the gold to Hreidmar, and with it crammed the otter's skin full, and set it up on the feet. They then had to heap up the gold and cover it; but when that was done, Hreidmar, stepping forward, observed a whisker, and required it to be covered; whereupon Odin drew forth the ring "Andvaranaut," and covered the hair. Loki said:

6. There is gold for thee, and thou hast a great redemption for my life. For thy son no blessing is decreed; of both it shall prove the bane.

Hreidmar.

7. Gifts thou hast given, friendly gifts thou hast given not; with a kind heart thou hast not given. Of your lives ye should have been deprived, had I foreknown that peril.

8. But that is worse, what I seem to know,—a strife of kinsmen for a woman. Princes yet unborn I think them to be, for whose hate that gold is destined.

9. The red gold, I trust, I shall possess while I am living: of thy threats I entertain no fear; so take yourselves hence home.

Fafnir and Regin demanded of Hreidmar their share of the blood-fine for their slain brother Otr, which he refused, and Fafnir stabbed his father with a sword while sleeping. Hreidmar called out to his daughters:

10. Lyngheid and Lofnheid! Know my life is departing. To many things need compels. *Lyngheid.*

Few sisters will, although they lose a father, avenge a brother's crime.

Hreidmar.

11. Then bring forth a daughter, wolf-hearted fury! If by a chief thou have not a son. Get for the maid a spouse, in thy great need; then will her son thy wrong avenge.

Hreidmar then died, and Fafnir took all the gold. Regin then requested to have his share of the patrimony, but met with a refusal from Fafnir. Regin thereupon sought counsel of his sister Lyngheid, how he might obtain his patrimony. She said:

12. Thou of thy brother shalt mildly demand thy patrimony and a better spirit. It is not seemly, that with the sword thou shouldst demand thy property of Fafnir.

The foregoing is what Regin related to Sigurd. One day, when he came to Regin's dwelling, he was kindly received, and Regin said:

13. Hither is come the son of Sigmund to our Hall, that man of energy: courage he has greater than I aged man: now of a conflict have I hope from the fierce wolf.

14. I will nurture the bold-hearted prince: now Yngvi's kinsman is to us come; he will be a king under the sun most powerful; over all lands will his destinies resound.

Sigurd was thence forward constantly with Regin, who related to him how Fafnir lay on Gnitaheid in the likeness of a serpent. He had an "Oegis-helm," at which all living beings were terror-stricken. Regin forged a sword for Sigurd, that was named Gram, and was so sharp that immersing it in the Rhine, he let a piece of wool down the stream, when it clove the fleece asunder as water. With that sword Sigurd clove in two Regin's anvil. After that Regin instigated Sigurd to slay Fafnir. He said:

15. Loud will laugh Hunding's sons, they who Eylimi of life deprived, if the prince is more desirous to seek red rings, than to avenge his father.

King Hialprek collected a fleet to enable Sigurd to avenge his father. They encountered a great storm, and were driven past a certain promontory. A man was standing on the cliff who said:

16. Who ride yonder, on Rævils horses, the towering billows, the roaring main: the sail-steeds are with sweat bedewed, the wave-coursers will not the wind withstand.

Regin.

17. Here am I and Sigurd in sea-trees; a fair wind is given us for death itself: higher than our prows the steep waves dash, the rolling horses plunge. Who is it that inquires?

Hnikar.

18. They called me Hnikar, when I Hugin gladdened, young Volsung! and battles fought. Now they mayest call me the ancient of the rock, Feng, or Fiolnir.—I desire a passage.

They turn to the land, the old man goes on board, and the storm abates. Sigurd said:

19. Tell me, Hnikar! since thou knowest the omens both of gods and men, which omens are the best—if to fight 'tis needful—at the swing of glaves?

Hnikar.

20. Good omens there are many, if men but knew them, at the swing of glaves, a faithful fellowship, I think, is the dark raven's, with the sworded warrior.

21. The second is, if, when thou art gone out, and about to depart, thou seest two renown-seeking men standing in the fore-court.

22. The third omen is, if wolves thou hearest howl under the ash-boughs, it will victory to thee announce over helmed warriors, if thou seest them go before thee.

23. No man should fight against the moon's late-shining sister. They have victory, who can see keenly at the play of swords, or to form the wedge-array.

24. Most perilous it is, if with thy foot thou strikest, when thou to battle goest. Wily Disir stand on either side of thee, and wish to see thee wounded.

25. Combed and washed let every brave man be, and at morning fed; for 'tis uncertain whither he at eve may come. 'Tis bad to succumb to fate.

Sigurd fought a great battle with Lyngvi, Hunding's son, and his brothers, in which Lyngvi and his three brothers fell. After the battle Regin said:

26. Now is the bloody eagle, with the trenchant blade, graven on the back of Sigmund's slayer. No son of king, who the earth reddens, and the raven gladdens, is more excellent.

Sigurd returned home to Hialprek, when Regin instigated him to slay Fafnir.

THE LAY OF FAFNIR.

Sigurd and Regin went up to Gnitaheid, and there found Fafnir's slot, or track, along which he crawled to the water. There on the way Sigurd made a large pit, and went down into it. When Fafnir crawled from the gold he blew forth venom, but it flew over Sigurd's head. When Fafnir crept over the pit, Sigurd with his sword pierced him to the heart. Fafnir shook himself, and beat with his head and tail. Sigurd leapt from the pit, and each looked at the other. Fafnir said:

1. Young fellow! young fellow! by what fellow art thou begot? of what people are thou the son? that thou in Fafnir reddenst thy glittering falchion? Thy sword has pierced my heart.

Sigurd concealed his name, because it was the belief in those times, that the words of dying persons were of great power, if they cursed an enemy by his name.

Sigurd.

2. Gofugt-dyr I am called, but I have wandered a motherless child; nor have I a father like the sons of men: alone I wander.

Fafnir.

3. If thou hast no father like the sons of men, by what wonder art thou begotten?

Sigurd.

4. My race, I tell thee, is to thee unknown, and my self also. Sigmund was my father named, my name is Sigurd, who with weapon have assailed thee.

Fafnir.

5. Who has incited thee? why hast thou suffered thyself to be incited to take my life? youth of the sparkling eyes! Thou hadst a cruel father— * * * *

Sigurd.

6. My heart incited me, my hands gave me aid, and my keen sword. Rarely a man is bold, when of mature age, if in childhood he was faint-hearted.

Fafnir.

7. I know if thou hadst chanced to grow in the lap of friends, they would have seen thee fierce in fight. Now thou art a captive, taken in war, and, 'tis said, slaves ever tremble.

Sigurd.

8. Why Fafnir! dost thou upbraid me that I am far from my paternal home? I am not a captive, although in war I was taken: thou hast found that I am free.

Fafnir.

9. Thou wilt account only as angry words all I to thee shall say, but I will say the truth. The jingling gold, and the gleed-red treasure, those rings, shall be thy bane.

Sigurd.

10. Treasure at command every one desires, ever till that one day; for at some time each mortal shall hence to Hel depart.

Fafnir.

11. The Norns' decree thou wilt hold in contempt as from a witless wight: In water thou shalt be drowned, if in wind thou rowest. All things bring peril to the fated.

Sigurd.

12. Tell me, Fafnir! as thou art wise declared, and many things to know: who those Norns are, who help in need, and from babes loose the mothers.

Fafnir.

13. Very diversely born I take those Norns to be: they have no common race. Some are of Æsir-race, some of Alfar-race, some are Dvalin's daughters.

Sigurd.

14. Tell me, Fafnir! as thou art wise declared, and many things to know, how that holm is called, where Surt and the Æsir will sword-liquor together mingle?

Fafnir.

15. Oskopnir it is called; there shall the gods with lances play; Bifrost shall be broken, when they go forth, and their steeds in the river swim.

16. An Oegis-helm I bore among the sons of men, while I o'er the treasures lay; stronger than all I thought myself to be; stronger I found not many!

Sigurd.

17. An Oegis-helm is no protection, where men impelled by anger fight: soon he finds, who among many comes, that no one is alone the boldest.

Fafnir.

18. Venom I blew forth, when on my father's great heritage I lay.

Sigurd.

19. Thou, glistening serpent! didst a great belching make, and wast so hard of heart. Fierceness so much the greater have the sons of men, when they possess that helm.

Fafnir.

20. Sigurd! I now counsel thee, do thou take my counsel; and hence ride home. The jingling gold, and the gleed-red treasure, those rings, shall be thy bane.

Sigurd.

21. Counsel regarding thee is taken, and I to the gold will ride, on the heath that lies. But lie thou, Fafnir! in the pangs of death, until Hel have thee!

Fafnir.

22. Regin betrayed me, he will thee betray, he of us both will be the bane. Fafnir must, I trow, let forth his life: thine was the greater might!

Regin had gone away while Sigurd slew Fafnir, but came back as Sigurd was wiping the blood from his sword. He said:

23. Hail to thee now, Sigurd! Now hast thou victory won and Fafnir slain: of all the men who tread the earth, thou art, I say, the bravest born.

Sigurd.

24. Uncertain 'tis to know, when we all come to gether, sons of victorious heroes, which is the bravest born. Many a one is bold, who sword has never broken in another's breast.

Regin.

25. Glad are thou now, Sigurd! and in thy gain rejoicing, while Gram, in the grass thou driest. My brother thou to death hast wounded, yet in some degree was I the cause.

Sigurd.

26. Thou didst me counsel, that I should ride o'er high fells hither. Treasure and life had still possess'd that glistening serpent, hadst thou my anger not excited.

Regin then approached Fafnir and cut out his heart with a sword named Ridill, and afterwards drank blood from his wound. He said:

27. Sit now, Sigurd!—but I must go to sleep—and Fafnir's heart hold to the fire. Of this refection I would fain partake, after that drink of blood.

Sigurd.

28. Thou wentst far off, while I in Fafnir my keen sword reddened. With my strength I strove against the serpent's might, while in the ling thou layest.

Regin.

29. Long hadst thou allowed in the ling to lie that Jotun old, hadst thou the sword not used that I forged for thee, thy keen-edged glave.

Sigurd.

30. Valour is better than might of sword, when foes embittered fight; for a brave man I have ever seen gain victory with a dull sword.

31. For the brave 'tis better than for the timid to join in the game of war; for the joyous it is better than for the sad, let come whatever may.

Sigurd took Fafnir's heart and roasted it on a stick. When he thought it roasted enough, and the blood frothed from it, he touched it with his finger, to try whether it were quite done. He burnt his finger and put it in his mouth; and when Fafnir's heart's blood touched his tongue he understood the language of birds. He heard the eagles chattering among the branches. One eagle said:

38. There sits Sigurd sprinkled with blood; Fafnir's heart at the fire he roasts. Wise methinks were the ring-dispenser, if he the glistening life-pulp ate.

Second eagle.

33. There lies Regin communing with himself; he will beguile the youth, who in him trusts: in rage he brings malicious words together, the framer of evil will avenge his brother.

Third eagle.

34. By the head shorter, let him the hoary babbler send hence to Hel; then can he all the gold possess alone, the mass that under Fafnir lay.

Fourth eagle.

35. He would, methinks, be prudent, if he could have your friendly counsel, my sisters! If he would bethink himself, and Hugin gladden. There I expect the wolf, where his ears I see.

Fifth eagle.

36. Not so prudent is that tree of battle, as I that martial leader had supposed, if he one brother lets depart, now he the other has of life bereft.

Sixth eagle.

37. He is most simple, if he longer spares that people's pest. There lies Regin, who has betrayed him.— He cannot guard against it.

Seventh eagle.

38. By the head shorter let him make the ice-cold Jotun, and of his rings deprive him; then of that treasure thou, which Fafnir owned, sole lord wilt be!

Sigurd.

39. Fate shall not so resistless be, that Regin shall my death-word bear; for the brothers both shall speedily go hence to Hel.

Sigurd cut off the head of Regin, and then ate Fafnir's heart, and drank the blood of both Regin and Fafnir. He then heard the eagles saying:

40. Bind thou, Sigurd! the red-gold rings. It is not kingly many things to fear. I a maid know by far the fairest, with gold adorned. Couldst thou but her obtain!

Second eagle.

41. To Giuki lead all-verdant ways; the fates point out to wayfarers where the good king a born daughter has; her wilt thou, Sigurd! purchase with bridal gifts.

Third eagle.

42. There stands a hall on the high Hindarfiall, without 'tis all with fire surrounded; sagacious men have it constructed of the resplendent radiance of the flood.

Fourth eagle.

43. On the fell I know a warrior maid to sleep, over her waves the linden's bane. Ygg whilom stuck a sleep-thorn in the robe of the maid who would heroes choose.

44. Thou, youth! mayest see the helmed maiden, her whom Vingskornir from battle bore. May not Sigrdrifa's slumber break the son of warriors, against the Norns' decrees.

Sigurd rode along Fafnir's track to his lair, which he found open. The doors and door-posts were of iron; of iron also were all the beams in the house; but the treasure was buried in the earth. Sigurd found there a great quantity of gold, and filled two chests with it. He took thence the Oegis-helm, a golden corslet, the sword named Hrotti, and many precious things, all which he laid on Grani; but the horse would not proceed until Sigurd had mounted on his back.

THE LAY OF SIGRDRIFA.

Sigurd rode up the Hindarfiall, and directed his course southwards towards Frankland. In the fell he saw a great light, as if a fire were burning, which blazed up to the sky. On approaching it, there stood a "skialdborg," and over it a banner. Sigurd went into the skialdborg, and saw a warrior lying within it asleep, completely armed. He first took the helmet off the warrior's head, and saw that it was a woman. Her corslet was as fast as if it had grown to her body. With his sword Gram he ripped the corslet from the upper opening downwards, and then through both sleeves. He then took the corslet off from her, when she awoke, sat up and, on seeing Sigurd, said:

1. What has my corslet cut? why from sleep have I started? who has cast from me the fallow bands?

Sigurd.

Sigmund's son has just now ript the raven's perch, with Sigurd's sword.

She.

2. Long have I slept, long been with sleep oppressed, long are mortals' sufferings! Odin is the cause that I have been unable to cast off torpor.

Sigurd sat down and asked her name. She then took a horn filled with mead, and gave him the *minnis-cup.*

She.

3. Hail to Day! Hail to the sons of Day! To Night and her daughter hail! With placid eyes behold us here, and here sitting give us victory.

4. Hail to the Æsir! Hail to the Asyniur! Hail to the bounteous earth! Words and wisdom give to us noble twain, and healing hands while we live.

She was named Sigrdrifa, and was a Valkyria. She said that two kings had made war on each other, one of whom was named Hialmgunnar; he was old and a great warrior, and Odin had promised him victory. The other was Agnar, a brother of Hoda, whom no divinity would patronize. Sigrdrifa overcame Hialmgunnar in battle; in revenge for which Odin pricked her with a sleep-thorn, and declared that henceforth she should never have victory in battle, and should be given in marriage. "But I said to him, that I had bound myself by a vow not to espouse any man who could be made to fear." Sigurd answers, and implores her to teach him wisdom, as she had intelligence from all regions:

Sigrdrifa.

5. Beer I bear to thee, column of battle! with might mingled, and with bright glory: 'tis full of song, and salutary saws, of potent incantations, and joyous discourses.

6. Sig-runes thou must know, if victory (sigr) thou wilt have, and on thy sword's hilt grave them; some on the chapes, some on the guard, and twice name the name of Ty.

7. Ol-(beer-) runes thou must know, if thou wilt not that another's wife thy trust betray, if thou in her confide. On the horn must they be graven, and on the hand's back, and Naud on the nail be scored.

8. A cup must be blessed, and against peril guarded, and garlick in the liquor cast: then I know thou wilt never have mead with treachery mingled.

9. Biarg- (help-) runes thou must know, if thou wilt help, and loose the child from women. In the palm they must be graven, and round the joints be clasped, and the Disir prayed for aid.

10. Brim- (sea-) runes thou must know, if thou wilt have secure afloat thy sailing steeds. On the prow they must be graven, and on the helm-blade, and with fire to the oar applied. No surge shall be so towering, nor waves so dark, but from the ocean thou safe shalt come.

11. Lim- (branch-) runes thou must know, if thou a leech wouldst be, and wounds know how to heal. On the bark they must be graven, and on the leaves of trees, of those whose boughs bent eastward.

12. Mal- (speech-) runes thou must know, if thou wilt that no one for injury with hate requite thee. Those thou must wind, those thou must wrap round, those thou must altogether place in the assembly, where people have into full court to go.

13. Hug- (thought-) runes thou must know, if thou a wiser man wilt be than every other. Those interpreted, those graved, those devised Hropt, from the fluid, which had leaked from Heiddraupnir's head, and from Hoddropnir's horn.

14. On a rock he stood, with edged sword, a helm on his head he bore. Then spake Mim's head its first wise word, and true sayings uttered.

15. They are, it said, on the shield graven, which stands before the shining god, on Arvakr's ear, and on Alsvid's hoof, on the wheel which rolls under Rognir's car, on Sleipnir's teeth, and on the sledge's bands.

16. On the bear's paw, and on Bragi's tongue, on the wolf's claws, and the eagle's beak, on bloody wings, and on the bridge's end, on the releasing hand, and on healing's track.

17. On glass and on gold, on amulets of men, in wine and in wort, and in the welcome seat, on Gungnir's point, and on Grani's breast, on the Norn's nail, and the owl's neb.

18. All were erased that were inscribed, and mingled with the sacred mead, and sent on distant ways: they are with the Æsir, they are with the Alfar, some with the wise Vanir, some human beings have.

19. Those are bok-runes, those are biarg-runes, and all ol-(beer-) runes, and precious megin- (power-) runes, for those who can, without confusion or corruption, turn them to his welfare. Use, if thou hast understood them, until the powers perish.

20. Now thou shalt choose, since a choice is offered thee, keen armed warrior! my speech, or silence: think over it in thy mind. All evils have their measure.

Sigurd.

21. I will not flee, though thou shouldst know me doomed. I am not born a craven. Thy friendly counsels all I will receive, as long as life is in me.

Sigrdrifa.

22. This I thee counsel first: that towards thy kin thou bear thee blameless. Take not hasty vengeance, although they raise up strife: that, it is said, benefits the dead.

23. This I thee counsel secondly: that no oath thou swear, if it be not true. Cruel bonds follow broken faith: accursed is the faith-breaker.

24. This I thee counsel thirdly: that in the assembly thou contend not with a fool; for an unwise man oft utters words worse than he knows of.

25. All is vain, if thou holdest silence; then wilt thou seem a craven born, or else truly accused. Doubtful is a servant's testimony, unless a good one thou gettest. On the next day let his life go forth, and so men's lies reward.

26. This I counsel thee fourthly: if a wicked sorceress dwells by the way, to go on is better than there to lodge, though night may overtake thee.

27. Of searching eyes the sons of men have need, when fiercely they have to fight: oft pernicious women by the way-side sit, who swords and valour deaden.

28. This I thee counsel fifthly: although thou see fair women on the benches sitting, let not their kindred's silver over thy sleep have power. To kiss thee entice no woman.

29. This I thee counsel sixthly: although among men pass offensive tipsy talk, never while drunken quarrel with men of war: wine steals the wits of many.

30. Brawls and drink to many men have been a heartfelt sorrow; to some their death, to some calamity: many are the griefs of men!

31. This I thee counsel seventhly: if thou hast disputes with a daring man, better it is for men to fight than to be burnt within their dwelling.

32. This I thee counsel eighthly: that thou guard thee against evil, and eschew deceit. Entice no maiden, nor wife of man, nor to wantonness incite.

33. This I thee counsel ninthly: that thou corpses bury, wherever on the earth thou findest them, whether from sickness they have died, or from the sea, or are from weapons dead.

34. Let a mound be raised for those departed; let their hands and head be washed, combed, and wiped dry, ere in the coffin they are laid: and pray for their happy sleep.

35. This I thee counsel tenthly: that thou never trust a foe's kinsman's promises, whose brother thou hast slain, or sire laid low. there is a wolf in a young son, though he with gold be gladdened.

36. Strifes and fierce enmities think not to be lulled, no more than deadly injury. Wisdom and fame in arms a prince not easily acquires, who shall of men be foremost.

37. This I counsel thee eleventhly: that thou at evil look, what course it may take. A long life, it seems to me the prince may   enjoy;—fierce disputes will arise.

Sigurd said: "A wiser mortal exists not, and I swear that I will possess thee, for thou art after my heart." She answered: "Thee I will have before all others, though I have to choose among all men." And this they confirmed with oaths to each other.

FRAGMENTS OF THE LAY OF SIGURD AND BRYNHILD.

One day, when Sigurd was come from the forest, his hawk flew to the window at which Brynhild sat employed on weaving. Sigurd ran after it, saw the lady, and appeared struck with her handiwork and beauty. On the following day Sigurd went to her apartment, and Alsvid stood outside the door shafting arrows. Sigurd said: "Hail to thee, lady!" or "How fares it with thee?" She answered: "We are well, my kindred and friends are living, but it is uncertain what any one's lot may be till their last day." He sat down by her. Brynhild said: "This seat will be allowed to few, unless my father comes." Sigurd answered: "Now is that come to pass which thou didst promise me." She said: "Here shalt thou be welcome." She then arose, and her four maidens with her, and, approaching him with a golden cup, bade him drink. He reached towards her and took hold of her hand together with the cup, and placed her by him, clasped her round the neck, kissed her, and said: "A fairer than thou was never born." She said: "It is not wise to place faith in women, for they so often break their promise." He said: "Better days will come upon us, so that we may enjoy happiness," Brynhild said: "It is not ordained that we shall live together, for I am a shield-maiden (skjaldmær)." Sigurd said: "Then will our happiness be best promoted, if we live together; for harder to endure is the pain which herein lies than from a keen weapon." Brynhild said: "I shall be called to the aid of warriors, but thou wilt espouse Gudrun, Giuki's daughter." Sigurd said: "No king's daughter shall ensnare me, therefore have not two thoughts on that sub ject; and I swear by the gods that I will possess thee and no other woman." She answered to the same effect. Sigurd thanked her for what she had said to him, and gave her a gold ring. He remained there a short time in great favour.

Sigurd now rode from Heimir's dwelling with much gold, until he came to the palace of King Giuki, whose wife was named Grimhild. They had three sons, Gunnar, Hogni, and Guthorm. Gudrun was the name of their daughter. King Giuki entreated Sigurd to stay there, and there he remained a while. All appeared low by the side of Sigurd. One evening the sorceress Grimhild rose and presented a horn to Sigurd, saying: "Joyful for us is thy presence, and we desire that all good may befal thee. Take this horn and drink." He took it and drank, and with that drink forgot both his love and his vows to Brynhild. After that, Grimhild so fascinated him that he was induced to espouse Gudrun, and all pledged their faith to Sigurd, and confirmed it by oaths. Sigurd gave Gudrun to eat of Fafnir's heart, and she became afterwards far more austere than before. Their son was named Sigmund.

Grimhild now counselled her son Gunnar to woo Brynhild, and consulted with Sigurd, in consequence of this design. Brynhild had vowed to wed that man only who should ride over the blazing fire that was laid around her hall. They found the hall and the fire burning around it. Gunnar rode Goti, and Hogni Holknir. Gunnar turns his horse towards the fire, but it shrinks back. Sigurd said: "Why dost thou shrink back, Gunnar?" Gunnar answers: "My horse will not leap this fire," and prays Sigurd to lend him Grani. "He is at thy service," said Sigurd. Gunnar now rides again towards the fire, but Grani will not go over. They then changed forms. Sigurd rides, having in his hand the sword Gram, and golden spurs on his heels. Grani runs forward to the fire when he feels the spur. There was now a great noise, as it is said:

1. The fire began to rage, and the earth to tremble, high rose the flame to heaven itself: there ventured few chiefs of people through that fire to ride, or to leap over.

2. Sigurd Grani with his word urged, the fire was quenched before the prince, the flame allayed before the glory-seeker with the bright saddle that Rok had owned.

Brynhild was sitting in a chair as Sigurd entered. She asks who he is, and he calls himself Gunnar Giuki's son. "And thou art destined to be my wife with thy father's consent. I have ridden through the flickering flame (vafrlogi) at thy requisition." She said: "I know not well how I shall answer this." Sigurd stood erect on the floor resting on the hilt of his sword. She rose embarrassed from her seat, like a swan on the waves, having a sword in her hand, a helmet on her head, and wearing a corslet. "Gunnar," said she, "speak not so to me, unless thou art the foremost of men; and then thou must slay him who has sought me, if thou hast so much trust in thyself." Sigurd said: "Remember now thy promise, that thou wouldst go with that man who should ride through the flickering flame." She acknowledged the truth of his words, stood up, and gave him a glad welcome. He tarried there three nights, and they prepared one bed. He took the sword Gram and laid it between them. She inquired why he did so. He said that it was enjoined him so to act towards his bride on their marriage, or he would receive his death. He then took from her the ring called Andvaranaut, and gave her another that had belonged to Fafnir. After this he rode away through the same fire to his companions, when Gunnar and he again changed forms, and they then rode home.

Brynhild related this in confidence to her foster-father Heimir, and said: "A king named Gunnar has ridden through the flickering flame, and is come to speak with me; but I told him that Sigurd alone might so do, to whom I gave my vow at Hindarfiall, and that he only was the man." Heimir said that what had happened must remain as it was. Brynhild said: "Our daughter Aslaug thou shalt rear up here with thee." Brynhild then went to her father, King Budli, and he with his daughter Brynhild went to King Giuki's palace. A great feasting was afterwards held, when Sigurd remembered all his oaths to Brynhild, and yet kept silence. Brynhild and Gunnar sat at the drinking and drank wine.

One day Brynhild and Gudrun went to the river Rhine, and Brynhild went farther out into the water. Gudrun asked why she did so? Brynhild answered: "Why shall I go on along with thee in this more than in anything else?" "I presume that my father was more potent than thine, and my husband has performed more valorous deeds, and ridden through the blazing fire. Thy husband was King Hialprek's thrall." Gudrun answered angrily: "Thou shouldst be wiser than to venture to vilify my husband, as it is the talk of all that no one like to him in every respect has ever come into the world; nor does it become thee to vilify him, as he was thy former husband, and slew Fafnir, and rode through the fire, whom thou thoughtest was King Gunnar; and he lay with thee, and took from thee the ring Andvaranaut, and here mayest thou recognize it." Brynhild then looking at the ring, recognized it, and turned pale as though she were dead. Brynhild was very taciturn that evening, and Gudrun asked Sigurd why Brynhild was so taciturn. He dissuaded her much from making this inquiry, and said that at all events it would soon be known.

On the morrow, when sitting in their apartment, Gudrun said: "Be cheerful, Brynhild! What is it that prevents thy mirth?" Brynhild answered: "Malice drives thee to this; for thou hast a cruel heart." "Judge not so," said Gudrun. Brynhild continued: "Ask about that only which is better for thee to know; that is more befitting women of high degree. It is good, too, for thee to be content, as all goes according to thy wishes." Gudrun said: "It is premature to glory in that: this forebodes something; but what instigates thee against us?" Brynhild answered: "Thou shalt be requited for having espoused

Sigurd; for I grudge thee the possession of him." Gudrun said: "We knew not of your secret." Brynhild answered: "We have had no secret, though we have sworn oaths of fidelity; and thou knowest that I have been deceived, and I will avenge it." Gudrun said: "Thou art better married than thou deservest to be, and thy violence must be cooled." "Content should I be," said Brynhild, "didst thou not possess a more renowned husband than I." Gudrun answered: "Thou hast as renowned a husband; for it is doubtful which is the greater king." Brynhild said: "Sigurd overcame Fafnir, and that is worth more than all Gunnar's kingdom, as it is said:

"Sigurd the serpent slew, and that henceforth shall be by none forgotten, while mankind lives: but thy brother neither dared through the fire to ride, nor over it to leap."

Gudrun said: "Grani would not run through the fire under King Gunnar: but he dared to ride." Brynhild said: "Let us not contend: I bear no good will to Grimhild." Gudrun said: "Blame her not; for she is towards thee as to her own daughter." Brynhild said: "She is the cause of all the evil which gnaws me. She presented to Sigurd the pernicious drink, so that he no more remembered me." Gudrun said: "Many an unjust word thou utterest, and this is a great falsehood." Brynhild said: "So enjoy Sigurd as thou hast not deceived me, and may it go with thee as I imagine." Gudrun said: "Better shall I enjoy him than thou wilt wish; and no one has said he has had too much good with me at any time." Brynhild said: "Thou sayest ill and wilt repent of it. Let us cease from angry words, and not indulge in useless prattle. Long have I borne in silence the grief that dwells in my breast: I have also felt regard for thy brother. But let us talk of other things." Gudrun said: "Your imagination looks far forward." Brynhild then lay in bed, and King Gunnar came to talk with her, and begged her to rise and give vent to her sorrow; but she would not listen to him. They then brought Sigurd to visit her and learn whether her grief might not be alleviated. They called to memory their oaths, and how they had been deceived, and at length Sigurd offered to marry her and put away Gudrun; but she would not hear of it. Sigurd left the apartment, but was so greatly affected by her sorrow that the rings of his corslet burst asunder from his sides, as is said in the Sigurdarkvida:

"Out went Sigurd from that interview into the hall of kings, writhing with anguish; so that began to start the ardent warrior's iron-woven sark off from his sides." Brynhild afterwards instigated Gunnar to murder Sigurd, saying that he had deceived them both and broken his oath. Gunnar consulted with Hogni, and revealed to him this conversation. Hogni earnestly strove to dissuade him from such a deed, on account of their oaths. Gunnar removed the difficulty, saying: "Let us instigate our brother Guthorm; he is young and of little judgment, and is, moreover, free of all oaths; and so avenge the mortal injury of his having seduced Brynhild." They then took a serpent and the flesh of a wolf, and had them cooked, and gave them to him to eat, and offered him gold and a large realm, to do the deed, as is said:

"The forest-fish they roasted, and the wolf's carcase took, while some to Guthorm dealt out gold; gave him Geri's flesh with his drink, and many other things steeped therein." With this food he became so furious, that he would instantly perpetrate the deed. On this it is related as in the Sigurdarkvida, when Gunnar and Brynhild conversed together.]

THE THIRD LAY OF SIGURD FAFNICIDE.

1. It was of old that Sigurd, the young Volsung, Giuki sought, after his conflict, received the pledge of friendship from the two brothers; oaths exchanged the bold of deed.

2. A maid they offered him, and treasures many, Gudrun, Giuki's youthful daughter. Drank and conversed, many days together, Sigurd the young and Giuki's sons.

3. Until they went to woo Brynhild, and with them Sigurd, the youthful Volsung, rode in company, who knew the way. He would have possessed her, if her possess he might.

4. Sigurd the southern laid a naked sword, a glittering falchion, between them; nor the damsel did he kiss, nor did the Hunnish king to his arm lift her. He the blooming maid to Giuki's son delivered.

5. She to herself of body was of no sin conscious, nor at her death-day, of any crime, that could be a stain, or thought to be: intervened therein the grisly fates.

6. Alone she sat without, at eve of day, began aloud with herself to speak: "Sigurd must be mine; I must die, or that blooming youth clasp in my arms."

7. "Of the words I have uttered I now repent; he is Gudrun's consort, and I am Gunnar's. The hateful Norns long suffering have decreed us."

8. Oftentimes she wandered, filled with evil thoughts, o'er ice and icebergs, every eve, when he and Gudrun had to their couch withdrawn, and Sigurd her in the coverings wrapt, the Hunnish king his wife caressed.

9. "Devoid I go of spouse and pleasure; I will beguile myself with vengeful thoughts."

10. By those fits of fury she was impelled to murder. "Thou, Gunnar! shalt wholly lose my land, and myself also. Never shall I be happy, king! with thee.

11. I will return thither from whence I came, to my near kindred, my relations; there will I remain, and slumber life away, unless thou Sigurd cause to be slain, and a king become than the other greater.

12. Let the son go together with the father, the young wolf may not longer be fostered. For whom will vengeance be the easier to appease, if the son lives?"

13. Wroth was Gunnar, and with grief borne down; in his mind revolved, sat the whole day; he knew not well, nor could devise, what were most desirable for him to do, or were most fitting to be done, when he should find himself of the Volsung bereft, and in Sigurd a great loss sustain.

14. Much he thought, and also long, that it did not often happen, that from their royal state women withdrew. Hogni he then to counsel summoned, in whom he placed the fullest trust.

15. "Of all to me Brynhild, Budli's daughter, is the dearest; she is the chief of women: rather will I my life lay down than that fair one's treasures lose.

16. "Wilt thou the prince for his wealth circumvent? good 'tis to command the ore of Rhine, and at ease over riches rule, and in tranquillity happiness enjoy."

17. This alone Hogni for answer gave: "It beseems us not so to do, by the sword to break sworn oaths, oaths sworn, and plighted faith.

18. "We know not on earth men more fortunate, while we four over the people rule, and the Hun lives, that warlike chief; nor on earth, a race more excellent, if we five sons long shall foster, and the good progeny can increase.

19. I know full well whence the causes spring: Brynhild's importunity is over-great.

20. We will Guthorm, our younger brother, and not over-wise, for the deed prepare: he is free from sworn oaths, sworn oaths, and plighted faith."

21. Easy it was to instigate the ferocious spirit: in the heart of Sigurd stood his sword.

22. On vengeance bent, the warrior in his chamber hurled his brand after the fierce assassin; to Guthorm flew dartlike Gram's gleaming steel from the king's hand.

23. Fell the murderer in two parts, arms and head flew far away, but his feet's part fell backwards on the place.

24. Sunk in sleep was Gudrun, in her bed, void of cares, by Sigurd's side: but she awoke of joys bereft, when in the blood of Frey's friend she swam.

25. So violently struck she her hands together, that the stout of heart rose in his bed. "Weep not, Gudrun! so cruelly, my blooming bride! thy brothers live.

26. An heir I have, alas! too young; he cannot flee from the hostile house; among themselves they recently have dark and evil counsels devised.

27. Never henceforth, although seven thou bear, will such a son to the trysting with them ride. Full well I know how this has befallen: Brynhild the sole cause is of all the evil.

28. Me the maiden loved more than any man; but towards Gunnar I sinned not; affinity I held sacred, and sworn oaths; thence forward I was called his consort's friend."

29. The woman gave forth sighs, and the king his life. So violently she struck her hands together, that the beakers on the wall responsive rang, and in the court the geese loudly screamed.

30. Laughed then Brynhild, Budli's daughter, once only, from her whole soul, when in her bed she listened to the loud lament of Giuki's daughter.

31. Then said Gunnar, the hawk-bearing prince: "Laugh not thereat, thou barbarous woman! glad on thy couch, as if good awaited thee. Why hast thou lost that beauteous colour? authoress of crime! Methinks to death thou art doomed.

32. Well dost thou deserve, above all women, that before thy eyes, we should lay Atli low, that thou shouldst see thy brother's blood-streaming sore, his gory wounds shouldst have to bind."

33. Then said Brynhild, Budli's daughter: "No one provokes thee, Gunnar! complete is thy work of death. Little does Atli thy hatred fear; his life will outlast thine, and his might be ever greater.

34. Gunnar! will tell thee, though thou well knowest it, how early we resolved on crimes. I was o'er-young and unrestrained, with wealth endowed, in my brother's house.

35. Nor did I desire to marry any man, before ye Giukungs rode to our dwelling, three on horseback, powerful kings: would that journey had never been!

36. Then myself I promised to the great king, who with gold sat on Grani's back. In eyes he did not you resemble, nor was at all in aspect like: yet ye thought yourselves mighty kings.

37. And to me apart Atli said, that he would not have our heritage divided, nor gold nor lands, unless I let myself be married, nor grant me any part of the acquired gold, which he to me a girl had given to possess, and to me a child in moneys counted.

38. Then distracted was my mind thereon, whether I should engage in conflict, and death dispense, valiant in arms, for my brother's quarrel. That would then be world-widely known, and to many a one bring heartfelt anguish.

39. Our reconciliation we let follow: to me it had been more pleasing the treasures to accept, the red-gold rings of Sigmund's son: nor did I another's gold desire; him alone I loved, none other. Menskogul had not a changing mind.

40. All this will Atli hereafter find, when he shall hear of my funeral rites completed; for never shall the heavy-hearted woman with another's husband pass her life. Then will my wrongs be all avenged."

41. Up rose Gunnar, prince of warriors, and round his consort's neck laid his hands; all drew nigh, yet each one singly, through honest feeling, to dissuade her.

42. She from her neck those about her cast; she let no one stay her from her long journey.

43. He then called Hogni to consultation. "I will that all our folk to the hall be summoned, thine with, mine—now 'tis most needful—to see if we can hinder my consort's fatal course, till from our speech a hindrance may come: then let us leave necessity to rule."

44. To him Hogni answer gave: "Let no one hinder her from the long journey, whence may she never born again return. Unblest she came on her mother's lap, born in the world for ceaseless misery, for many a man's heartfelt sorrow."

45. Downcast he from the meeting turned to where the lady treasures distributed. She was viewing all she owned: hungry female thralls and chamber-women. She put on her golden corslet—no good meditated—ere herself she pierced, with the sword's point.

46. On the pillow she turned to> the other side, and, wounded with the glave, on her last counsels thought.

47. "Now let come those who desire gold, and aught less precious, to receive from me. To every one I give a gilded necklace, needle-work and coverlets, splendid weeds."

48. All were silent, thought on what to do, and all together answer gave: "Too many are there dead: we will yet live, still be hungry hall-servants, to do what fitting is."

49. At length after reflection, the lady linen-clad, young in years, words in answer uttered: "I desire that none, dead to entreaty, should by force, for our sake, lose their life.

50. Yet o'er your bones will burn fewer ornaments, Menia's good meal, when ye go hence me to seek.

51. Gunnar! sit down, I will tell to thee, that of life now hopeless is thy bright consort. Thy vessel will not be always afloat, though I shall have my life resigned.

52. With Gudrun thou wilt be reconciled, sooner than thou thinkest: that wise woman has by the king sad memorials, after her consort's death.

53. There is born a maid, which her mother rears; brighter far than the clear day, than the sun's beam, will Svanhild be.

54. Gudrun thou wilt give to an illustrious one, a warrior, the bane of many men: not to her wish will she be married; Atli will come her to espouse, Budli's son, my brother.

55. Much have I in memory how I was treated, when ye me so cruelly had deceived: robbed I was of happiness, while my life lasted.

56. Thou wilt desire Oddrun to possess, but Atli will permit it not; in secret ye will each other meet. She will love thee, as I had done, if us a better fate had been allotted.

57. Thee will Atli barbarously treat; in the narrow serpent-den wilt thou be cast.

58. It will too come to pass, not long after, that Atli will his soul resign, his prosperity, and cease to live; for Gudrun in her vengeance him in his bed will slay, through bitterness of spirit, with the sword's sharp edge.

59. More seemly would appear our sister Gudrun, had she in death her first consort followed, had but good counsel been to her given, or she a soul possessed resembling mine—

60. Faintly I now speak—but for our sake she will not lose her life. She will be borne on towering billows to King Jonakr's paternal soil. Doubts will be in the resolves of Jonakr's sons.

61. She will Svanhild send from the land, her daughter, and Sigurd's. Her will destroy Bikki's counsel; for Jormunrek for evil lives. Then will have passed away all Sigurd's race, and Gudrun's tears will be the more.

62. One prayer I have to thee yet to make, in this world 'twill be my last request: Let in the plain be raised a pile so spacious, that for us all like room may be, for those who shall have died with Sigurd.

63. Bedeck the pile about with shields and hangings, a variegated corpse-cloth, and multitude of slain. Let them burn the Hun on the one side of me;

64. Let them with the Hun burn on the other side, my household slaves, with collars splendid, two at our heads, and two hawks; then will all be equally distributed.

65. Let also lie between us both the sword with rings adorned, the keen-edged iron, so again be placed, as when we both one couch ascended, and were then called by the name of consorts.

66. Then will not clang against his heel the hall's bright gates, with splendid ring, if my train him hence shall follow. Then will our procession appear not mean.

67. For him will follow five female thralls, eight male slaves of gentle birth, fostered with me, and with my patrimony, which to his, daughter Budli gave.

68. Much I have said, and more would say, if the sword would grant me power of speech. My voice fails, my wounds swell: truth only I have uttered; so I will cease."

FRAGMENTS OF THE LAY OF BRYNHILD.

Gunnar.

1. "Why art thou, Brynhild! Budli's daughter! absorbed in evil and murderous thoughts? What injury has Sigurd done thee, that thou the hero wilt of life bereave?"

Brynhild.

2. "Sigurd to me oaths has sworn, oaths sworn, all falsehoods. He at a time deceived me when he should have been of all oaths most observant."

Hogni.

3. "Thee Brynhild has in anger instigated evil to perpetrate, harm to execute. She grudges Gudrun her happy marriage, and thee, possession of herself." * * *

4. Some a wolf roasted, some a snake cut up, some to Guthorm served the wolf, before they might, eager for crime, on the mighty man lay their hands.

5. Without stood Gudrun, Giuki's daughter, and these words first of all uttered: "Where is now Sigurd, lord of warriors, seeing that my kinsmen foremost ride?"

6. Hogni alone to her answer gave: "Asunder have we Sigurd hewed with our swords; his grey steed bends o'er the dead chief."

7. Then said Brynhild, Budli's daughter: "Well shall ye now enjoy arms and lands. Sigurd would alone over all have ruled, had he a little longer life retained.

8. Unseemly it had been that he should so have ruled over Giuki's heritage and the Goths' people, when he five sons, for the fall of hosts, eager for warfare, had begotten."

9. Then laughed Brynhild—the whole burgh resounded—once only from her whole heart: "Well shall ye enjoy lands and subjects, now the daring king ye have caused to fall."

10. Then said Gudrun, Giuki's daughter: "Much thou speakest, things most atrocious: may fiends have Gunnar, Sigurd's murderer! Souls malevolent vengeance awaits."

11. Sigurd had fallen south of Rhine: loud from a tree a raven screamed: "With your blood will Atli his sword's edges redden; the oaths ye have sworn your slaughter shall dissolve."

12. Evening was advanced, much was drunken, then did pleasant talk of all kinds pass: all sank in sleep, when to rest they went. Gunnar alone was wakeful longer than all:

13. He began his foot to move, and much with himself to speak; the warlike chief in his mind pondered, what during the conflict the raven and the eagle were ever saying, as they rode home.

14. Brynhild awoke, Budli's daughter, daughter of Skioldungs, a little ere day: "Urge me or stay me— the mischief is perpetrated—my sorrow to pour forth, or to suppress it."

15. All were silent at these words; few understood the lady's conduct, that weeping she should begin to speak of what she laughing had desired.

16. "In my dream, Gunnar! all seemed so horrid, in the chamber all was dead; my bed was cold; and thou, king! wast riding of joy bereft, with fetters loaded, to a hostile host. So will ye all, race of Niflungs! be of power deprived, perjurers as ye are!

17. Ill Gunnar! didst thou remember, when blood ye in your footsteps both let flow; now hast thou him ill for all that requited, because he would prove himself foremost.

18. Then was it proved, when the hero had ridden to see me, to woo me, how the warlike chief whilom held sacred his oath towards the youthful prince.

19. Laid his sword, with gold adorned, the illustrious king between us both: outward its edges were with fire wrought, but with venom drops tempered within."

From this lay, in which the death of Sigurd is related, it appears that he was slain without doors, while some relate that he was slain sleeping in his bed: but the Germans say he was slain out in the forest; and it is told in the "Gudrunarkvida hin Forna," that Sigurd and the sons of Giuki had ridden to the public assembly (thing) when he was slain. But it is said by all, without exception, that they broke faith with him, and attacked him while lying down and unprepared.

THE FIRST LAY OF GUDRUN.

Gudrun sat over Sigurd dead; she wept not as other women, although ready to burst with sorrow. Both men and women, came to console her, but that was not easy. It is said by some that Gudrun had eaten of Fafnir's heart, and therefore understood the talk of birds. This is also sung of Gudrun:

1. Of old it was that Gudrun prepared to die, when she sorrowing over Sigurd sat. No sigh she uttered, nor with her hands beat, nor wailed, as other women.

2. Jarls came forward of great sagacity, from her sad state of mind to divert her. Gudrun could not shed a tear, such was her affliction; ready she was to burst.

3. Sat there noble wives of jarls, adorned with gold, before Gudrun; each of them told her sorrows, the bitterest she had known.

4. Then said Giaflaug, Giuki's sister: "I know myself to be on earth most joyless: of five consorts I the loss have suffered; of two daughters, sisters three, and brothers eight; I alone live."

5. Gudrun could not shed a tear, such was her affliction for her dead consort, and her soul's anguish for the king's fall.

6. Then said Herborg, Hunaland's queen: "I a more cruel grief have to recount: my seven sons, in the south land, my spouse the eighth, in conflict fell.

7. My father and my mother, my brothers four, on the sea the wind deluded; the waves struck on the ship's timbers.

8. Their last honours 'twas mine to pay, 'twas mine to see them tombed, their funeral rites to prepare was mine. All this I underwent in one half-year, and to me no one consolation offered.

9. Then I became a captive, taken in war, at the close of the same half-year. Then had I to adorn, and tie the shoes, of the hersir's wife, each morn.

10. From jealousy she threatened me, and with hard blows drove me: nowhere master found I a better, but mistress no where a worse."

11. Gudrun could not shed a tear, such was her affliction for her dead consort, and her soul's anguish for the king's fall.

12. Then said Gullrond, Giuki's daughter: "Little canst thou, my fosterer, wise as thou art, with a young wife fittingly talk." The king's body she forbade to be longer hidden.

13. She snatched the sheet from Sigurd's corpse, and turned his cheek towards his wife's knees: "Behold thy loved one, lay thy mouth to his lip, as if thou wouldst embrace the living prince."

14. Gudrun upon him cast one look: she saw the prince's locks dripping with blood, the chief's sparkling eyes closed in death, his kingly breast cleft by the sword.

15. Then sank down Gudrun back on her pillow, her head-gear was loosed, her cheeks grew red, and a flood of tears fell to her knees.

16. Then wept Gudrun, Giuki's daughter, so that the tears spontaneously flowed, and at the same time screamed the geese in the court, the noble birds, which the lady owned.

17. Then spake Gullrond, Giuki's daughter: "Your loves I know were the most ardent among living beings upon earth: thou hadst delight nowhere, sister mine! save with Sigurd."

18. Then said Gudrun, Giuki's daughter: "Such was my Sigurd among Giuki's sons, as is the garlick out from the grass which grows, or a bright stone on a thread drawn, a precious gem on kings.

19. I also seemed to the prince's warriors higher than any of Herian's Disir; now I am as little as the leaf oft is in the storm-winds, after the chieftain's death.

20. Sitting I miss, and in my bed, my dearest friend. Giuki's sons have caused, Giuki's sons have caused my affliction, and their sister's tears of anguish.

21. So ye desolate the people's land, as ye have kept your sworn oaths. Gunnar! thou wilt not the gold enjoy; those rings will be thy bane, for the oaths thou to Sigurd gavest.

22. Oft in the mansion was the greater mirth, when my Sigurd Grani saddled, and Brynhild they went to woo, that which accursed, in an evil hour!"

23. Then said Brynhild, Budli's daughter: "May the hag lack spouse and children, who thee, Gudrun! has caused to weep, and this morning given thee runes of speech!"

24. Then said Gullrond, Giuki's daughter: "Cease, thou loathed of all! from those words. The evil destiny of princes thou hast ever been; thee every billow drives of an evil nature; thou sore affliction of seven kings, the greatest bane of friendship among women!"

25. Then said Brynhild, Budli's daughter: "Atli my brother, Budli's offspring, is the sole cause of all the evil;

26. When in the hall of the Hunnish folk, with the king we beheld the fire of the serpent's bed. Of that journey, I have paid the penalty, that sight I have ever rued."

27. She by a column stood, the wood violently clasped. From the eyes of Brynhild, Budli's daughter, fire gleamed forth; venom she snorted, when she beheld the wounds of Sigurd.

Gudrun then went away to the forest and deserts, and travelled to Denmark, where she stayed seven half-years with Thora, Hakon's daughter. Brynhild would not outlive Sigurd. She caused her eight thralls and five female slaves to be killed, and then slew herself with a sword, as it is related in the "Sigurdarkvida in Skemma" (the Short Lay of Sigurd).

BRYNHILD'S HEL-RIDE.

After Brynhild's death two piles were made, one for Sigurd, which was the first burnt; but Brynhild was burnt afterwards, and she was in a chariot, which was hung with precious tapestry; so that it was said that Brynhild drove in a chariot on the way to Hel, and passed through a place in which a giantess dwelt. The giantess said:

1. "Thou shalt not pass through my stone-supported dwelling place. Better had it beseemed thee to work broidery, than to seek after another's husband.

2. Why dost thou, vagrant woman! from Valland, my dwelling visit? Thou hast, golden dame! if thou desirest to know, gentle one! from thy hands washed human blood."

Brynhild.

3. "Upbraid me not, woman of the rock! although I have in warfare been. Of us, I trow, I shall the better seem, wherever men our conditions know."

Giantess.

4. "Thou, Brynhild! Budli's daughter! wast in evil hour born in the world; thou hast been the bane of Giuki's children, and their happy house subverted."

Brynhild.

5. "From my chariot I will truly tell thee, thou witless crone! if thou desirest to know, how Giuki's heirs made me both lovelorn and perjured.

6. The bold-hearted king caused the garbs of us eight sisters under an oak to be borne. Twelve years old was I, if thou desirest to know, when to the youthful king oaths I gave.

7. By all in Hlymdalir I was called Hild with the helm, by all who knew me.

8. Then caused I next, in the Gothic realm, the old Hialmgunnar to Hel to journey: I gave victory to the youthful brother of Oda, whereat Odin became hostile to me.

9. He with shields encompassed me, red and white, in Skatalund; their surfaces enclosed me; him he ordained my sleep to break, who in no place could be made to fear.

10. He made around my hall, towards the south, towering burn the destroyer of all wood: then bade that man only over it to ride, who me the gold should bring, that under Fafnir lay.

11. On Grani rode the chief, the gold-disperser, to where my foster-father ruled o'er the dwellings. He alone seemed there to all superior, the Danish warrior, of the court.

12. We slept and were content in the same bed, as if he had my born brother been; neither of us might on the other, for eight nights, lay a hand.

141

13. Reproached me Gudrun, Giuki's daughter, that I had slept in Sigurd's arms; then was I made aware of what I fain would not,—that they had deceived me, when a mate I took.

14. To calamities all too lasting men and women, ever will be while living born. We two shall now, Sigurd and I pass our life together. Sink thou of giant-kind!"

THE SLAUGHTER OF THE NIFLUNGS.

Gunnar and Hogni then took all the gold, Fafnir's heritage. Dissension prevailed afterwards between the Giukungs and Atli. He charged them with being the cause of Brynhild's death. By way of reconciliation, it was agreed that they should give him Gudrun in marriage, to whom they administered an oblivious potion, before she would consent to espouse Atli. Atli had two sons, Erp and Eitil, but Svanhild was the daughter of Sigurd and Gudrun. King Atli invited Gunnar and Hogni to his residence, and sent to them Vingi, or Knefrod. Gudrun was aware of treachery, and sent them word in runes not to come; and to Hogni, as a token, she sent the ring Andvaranaut, in which she had tied some wolf's hair. Gunnar had sought the hand of Oddrun, Atli's sister, but did not obtain it. He then married Glaumvor, and Hogni took Kostbera to wife. Their sons were Solar, Snævar, and Giuki. When the Giukungs came to Atli, Gudrun besought his sons to intercede for their lives, but they would not. The heart of Hogni was cut out, and Gunnar was cast into a pen of serpents. He struck his harp and lulled the serpents, but an adder stung him to the liver.

THE SECOND LAY OF GUDRUN.

King Theodric was with Atli, and had there lost the greater number of his men. Theodric and Gudrun mutually bewailed their afflictions. She related to him and said:

1. A maid above all maids I was; my mother reared me bright in her bower; my brothers I much loved, until me Giuki, with gold adorned, with gold adorned, to Sigurd gave.

2. Such was Sigurd above Giuki's sons, as the green leek is, springing from the grass, or the high-limbed hart above the savage beasts, or gleed-red gold above grey silver.

3. Until my brothers the possession grudged me of a consort to all superior. They could not sleep, nor on affairs deliberate, before they Sigurd had caused to die.

4. Grani to the assembly ran, his tramp was to be heard; but Sigurd then himself came not. All the saddle-beasts were splashed with blood, and with sweating faint, from the murderers.

5. Weeping I went to talk to Grani, with humid cheeks, I prayed the steed to tell: then Grani shuddered, in the grass bowed down his head. The steed knew that his master was no more.

6. Long I wandered, long was my mind distracted, ere of the people's guardian I inquired for my king.

7. Gunnar hung his head, but Hogni told me of Sigurd's cruel death. "Beyond the river slaughtered lies Guthorm's murderer, and to the wolves given.

8. Yonder behold Sigurd, towards the south, there thou wilt hear the ravens croak, the eagles scream, in their feast exulting; the wolves howling round thy consort."

9. "Why wilt thou, Hogni! to a joyless being such miseries recount? May thy heart by ravens be torn and scattered over the wide world, rather than thou shouldst walk with men."

10. Hogni answered, for once cast down, from his cheerful mood by intense trouble: "Gudrun! thou wouldst have greater cause to weep, if the ravens should tear my heart."

11. Alone I turned from that interview to the wolves' scattered leavings. No sigh I uttered, nor with my hands beat, nor wailed, as other women, when I heartbroken sat by Sigurd.

12. Night seemed to me of blackest darkness, when I sorrowing sat by Sigurd. Better by far it seemed to me had the wolves taken my life, or I had been burnt as a birchen tree.

13. From the fell I journeyed five long days and nights, until the lofty hall of Half I recognized. Seven half-years I with Thora stayed, Hakon's daughter, in Denmark.

14. She for my solace wrought in gold southern halls, and Danish swans.

15. We had in pictures the game of warriors, and in handiworks a prince's nobles; red shields, Hunnish heroes, a sworded host, a helmed host, a prince's following.

16. Sigmund's ships from the land sailing, with gilded heads, and carved prows. We on our canvas wrought how Sigar and Siggeir both contended southward in Fyen.

17. When Grimhild, the Gothic woman, heard how greatly I was afflicted, she cast aside her needle-work, and her sons called oft and earnestly, that she might know, who for her son would their sister compensate, or for her consort slain the blood-fine pay?

18. Gunnar was ready gold to offer, for the injuries to atone, and Hogni also. * * * She then inquired who would go the steeds to saddle, the chariot to drive, on horseback ride, the hawk let fly, arrows shoot from the yew bow?

19. Valdar and the Danes with Jarizleif, Eymod the third with Jarizkar, then entered, to princes like. Red mantles had the Langbard's men, corslets ornamented, towering helms; girded they were with falchions, brown were their locks.

20. For me each one would choose precious gifts, precious gifts, and to my heart would speak, if for my many woes they might gain my confidence, and I would in them trust.

21. Grimhild to me brought a potion to drink cold and bitter, that I my injuries might forget; it was mingled with Urd's power, with cold sea-water, and with Son's blood.

22. In that horn were characters of every kind graven and red-hued; nor could I comprehend them: the long lyng-fish of the Haddings' land, an uncut ear of corn: the wild-beasts' entrance.

23. In that potion were many ills together, a herb from every wood, and the acorn, the fire-stead's dew, entrails of offerings, swine's liver seethed; for that deadens strife.

24. And then I forgot, when I had taken it, all the king's words in the hall spoken. There to my feet three kings came, before she herself sought to speak with me.

25. "Gudrun! I will give thee gold to possess, of all the riches much of thy dead father; rings of red gold, Hlodver's halls, all the hangings left by the fallen king.

26. Hunnish maids, those who weave tapestry, and in bright gold work, so that it may delight thee. Over Budli's wealth thou alone shalt rule, adorned with gold, and given to Atli."

27. "I will not have any man, nor Brynhild's brother marry: it beseems me not with Budli's son to increase a race, or life enjoy."

28. "Take care not to pay the chiefs with hate; for 'tis we who have been the aggressors: so shouldst thou act as if yet lived Sigurd and Sigmund, if sons thou bearest."

29. "Grimhild! I cannot in mirth indulge, nor, for my hero's sake, cherish a hope, since the bloodthirsty raven have together cruelly drunk my Sigurd's heart's blood."

30. "Him of all I have found to be a king of noblest race, and in much most excellent: him shalt thou have until age lays thee low, or mateless be, if him thou wilt not take."

31. "Cease to offer that cup of ills so pertinaciously, that race to me: he will Gunnar's destruction perpetrate, and will cut out Hogni's heart. I will not cease until the exulting strife-exciter's life I shall have taken."

32. Weeping Grimhild caught the words, by which to her sons Gudrun foreboded evil, and to her kindred dire misfortunes. "Lands I will also give thee, people and followers, Vinbiorg and Valbiorg, if thou wilt accept them; for life possess them, and be happy, daughter!"

33. "Him then I will choose among the kings, and from my relatives reluctantly receive him. Never will he be to me a welcome consort, nor my brothers' bale a protection to our sons."

34. Forthwith on horseback was each warrior to be seen; but the Walish women were in chariots placed. For seven days o'er a cold land we rode; but the second seven, we beat the waves; and the third seven, we reached dry land.

35. There the gate-wards of the lofty burgh the latticed entrance opened, ere the court we entered.

36. Atli waked me, but I seemed to be full of evil thoughts, for my kinsmen's death.

37. "So me just now have the Norns waked,—a grateful interpretation I fain would have. Methought that thou, Gudrun! Giuki's daughter! with a treacherous sword didst pierce me through."

38. "Fire it forebodes, when one of iron dreams, arrogance and pleasure, a woman's anger. Against evil I will go burn thee, cure and medicate thee, although to me thou art hateful."

39. "Seemed to me here in the garden that young shoots had fallen, which I wished to let grow: torn up with their roots, reddened with blood, to table they were brought, and offered me to eat.

40. "Seemed to me that hawks flew from my hand, lacking their quarry, to the house of woes; seemed to me I ate their hearts with honey swollen with blood, with sorrowing mind.

41. "Seemed to me from my hand whelps I let slip; lacking cause of joy, both of them howled: seemed to me their bodies became dead carcases: of the carrion I was compelled to eat."

42. "There will warriors round thy couch converse, and of the white-locked ones take off the head; death-doomed they are within a few nights, a little ere day: thy court will eat of them."

43. "Lie down I would not, nor sleep after, obstinate in my fate—That I will execute!"

THE THIRD LAY OF GUDRUN.

Atli had a serving-woman named Herkia, who had been his concubine. She informed Atli that she had seen Thiodrek and Gudrun together; whereat Atli was much afflicted. Then Gudrun said:

1. What ails thee ever, Atli! Budli's son! Hast thou sorrow in thy heart? Why never laughest thou? To thy jarls it would seem more desirable, that thou with men wouldst talk, and on me wouldst look.

Atli.

2. It grieves me, Gudrun! Giuki's daughter! that in my palace here, Herkia has said, that thou and Thiodrek have under one covering slept, and wantonly been in the linen wrapt.

Gudrun.

3. For all this charge 1 will give my oaths by the white sacred stone, that with me and Thiodrek nothing has passed, which to man and wife only belongs;

4. Save that 1 embraced the prince of armies, the honoured king, a single time. Other were our cogitations, when sorrowful we two sat to converse.

5. Hither came Thiodrek, with thirty warriors; now there lives not one of those thirty men. Surround me with thy brothers, and with mailed warriors; surround me with all thy noblest kinsmen.

6. Send to Saxi the Southmen's prince; he can hallow the boiling cauldron."

7. Seven hundred men entered the hall, ere in the cauldron the queen dipt her hand.

8. "Now Gunnar comes not, nor call 1 Hogni: 1 shall not see again my loved brothers: with his sword would Hogni such wrong avenge: now 1 must myself purify from crime."

9. She to the bottom, plunged her snow-white hand, and up she drew the precious stones. "See now, ye men! I am proved guiltless in holy wise, boil the vessel as it may."

10. Laughed then Atli's heart within his breast, when he unscathed beheld the hand of Gudrun. "Now must Herkia to the cauldron go, she who Gudrun had hoped to injure." No one has misery seen who saw not that, how the hand there of Herkia was burnt. They then the woman led to a foul slough. So were Gudrun's wrongs avenged.

ODDRUN'S LAMENT.

There was a king named Heidrek, who had a daughter named Borgny. Her lover was named Vilmund. She could not give birth to a child until Oddrun, Atli's sister, came. She had been the beloved of Gunnar, Giuki's son. Of this story it is here sung:

1. I have heard tell, in ancient stories how a damsel came to the eastern land: no one was able, on the face of earth, help to afford to Heidrek's daughter.

2. When Oddrun, Atli's sister, heard that the damsel had great pains, from the stall she led her well-bridled steed, and on the swart one the saddle laid.

3. She the horse made run on the smooth, dusty way, until she came to where a high hall stood. She the saddle snatched from the hungry steed, and in she went along the court, and these words first of all uttered:

4. "What is most noteworthy in this country? or what most desirable in the Hunnish land?"

Borgny.

5. Here lies Borgny with pains overwhelmed, thy friend, Oddrun! See if thou canst help her.

Oddrun.

6. What chieftain has on thee brought this dishonour? Why so acute are Borgny's pains?

Borgny.

7. Vilmund is named the falcon-bearer's friend: he the damsel wrapt in a warm coverlet five whole winters, so that from her father she was hidden.

8. They, I ween, spoke not more than this: kindly she went to sit at the damsel's knee. Vehemently sang Oddrun, fervently sang Oddrun songs of power over Borgny.

9. A girl and boy might then tread the mould-way, gentle babes, born of Hogni's bane. Then began to speak the death-sick damsel, who before had no word uttered.

10. "So may thee help the benignant genii, Frigg and Freyia, and other gods besides, as thou hast from me peril removed!"

11. "I was not inclined to give thee help, because thou never wast of succour worthy: I vowed, and have performed what I then said—when the princes the heritage divided, that I would ever help afford."

Borgny.

12. Mad art thou, Oddrun! and hast lost thy wits, when in hostile spirit most of thy words thou utterest; for I have been thy companion upon the earth, as if from brothers we both were born.

Oddrun.

13. I remember yet what thou one evening saidst, when I for Gunnar, a compotation made. Such a case, saidst thou, would not thenceforth happen, to any maiden, save to me alone."

14. Then sat down the sorrowing lady to tell her woes, from her great grief:

15. "I was nurtured in the kingly hall, I was the joy of many in the council of men. Life I enjoyed, and my father's wealth, five winters only, while my father lived.

16. These last words the noble-hearted king strove to utter, ere he departed hence.

17. He bade me be endowed with ruddy gold, and in the south be given to Grimhild's son. He said no maiden could more excellent in the world be born, if fate willed it not otherwise.

18. Brynhild in her bower was occupied in broidery: she had people and lands around her. Earth slumbered, and the heavens above, when Fafnir's bane her burgh first saw.

19. Then was conflict waged with the Walish sword, and the burgh taken which Brynhild owned. It was not long—which was not surprising—ere she discovered all those frauds.

20. These she caused cruelly to be avenged, so that we all have great afflictions. Known it will be through every land of men, that she caused herself to die with Sigurd.

21. But I for Gunnar, rings' dispenser, love conceived, such as Brynhild should. But he Brynhild bade a helmet take, said she a Valkyria should become.

22. They forthwith offered ruddy rings to my brother, and indemnity not small. He besides offered for me fifteen vills, and the load of Grani's sides, if he would accept them.

23. But Atli said he never would a marriage-gift receive from Giuki's son. Still we could not our loves withstand, but I my head must lay upon the ring-breaker.

24. Many things said my relations; declared they had surprised us both together; but Atli said, that I would not crime commit, nor scandal perpetrate. But such should no one for another ever deny, when love has part.

25. Atli sent his emissaries about the Murkwood, that he might prove me; and they came to where they ought not to have come, to where we had one couch prepared.

26. To the men we offered red-gold rings, that they it might not to Atli tell; but they forthwith hastened home, and it quickly to Atli told.

27. But they from Gudrun carefully concealed it, yet rather by half she should have known it.

28. A sound was heard of gold-shod hoofs, when into the court rode Giuki's heirs. * * * Of Hogni they the heart cut out, and into a serpent-pen the other cast.

29. I had gone yet once again to Geirmund, to prepare a banquet. * * * The brave king began the harp to sound; for the prince of noble race hoped that I to his aid might come.

30. I it heard from Hlesey, how of trouble there the harp-strings sang.

31. I my thralls bade all be ready: I the prince's life would save. The vessel we let float past the forest, until I saw all Atli's courts.

32. Then came Atli's miserable mother crawling forth:—may she perish!—she Gunnar pierced to the heart; so that the hero I could not save.

33. Oftentimes I wonder, woman gold-adorned! how I after can life retain; for I seemed the formidable sword-dispenser as myself to love:

34. Thou sitst and listenest, while I recount to thee many an evil fate, my own and theirs." Each one lives as he best may. Now is ended *Oddrun's lament.*

THE LAY OF ATLI.

Gudrun, Giuki's daughter, avenged her brothers, as is well known. She first killed Atli's sons, and afterwards Atli himself, and burnt the palace with all the household. On these events was this lay composed.

1. Atli sent riding a messenger to Gunnar, a crafty man, Knefrud was his name. To Giuki's courts he came, and to Gunnar's hall, to the seats of state, and the glad potation:

2. There drank the courtiers wine in their Valhall—but the guileful ones silence kept—the Huns' wrath they feared. Then said Knefrud, with chilling voice:—the southern warrior on a high bench sat—

3. "Atli has sent me hither on his errand riding on a bit-griping steed, through the unknown Murkwood, to pray you, Gunnar! that to his bench ye come, with helms of state, Atli's home to visit.

4. "Shields ye there can choose, and smooth-shaven spears, gold-red helms, and of Huns a multitude, silver-gilt saddle-cloths, sarks gory-red, the dart's obstruction, and bit-griping steeds.

5. "The plain he will also give you, the broad Gnita heid, whistling javelins, and gilded prows, vast treasures, and Danp's towns, with that famed forest, which men the Murkwood call."

6. Gunnar his head then turned, and to Hogni said: "What counselest thou, bold warrior? now suchlike we hear? Of no gold I knew on Gnita's heath, to which we possess not other equal.

7. "Seven halls have we filled with swords, of each of which the hilt is gold. My horse I know the best, and my sword the keenest; my bow adorns my seat, my corslets are of gold, my helm and shield the brightest, brought from the hall of Kiar: mine alone are better than all the Hunnish ones.

8. "What thinkest thou the woman means, by sending us a ring in a wolf's clothing wrapt? I think that she caution enjoins. Wolf's hair I found twined in the red-gold ring: wolfish is the way we on our errand ride."

9. No sons pursuaded Gunnar, nor other kinsman, interpreters nor counsellors, nor those who potent were. Then spake Gunnar, as beseemed a king, great in his mead-hall, from his large soul:

10. "Rise now up, Fiornir! let along the benches pass the golden cups of heroes, from the attendants' hands.

11. "The wolf shall rule the Niflungs' heritage, O bearded sages! if Gunnar perish; black-coated bears earth's fruit tear with their teeth, to the dogs' delight, if Gunnar come not back."

12. Honoured men, weeping led the land's ruler from the Huns' court. Then said Hogni's youthful heir: "Go now, prudent and prosperous, whither your wishes lead."

13. The warriors made their bit-griping steeds over the mountains fly, through the unknown Murkwood. The whole Hunnish forest trembled where'er the warriors rode; over the shrubless, all-green plains they sped.

14. Atli's land they saw, and the high watch-towers; Bikki's people stood on that lofty fortress; the south people's hall was round with benches set, with well-bound bucklers, and white shields, the javelin's obstruction. There Atli drank wine in his Valhall: his guards sat without, Gunnar and his men to watch, lest they there should come with yelling dart, to excite their prince to conflict.

15. Their sister forthwith saw, when the hall they had entered, her brothers both—beer had she little drunken—"Betrayed art thou now, Gunnar! though strong, how wilt thou contend with the Huns' deadly wiles? Go quickly from this hall!

16. "Better hadst thou, Gunnar! in corslet come, than with helm of state, to see the home of Atli; thou in the saddle wouldst have sat whole sun-bright days, and o'er the pallid dead let the Norns weep, the Hunnish shield-maids misery suffer; but Atli himself thou shouldst into the serpent-pen have cast; but now the serpent-pen is for you two reserved."

17. "Sister! 'tis now too late the Niflungs to assemble, long 'tis to seek the aid of men, of valiant heroes, over the rugged fells of Rhine."

18. Then the Burgundians' friends Gunnar seized, in fetters laid, and him fast bound.

19. Hogni hewed down seven, with the keen sword, but the eighth he thrust into the raging fire. So should a valiant man defend himself from foes.

20. Hogni had Gunnar's hands protected. The bold chief they asked, if the Goths' lord would with gold his life redeem?

21. "Hogni's heart in my hand shall lie, cut bloody from the breast of the valiant chief, the king's son, with a dull-edged knife." * * * They the heart cut out from Hialli's breast; on a dish bleeding laid it, and it to Gunnar bare.

23. Then said Gunnar, lord of men: "Here have I the heart of the timid Hialli, unlike the heart of the bold Hogni; for much it trembles as in the dish it lies: it trembled more by half, while in his breast it lay."

24. Hogni laughed, when to his heart they cut the living crest-crasher; no lament uttered he. All bleeding on a dish they laid it, and it to Gunnar bare.

25. Calmly said Gunnar, the warrior Niflung: "Here have I the heart of the bold Hogni, unlike the heart of the timid Hialli; for it little trembles, as in the dish it lies: it trembled less, while in his breast it lay.

26. "So far shalt thou, Atli! be from the eyes of men as thou wilt from the treasures be. In my power alone is all the hidden Niflungs' gold, now that Hogni lives not.

27. "Ever was I wavering, while we both lived; now am I so no longer, as I alone survive. Rhine shall possess men's baleful metal, the mighty stream, the As-known Niflungs' heritage. In the rolling water the choice rings shall glitter, rather than on the hands of the Huns' children shine.

28. "Drive your wheel-chariots, the captive is now in bonds."

29. Atli the mighty, their sister's husband, rode with resounding steeds, with strife-thorns surrounded. Gudrun perceived the heroes' peril, she from tears refrained, on entering the hall of tumult.

30. "So be it with thee, Atli! as towards Gunnar thou hast held the oft-sworn oaths, formerly taken— by the southward verging sun, and by Sigty's hill, the secluded bed of rest, and by Ullr's ring." Yet thence the more did the bit-shaker the treasure's guardian, the warrior chief, drag to death.

31. The living prince then did a host of men into a pen cast down, which was within with serpents over-crawled. But Gunnar there alone a harp in wrathful mood with his hand struck: the strings resounded. So should a daring chief, a ring-dispenser, gold from men withhold.

32. Atli turned his brass-shod steed, his home to revisit, back from the murder. Din was in the court with horses thronged, men's weapon-song, from the heath they were come.

33. Out then went Gudrun, Atli to meet, with a golden cup to do her duty to the king. "Thou canst, O King! joyful in thy hall receive from Gudrun the arms of the departed."

34. The drinking-cups of Atli groaned with wine heavy, when in the hall together the Huns were counted. Long-bearded, bold, the warriors entered.

35. Hastened the bright-faced dame to bear their potions to them, the wondrous lady to the chiefs; and reluctantly to the pallid Atli the festal dainties offered, and uttered words of hate.

36. "Thou, swords' dispenser! hast thy two sons' hearts, slaughter-gory, with honey eaten. I resolved that thou, bold chief! shouldst of a human dish eat at thy feasting, and to the place of honour send it. Henceforth thou wilt not to thy knees call Erp and Eitil, joyous with beer the two: thou wilt not henceforth, see them from thy middle seat, gold-dispersing, javelins shafting, manes clipping, or horses urging."

38. Uproar was on the benches, portentous the cry of men, noise beneath the costly hangings. The children of the Huns wept, all wept save Gudrun, who never wept, or for her bear-fierce brothers, or her dear sons, young, simple, whom she had borne to Atli.

39. Gold scattered the swan-fair dame; with ruddy rings the household gifted. Fate she let ripen, but the bright gold flow. The woman spared not the treasure-houses.

40. Atli incautious had himself drunk weary; weapon he had none, nor was 'gainst Gudrun guarded. Oft had their sport been better, when they lovingly embraced each other before the nobles.

41. With the sword's point she gave the bed of blood to drink with death-bent hand, and the dogs loosed, out at the hall-door drove them, and the lady wakened the household with burning brand. That vengeance she for her brothers took.

42. To fire she then gave all that were therein, and from her brothers' murder were from the dark den returned. The old structures fell, the treasure-houses smoked, the Budlungs' dwelling. Burnt too were the shield-maids within, their lives cut short; in the raging fire they sank.

43. Of this enough is said. No such woman will henceforth arms again bear, to avenge her brothers. That bright woman had to three kings of men the death-doom borne, before she died.

Yet more clearly is this told in "Atlamalum inum Groenlenzkum" (the Groenland lay of Atli).

THE GROENLAND LAY OF ATLI.

1. Of those misdeeds men have heard tell, when warriors of old a compact made, which by pledges they confirmed, a secret consultation held: terrible it was to them after, and to Giuki's sons likewise, who were betrayed.

2. The warriors' fate ripened, they were death-doomed: ill advised was Atli, though he possessed sagacity: he felled a mighty column, strove hardly against himself; with speed he messengers despatched, that his wife's brothers should come quickly.

3. Wise was the house-dame, prudently she thought; the words in order she had heard, that in secret they had said: the sage lady was at a loss: fain would she help them; they o'er the sea must sail, but she herself could not go.

4. Runes she graved, Vingi them falsified, before he gave them from him; of ill he was the bearer. Then departed Atli's messengers, through the branched firth, for where the bold warriors dwelt.

5. They with beer were cheered, and fires they kindled, naught thought they of guile, when they were come; they the gifts accepted, which the prince sent them, on a column hung them, and of no evil thought.

6. Then came Kostbera, she was Hogni's wife, a woman greatly cautious, and them both greeted. Glad was also Glaumvor, Gunnar's consort, the prudent dame her duty forgot not, she to the guests' need attended.

7. Hogni they home invited, if he would be pleased to go. Treachery was manifest, had they but reflected! Gunnar then promised, if only Hogni would, but Hogni refused what the other proposed.

8. The noble dames bore mead, of many things there was abundance, many horns passed round, until it seemed they had full drunken.

9. The household prepared their couches, as to them seemed best. Cunning was Kostbera, she could runes interpret; she the letters read by the bright fire;—her tongue she had to guard between both her gums—so perverted were they, it was difficult to understand them.

10. To their bed they went, she and Hogni. The gentle lady dreamed, and concealed it not, to the prince wisely said it as soon as she awoke.

11. "From home thou art going, Hogni! give ear to counsel; few are fully prudent: go another time.

12. I have the runes interpreted, which thy sister graved: that fair dame has not this time invited thee. At one thing I wonder most, I cannot even conceive, why so wise a woman so confusedly should grave; for it is so set down as if it intimated death to you both, if you should straightway come. Either she has left out a letter, or others are the cause."

13. "They are," said Hogni, "all suspicious; I have no knowledge of them, nor will I into it inquire, unless we have to make requital. The king will gift us with gleed-red gold. I never fear, though we may hear of terror."

14. "Tottering ye will go, if thitherward ye tend. No kind entertainment there will ye at this time find. Hogni! I have dreamed, I will not conceal it: in an evil hour ye will go, or so at least I fear."

15. "Methought thy coverlet was with fire consumed; that the towering flame rushed through my dwelling."

Hogni.

16. "Here lie linen cloths, which thou hadst little noticed: these will quickly burn where thou the coverlet sawest."

Kostbera.

17. "Methought a bear came in, and broke down the columns; and so his talons shook, that we were terror-stricken; by his mouth held many of us, so that we were helpless: there, too, was a din far from little."

Hogni.

18. "A tempest there will be furious and sudden: the white bear thou sawest will be a storm from the east."

Kostbera.

19. "Methought an eagle flew herein, all through the house: that will largely concern us. He sprinkled all with blood: from his threats I thought it to be the 'ham' of Atli."

Hogni.

20. "We often slaughter largely, and then red we see: often are oxen meant, when we of eagles dream. Sound is the heart of Atli, dream thou as thou mayest." With this they ended: all speeches have an end.

21. The high-born awoke, there the like befell: Glaumvor had perceived that her dreams were ill-boding, adverse to Gunnar's going to and fro.

22. "Methought a gallows was for thee erected, thou wentest to be hanged, that serpents ate thee, that I inter'd thee living, that the Powers' dissolution came—Divine thou what that portends.

23. "Methought a bloody glave from thy sark was drawn—ill 'tis such a dream to a consort to recount—methought a lance was thrust through thy middle: wolves howled on every side."

Gunnar.

24. "Where dogs run they are wont to bark: oft bodes the bay of dogs the flight of javelins."

Glaumvor.

25. "Methought a river ran herein, through the whole house, that it roared violently, rushed o'er the benches, brake the feet of you brothers twain; nothing the water spared: something will that portend!

26. "Methought dead women in the night came hither; not ill-clad were they: they would choose thee, forthwith invited thee to their seats. I ween thy Disir have forsaken thee."

Gunnar.

27. "Too late it is to speak, it is now so resolved; from the journey we shall not shrink, as it is decreed to go: very probable it seems that our lives will be short."

28. When colours were discernible, those on journey bent all rose up: the others fain would stay them. The five journeyed together, of "hus-carls" there were present twice that number—it was ill devised—Snævar and Solar, they were Hogni's sons; Orkning he was named, who them accompanied, a gentle shield-bearer was he, the brother of Hogni's wife.

29. They went fair-appointed, until the firth them parted: ever would their wives have stayed them, they would not be stayed.

30. Glaumvor then spake, Gunnar's consort, Vingi she addressed, as to her seemed fitting: "I know not whether ye will requite us as we would: with treachery came the guest, if aught of ill betide."

31. Then Vingi swore, little spared he himself: "May him the Jotuns have, if towards you he lies! the gallows hold him, if aught against peace he meditates!"

32. Bera took up the word, she of gentle soul: "Sail ye prosperous, and may success attend you: may it be as I pray, and if nothing hinder!"

33. Hogni answered—he to his kin meant well—"Be of good cheer, ye prudent! whatever may befall. Many say the same, though with great difference; for many little care how they depart from home."

34. On each other then they looked before they parted: then, I ween, their fates were severed, and their ways divided.

35. Vigorously they rowed, their bark was well nigh riven; backward bending the waves they beat, ardently plied: their oar-bands were broken, the rowlocks shattered. They made not the vessel fast before they quitted it.

36. A little after—I will the end relate—they saw the mansion stand that Budli had possessed. Loud creaked the latticed gates, when Hogni knocked.

37. Then said Vingi, what he had better not, "Go far from the house, 'tis perilous to enter; I quickly enticed you to perdition; ye shall forthwith be slain. With fair words I prayed your coming, though guile was under them. But just bide here, while a gallows I prepare."

38. Hogni answered—little thought he of yielding, or of aught fearful that was to be proved:—"Think not to frighten us: try that seldom. If one word thou addest, thou wilt thy harm prolong."

39. They rushed on Vingi, and struck him dead, laid on their axes, while life within him throbbed.

40. Atli his men assembled, in their byrnies they issued forth, went prepared so that a fence was between them. Words they bandied, all with rage boiling: "Already had we resolved to take your lives away."

Hogni.

41. "It looks but ill, if ye before have counselled: e'en now ye are unprepared, and we one have felled, smitten to death: one of your host was he."

42. Furious they became, when those words they heard; their fingers they stretched forth, and their bowstrings seized; sharply shot, and with shields themselves protected.

43. In then came the tale of what without was passing; loud before the hall they a thrall heard speak.

44. Then incensed was Gudrun, when the sad news she heard: adorned with necklaces, she tore them all asunder; so hurled the silver, that the rings in shivers flew.

45. Then she went out, not gently moved the doors; went forth, void of fear, and the comers hailed, turned to the Niflungs: that was her last greeting, truth attended it; more words she said:

46. "I sought by symbols to prevent your leaving home,—fate may no one resist—and yet must you come hither." Wisely she asked: might they not be appeased? No one consented, all answered no.

47. Saw then the high-born lady that a hard game they played; a deadly deed she meditated, and her robe dashed aside, a naked falchion seized, and her kinsmen's lives defended: skilful she was in warfare, where her hand she applied.

48. Giuki's daughter caused two warriors to fall; Atli's brother she struck down,—he must henceforth be borne—so she the conflict managed, that she his foot struck off. Another too she smote, so that he never rose, to Hel she sent him: her hand trembled not.

49. A conflict then ensued, which was widely famed, but that excelled all else which Giuki's sons performed. So 'tis said the Niflungs, while yet they lived, with swords maintained the fight, corslets rent, helmets hewed, as their hearts prompted.

50. At morning most they fought, until mid-day had passed; all early morn, and the forenoon, ere the fight was ended, the field flowed with blood, until eighteen had fallen: Bera's two sons, and her brother, had them overcome.

51. Then the fierce Atli spoke, wroth though he was: "'Tis ill to look around; this is long of you. We were thirty warlike thanes, eleven survive: the chasm is too great. We were five brothers, when Budli died; now has Hel the half, two lie slain.

162

52. "A great affinity I obtained, that I cannot deny, pernicious woman! of which I have no benefit: peace we have seldom had, since thou among us camest. Of kinsmen ye have bereft me, of riches often wronged. To Hel my sister ye have sent; that is to me most bitter."

Gudrun.

53. "This thou callest to mind, Atli! but thou so first didst act: my mother thou didst take, and for her treasures murder; my gifted niece with hunger thou didst cause to perish. Laughable to me it seems, when thou sorrows dost recount. The gods are to be thanked, that it goes ill with thee."

Atli.

54. Jarls! I exhort you the sorrow to augment of that presumptuous woman: I would fain see it. Strive so to do, that Gudrun may lament. Might I but see that in her lot she joys not!

55. Take ye Hogni, and with a knife hack him: cut out his heart: this ye shall do. Gunnar the fierce of soul to a gallows fasten; do the work thoroughly, lure up the serpents.

Hogni.

56. Do as thou listest, glad I will await it; stout I shall prove myself: I have ere now things much harder proved. Ye had a hindrance while unscathed we were: now are we so wounded that our fate thou mayest command.

57. Beiti spake,—he was Atli's steward—Take we Hialli, but Hogni let us save. Let us do half the work; he is death-worthy. As long as he lives a slug he will ever be.

58. Terrified was the kettle-watcher, the place no longer held him: he could be a whiner, he clomb into every nook: their conflict was his bane, as he the penalty must pay; and the day sad, when he must from the swine die, from all good things, which he had enjoyed.

59. Budli's cook they took, and the knife brought towards him. Howled the wretched thrall, ere the point he felt; declared that he had time the gardens to manure, the vilest offices to do, if from death he might escape. Joyful indeed was Hialli, could he but save his life.

60. Hogni all this observed—few so act, as for a slave to intercede, that he may escape!—"Less 'tis, I say, for me to play this game myself. Why shall we here desire to listen to that screaming?"

61. Hands on the good prince they laid. Then was no option for the bold warriors, the sentence longer to delay. Then laughed Hogni; heard the sons of day how he could hold out: torment he well endured!

62. A harp Gunnar took, with his foot-branches touched it. He could so strike it, that women wept, and the men sobbed, who best could hear it. He the noble queen counselled: the rafters burst asunder.

63. There died the noble, as the dawn of day; at the last they caused their deeds to live.

64. Atli thought himself great: over them both he strode, to the sagacious woman told the evil, and bitterly reproached her. "It is now morning, Gudrun! thy loved ones thou hast lost; partly thou art the cause that it has so befallen."

Gudrun.

65. Joyful art thou, Atli! slaughter to announce: repentance shall await thee, when thou hast all proved. That heritage shall be left thee—that I can tell thee—that ill shall never from thee go, unless I also die.

Atli.

66. That I can prevent; another course I see, easier by half: the good we oft reject. With slaves I will console thee, with things most precious, with snow-white silver, as thou thyself mayest desire.

Gudrun.

67. Of that there is *no* hope; I will all reject; atonement I have spurned for smaller injuries. Hard I was ever thought, now will that be aggravated. I every grudge concealed, while Hogni lived.

68. We were both nurtured in one house; many a play we played, and in the wood grew up; Grimhild us adorned with gold and necklaces; for my brothers' death never wilt thou indemnify me, nor ever do what shall to me seem good.

69. Mens' too great power women's lot oppresses; on the knee the hand sinks, if the arms wither; the tree inclines, if its root-fibres are severed. Now, Atli! thou mayest alone over all here command.

70. Most unwise it was, when to this the prince gave credit: the guile was manifest, had he been on his guard. Dissembling then was Gudrun, against her heart she could speak, made herself gay appear, with two shields she played.

71. A banquet she would prepare, her brothers' funeral feast; the same would Atli also for his own do.

72. With this they ended; the banquet was prepared; the feasting was too luxurious. The woman great of heart was stern, she warred on Budli's race; on her spouse she would cruel vengeance wreak.

73. The young ones she enticed, and on a block laid them, the fierce babes were terrified, and wept not, to their mother's bosom crept, asked what she was going to do.

74. "Ask no questions, both I intend to kill; long have I desired to cut short your days."

75. "Slay as thou wilt thy children, no one hinders it; thy rage will have short peace, if thou destroyest us in our blooming years, thou desperate woman!" It fell out accordingly: she cut the throats of both.

76. Atli oft inquired whither his boys were gone to play, as he nowhere saw them?

Gudrun.

77. Over I am resolved to go, and to Atli tell it. Grimhild's daughter will not conceal it from thee. Little glad, Atli! wilt thou be, when all thou learnest; great woe didst thou raise up, when thou my brother slewest.

78. Very seldom have I slept since they fell. Bitterly I threatened thee: now I have reminded thee. "It is now morning," saidst thou: I yet it well remember; and it now is eve, when thou the like shalt learn.

79. Thou thy sons hast lost, as thou least shouldest; know that their skulls thou hast had for beer-cups; thy drink I prepared, I their red blood have shed.

80. I their hearts took, and on a spit staked them, then to thee gave them. I said they were of calves,—it was long of thee alone—thou didst leave none, voraciously didst devour, well didst ply thy teeth.

81. Thy children's fate thou knowest, few a worse awaits. I have my part performed, though in it glory not.

Atli.

82. Cruel wast thou, Gudrun! who couldst so act, with thy children's blood my drink to mingle. Thou hast destroyed thy offspring, as thou least shouldest; and to myself thou leavest a short interval from ill.

Gudrun.

83. I could still desire thyself to slay; rarely too ill it fares with such a prince. Thou hast already perpetrated crimes unexampled among men of frantic cruelty, in this world: now thou hast added what we have just witnessed. A great misdeed hast thou committed, thy death-feast thou hast prepared.

Atli.

84. On the pile thou shalt be burnt, but first be stoned; then wilt thou have earned what thou hast ever sought.

Gudrun.

85. Tell to thyself such griefs early to-morrow: by a fairer death I will pass to another light.

86. In the same hall they sat, exchanged hostile thoughts, bandied words of hate: each was ill at ease.

87. Hate waxed in a Hniflung, a great deed he meditated; to Gudrun he declared that he was Atli's deadly foe.

88. Into her mind came Hogni's treatment; happy she him accounted, if he vengeance wreaked. Then was Atli slain, within a little space; Hogni's son him slew, and Gudrun herself.

89. The bold king spake, roused up from sleep; quickly he felt the wounds, said he no binding needed. "Tell me most truly who has slain Budli's son. I am hardly treated: of life I have no hope."

Gudrun.

90. I, Grimhild's daughter, will not from thee hide, that I am the cause that thy life passes away; but partly Hogni's son, that thy wounds make thee faint.

Atli.

91. To the slaughter thou hast rushed, although it ill beseemed thee; 'tis bad to circumvent a friend, who well confided in thee. Besought I went from home, to woo thee, Gudrun!

92. A widow thou was left, fierce thou wast accounted, which was no falsehood, as we have proved. Hither home thou earnest, us a host of men attended; all was splendid on our journey.

93. Pomp of all kinds was there, of illustrious men, beeves in abundance: largely we enjoyed them. Of all things there was plenty partaken of by many.

94. A marriage gift to my bride I gave, treasures for her acceptance, thralls thrice ten, seven fair female slaves: in such things was honour; silver there was yet more.

95. All seemed to thee as it were naught, while the lands untouched lay, which Budli had left me. So didst thou undermine, dist allow me nothing to receive. Thou didst my mother let often sit weeping: with heart content I found not one of my household after.

Gudrun.

96. Now, Atli! thou liest, though of that I little reck. Gentle I seldom was, yet didst thou greatly aggravate it. Young brothers ye fought together, among yourselves contended; to Hel went the half from thy house: all went to ruin that should be for benefit.

97. Brothers and sisters we were three, we thought ourselves invincible: from the land we departed, we followed Sigurd. We roved about, each steered a ship; seeking luck we went, till to the east we came.

98. The chief king we slew, there a land obtained, the "hersar" yielded to us; that manifested fear. We from the forest freed him whom we wished harmless, raised him to prosperity who nothing had possessed.

99. The Hun king died, then suddenly my fortune changed: great was the young wife's grief, the widow's lot was hers. A torment to me it seemed to come living to the house of Atli. A hero had possessed me: sad was that loss!

100. Thou didst never from a contest come, as we had heard, where thou didst gain thy cause, or others overcome; ever wouldst thou give way, and never stand, lettest all pass off quietly, as ill beseemed a king.

Atli.

101. Gudrun! now thou liest. Little will be bettered the lot of either: we have all suffered. Now act thou, Gudrun! of thy goodness, and for our honour, when I forth am borne.

Gudrun.

102. I a ship will buy, and a painted cist; will the winding-sheet well wax, to enwrap thy corpse; will think of every requisite, as if we had each other loved.

103. Atli was now a corpse, lament from his kin arose: the illustrious woman did all she had promised. The wise woman would go to destroy herself; her days were lengthened: she died another time.

104. Happy is every one hereafter who shall give birth to such a daughter famed for deeds, as Giuki begat: ever will live, in every land, their oft-told tale, wherever people shall give ear.

GUDRUN'S INCITEMENT.

Having slain Atli, Gudrun went to the sea-shore. She went out into the sea, and would destroy herself, but could not sink. She was borne across the firth to the land of King Jonakr, who married her. Their sons were Sorii, Erp, and Hamdir. There was reared up Svanhild, the daughter of Sigurd. She was given in marriage to Jormunrek the Powerful. With him lived Bikki, who counselled Randver, the king's son, to take her. Bikki told that to the king, who caused Randver to be hanged, and Svanhild trodden under horses' feet. When Gudrun heard of this she said to her sons:—

1. Then heard I tell of quarrels dire, hard sayings uttered from great affliction, when her sons the fierce-hearted Gudrun, in deadly words, to slaughter instigated.

2. "Why sit ye here? why sleep life away? why does it pain you not joyous words to speak, now Jormunrek your sister young in years has with horses trodden, white and black, in the public way, with grey and way-wont Gothic steeds?

3. Ye are not like to Gunnar and the others, nor of soul so valiant as Hogni was. Her ye should seek to avenge, if ye had the courage of my brothers, or the fierce spirit of the Hunnish kings."

4. Then said Hamdir, the great of heart: "Little didst thou care Hogni's deed to praise, when Sigurd he from sleep awaked. Thy blue-white bed-clothes were red with thy husband's gore, with death-blood covered.

5. "For thy brothers thou didst o'er-hasty vengeance take, dire and bitter, when thou thy sons didst murder. We young ones could on Jormunrek, acting all together, have avenged our sister.

6. "Bring forth the arms of the Hunnish kings: thou hast us stimulated to a sword-mote."

7. Laughing Gudrun to the storehouse turned, the kings' crested helms from the coffers drew, their ample corslets, and to her sons them bore. The young heroes loaded their horses' shoulders.

8. Then said Hamdir, the great of heart: "So will no more come his mother to see, the warrior felled in the Gothic land, so that thou the funeral-beer after us all may drink, after Svanhild and thy sons."

9. Weeping Gudrun, Giuki's daughter, sorrowing went, to sit in the fore-court, and to recount, with tear-worn cheeks, sad of soul, her calamities, in many ways.

10. "Three fires I have known, three hearths I have known, of three consorts I have been borne to the house. Sigurd alone to me was better than all, of whom my brothers were the murderers.

11. "Of my painful wounds I might not complain; yet they even more seemed to afflict me, when those chieftains to Atli gave me.

12. "My bright boys I called to speak with me; for my injuries I could not get revenge, ere I had severed the Hniflungs' heads.

13. "To the sea-shore I went, against the Norns I was embittered; I would cast off their persecution; bore, and submerged me not the towering billows; up on land I rose, because I was to live.

14. "To the nuptial couch I went—as I thought better for me,—for the third time, with a mighty king. I brought forth offspring, guardians of the heritage, guardians of the heritage, Jonakr's sons.

15. "But around Svanhild bond-maidens sat; of all my children her I loved the best. Svanhild was, in my hall, as was the sun-beam, fair to behold.

16. "I with gold adorned her, and with fine raiment, before I gave her to the Gothic people. That is to me the hardest of all my woes, that Svanhild's beauteous locks should in the mire be trodden under horses' feet.

17. "But that was yet more painful, when my Sigurd they ingloriously slew in his bed; though of all most cruel, when of Gunnar the glistening serpents to the vitals crawled; but the most agonizing, which to my heart flew, when the brave king's heart they while quick cut out.

18. "Many griefs I call to memory, many ills I call to memory. Guide, Sigurd! thy black steed, thy swift courser, hither let it run. Here sits no son's wife, no daughter, who to Gudrun precious things may give.

19. "Remember, Sigurd! what we together said, when on our bed we both were sitting, that thou, brave one, wouldst come to me from Hel's abode, but I from the world to thee.

20. "Raise, ye Jarls! an oaken pile; let it under heaven the highest be. May it burn a breast full of woes! the fire round my heart its sorrows melt!"

21. May all men's lot be bettered, all women's sorrow lessened, to whom this tale of woes shall be recounted.

THE LAY OF HAMDIR.

1. In that court arose woeful deeds, at the Alfar's doleful lament; at early morn, men's afflictions, troubles of various kinds; sorrows were quickened.

2. It was not now, nor yesterday, a long time since has passed away,—few things are more ancient, it was by much earlier—when Gudrun, Giuki's daughter, her young sons instigated Svanhild to avenge.

3. "She was your sister, her name Svanhild, she whom Jormunrek with horses trod to death, white and black, on the public way, with grey and way-wont Gothic steeds.

4. "Thenceforth all is sad to you, kings of people! Ye alone survive,

5. "Branches of my race. Lonely I am become, as the asp-tree in the forest, of kindred bereft, as the fir of branches; of joy deprived, as is the tree of foliage, when the branch-spoiler comes in the warm day."

6. Then spake Hamdir, the great of soul, "Little, Gudrun! didst thou care Hogni's deed to praise, when Sigurd they from sleep awaked On the bed thou satst, and the murderers laughed.

7. "Thy bed-clothes, blue and white, woven by cunning hands, swam in thy husband's gore. When Sigurd perished, o'er the dead thou satst, caredst not for mirth—so Gunnar willed it.

8. "Atli thou wouldst afflict by Erp's murder, and by Eitil's life's destruction: that proved for thyself the worse: therefore should every one so against others use, for life's destruction, a sharp-biting sword, that he harm not himself."

9. Then said Sorli—he had a prudent mind—"I with my mother will not speeches exchange: though words to each of you to me seem wanting. What, Gudrun! dost thou desire, which for tears thou canst not utter?

10. "For thy brothers weep, and thy dear sons, thy nearest kin, drawn to the strife: for us both shalt thou, Gudrun! also have to weep, who here sit fated on our steeds, far away to die."

11. From the court they went, for conflict ready. The young men journeyed over humid fells, on Hunnish steeds, murder to avenge.

12. Then said Erp, all at once—the noble youth was joking on his horse's back—"Ill 'tis to a timid man to point out the ways." They said the bastard was over bold.

13. On their way they had found the wily jester. "How will the swarthy dwarf afford us aid?"

14. He of another mother answered: so he said aid he would to his kin afford, as one foot to the other .

15. "What can a foot to a foot give; or, grown to the body, one hand the other?"

16. From the sheath they drew the iron blade, the falchion's edges, for Hel's delight. They their strength diminished by a third part, they their young kinsman caused to earth to sink.

17. Their mantles then they shook, their weapons grasped; the high-born were clad in sumptuous raiment.

18. Forward lay the ways, a woeful path they found, and their sister's son wounded on a gibbet, wind-cold outlaw-trees, on the town's west. Ever vibrated the ravens' whet: there to tarry was not good.

19. Uproar was in the hall, men were with drink excited, so that the horses' tramp no one heard, until a mindful man winded his horn.

20. To announce they went to Jormunrek that were seen helm-decked warriors. "Take ye counsel, potent ones are come; before mighty men ye have on a damsel trampled."

21. Then laughed Jormunrek, with his hand stroked his beard, asked not for his corslet; with wine he struggled, shook his dark locks, on his white shield looked, and in his hand swung the golden cup.

22. "Happy should I seem, if I could see Hamdir and Sorli within my hall. I would them then with bowstrings bind, the good sons of Giuki on the gallows hang."

23. Then said Hrodrglod, on the high steps standing; "Prince" said she to her son—for that was threatened which ought not to happen—"shall two men alone bind or slay ten hundred Goths in this lofty burgh?"

24. Tumult was in the mansion, the beer-cups flew in shivers, men lay in blood from the Goths' breasts flowing.

25. Then said Hamdir, the great of heart: "Jormunrek! thou didst desire our coming, brothers of one mother, into thy burgh: now seest thou thy feet, seest thy hands Jormunrek! cast into the glowing fire."

26. Then roared forth a godlike mail-clad warrior, as a bear roars: "On the men hurl stones, since spears bite not, nor edge of sword, nor point, the sons of Jonakr."

27. Then said Hamdir, the great of heart: "Harm didst thou, brother! when thou that mouth didst ope. Oft from that mouth bad counsel comes."

28. "Courage hast thou, Hamdir! if only thou hadst sense: that man lacks much who wisdom lacks.

29. "Off would the head now be, had but Erp lived, our brother bold in fight, whom on the way we slew, that warrior brave—me the Disir instigated—that man sacred to us, whom we resolved to slay. "I ween not that ours should be the wolves' example, that with ourselves we should contend, like the Norns' dogs, that voracious are in the desert nurtured."

30. "Well have we fought, on slaughtered Goths we stand, on those fallen by the sword, like eagles on a branch. Great glory we have gained, though now or to-morrow we shall die. No one lives till eve against the Norns' decree."There fell Sorli, at the mansion's front; but Hamdir sank at the house's back. This is called the Old Lay of Hamdir.

THE YOUNGER EDDAS OF STURLESON.

THE DELUDING OF GYLFI.

GEFJON'S PLOUGHING.

I. King Gylfi ruled over the land which is now called Svithiod (Sweden). It is related of him that he once gave a wayfaring woman, as a recompense for her having diverted him, as much land in his realm as she could plough with four oxen in a day and a night. This woman was, however, of the race of the Æsir, and was called Gefjon. She took four oxen from the north, out of Jotunheim (but they were the sons she had had with a giant), and set them before a plough. Now the plough made such deep furrows that it tore up the land, which the oxen drew westward out to sea until they came to a sound. There Gefjon fixed the land, and called it Sælund. And the place where the land had stood became water, and formed a lake which is now called "The Water" (Laugur), and the inlets of this lake correspond exactly with the headlands of Sealund. As Skald Bragi the Old saith:—

"Gefjon drew from Gylfi,Rich in stored up treasure,The land she joined to Denmark.Four heads and eight eyes bearing,While hot sweat trickled down them,The oxen dragged the reft massThat formed this winsome island."

GYLFI'S JOURNEY TO ASGARD.

2. King Gylfi was renowned for his wisdom and skill in magic. He beheld with astonishment that whatever the Æsir willed took place; and was at a loss whether to attribute their success to the superiority of their natural abilities, or to a power imparted to them by the mighty gods whom they worshipped. To be satisfied in this particular, he resolved to go to Asgard, and, taking upon himself the likeness of an old man, set out on his journey. But th Æsir, being too well skilled in divination not to foresee his design, prepared to receive him with various illusions. On entering the city Gylfi saw a very lofty mansion, the roof of which, as far as his eye could reach, was covered with golden shields. Thiodolf of Hvina thus alludes to Valhalla being roofed with shields.

"Warriors all care-worn,(Stones had poured upon them),On their backs let glistenValhalla's golden shingles."

At the entrance of the mansion Gylfi saw a man who amused himself by tossing seven small-swords in the air, and catching them as they fell, one after the other. This person having asked his name, Gylfi said that he was called Gangler, and that he came from a long journey, and begged for a night's lodging. He asked, in his turn, to whom this mansion belonged. The other told him that it belonged to their king, and added, "But I will lead thee to him, and thou shalt thyself ask him his name." So saying he entered the hall, and as Gylfi followed the door banged to behind him. He there saw many stately rooms crowded with people, some playing, some drinking, and others fighting with various weapons. Gangler, seeing a multitude of things, the meaning of which he could not comprehend, softly pronounced the following verse (from the Havamal, st. i.):—

"Scan every gateEre thou go on,With greatest caution;

For hard to say 'tisWhere foes are sittingIn this fair mansion."

He afterwards beheld three thrones raised one above another, with a man sitting on each of them. Upon his asking what the names of these lords might be, his guide answered: "He who sitteth on the lowest throne is a king; his name is Har (the High or Lofty One); the second is Jafnhar (i.e. equal to the High); but he who sitteth on the highest throne is called Thridi (the Third)." Har, perceiving the stranger, asked him what his errand was, adding that he should be welcome to eat and drink without cost, as were all those who remained in Hava Hall. Gangler said he desired first to ascertain whether there was any person present renowned for his wisdom.

"If thou art not the most knowing," replied Har, "I fear thou wilt hardly return safe. But go, stand there below, and propose thy questions, here sits one who will be able to answer them."

3. Gangler thus began his discourse:—"'Who is the first, or eldest of the gods?"

"In our language," replied Har, "he is called Alfadir (All-Father, or the Father of all); but in the old Asgard he had twelve names."

"Where is this God?" said Gangler; "what is his power? and what hath he done to display his glory?"

"He liveth," replied Har, "from all ages, he governeth all realms and swayeth all things great and small."

"He hath formed," added Jafnhar, "heaven and earth, and the air, and all things thereunto belonging."

"And what is more," continued Thridi, "he hath made man, and given him a soul which shall live and never perish though the body shall have mouldered away, or have been burnt to ashes. And all that are righteous shall dwell with him in the place called Gimli, or Vingolf; but the wicked shall go to Hel, and thence to Niflhel, which is below, in the ninth world."

"And where did this god remain before he made heaven and earth?" demanded Gangler.

"He was then," replied Har, "with the Hrimthursar."

4. "But with what did he begin, or what was the beginning of things?" demanded Gangler.

"Hear," replied Har, "what is said in the Voluspa."

"'Twas time's first dawn,When nought yet was,Nor sand nor sea,Nor cooling wave;Earth was not there,

Nor heaven above.Nought save a voidAnd yawning gulf.But verdure none.'"

"Many ages before the earth was made," added Jafnhar, "was Niflheim formed, in the middle of which lies the spring called Hvergelmir, from which flow twelve rivers, Gjoll being the nearest to the gate of the abode of death."

"But, first of all," continued Thridi, "there was in the southern region (sphere) the world called Muspell. It is a world too luminous and glowing to be entered by those who are not indigenous there. He who sitteth on its borders (or the land's-end) to guard it is named Surtur. In his hand he beareth a flaming falchion, and at the end of the world shall issue forth to combat, and shall vanquish all the gods, and consume the universe with fire."

5. "Tell me," said Gangler, "what was the state of things ere the races mingled, and nations came into being."

"When the rivers that are called Elivagar had flowed far from their sources," replied Har, "the venom which they rolled along hardened, as does dross that runs from a furnace, and became ice. When the rivers flowed no longer, and the ice stood still, the vapour arising from the venom gathered over it, and froze to rime, and in this manner were formed, in Ginnungagap, many layers of congealed vapour, piled one over the other."

"That part of Ginnungagap," added Jafnhar, "that lies towards the north was thus filled with heavy masses of gelid vapour and ice, whilst everywhere within were whirlwinds and fleeting mists. But the southern part of Ginnungagap was lighted by the sparks and flakes that flew into it from Muspellheim."

"Thus," continued Thridi, "whilst freezing cold and gathering gloom proceeded from Niflheim, that part of Ginnungagap looking towards Muspellheim was filled with glowing radiancy, the intervening space remaining calm and light as wind-still air. And when the heated blast met the gelid vapour it melted it into drops, and, by the might of him who sent the heat, these drops quickened into life, and took a human semblance. The being thus formed was named Ymir, but the Frost-giants call him Orgelmir. From him descend the race of the Frost-giants (Hrimthursar), as it is said in the Voluspa, 'From Vidolf come all witches; from Vilmeith all wizards; from Svarthofdi all poison-seethers; and all giants from Ymir.' And the giant Vafthrûdnir, when Gangrad asked, 'Whence came Orgelmir the first of the sons of giants?' answered, 'The Elivagar cast out drops of venom that quickened into a giant. From him spring all our race, and hence are we so strong and mighty.'"

"How did the race of Ymir spread itself?" asked Gangler; "or dost thou believe that this giant was a god?"

"We are far from believing him to have been a god," replied Har, "for he was wicked as are all of his race, whom we call Frost-giants. And it is said that, when Ymir slept, he fell into a sweat, and from the pit of his left arm was born a man and a woman, and one of his feet engendered with the other a son, from whom descend the Frost-giants, and we therefore call Ymir the old Frost-giant."

6. "Where dwelt Ymir, and on what did he live?" asked Gangler.

"Immediately after the gelid vapours had been resolved into drops," replied Kar, "there was formed out of them the cow named Audhumla. Four streams of milk ran from her teats, and thus fed she Ymir."

"But on what did the cow feed?" questioned Gangler.

"The cow," answered Har, "supported herself by licking the stones that were covered with salt and hoar frost. The first day that she licked these stones there sprang from them, towards evening, the hairs of a man, the second day a head, and on the third an entire man, who was endowed with beauty, agility and power. He was called Bur, and was the father of Bor, who took for his wife Besla, the daughter of the giant Bolthorn. And they had three sons, Odin, Vili, and Ve; and it is our belief that this Odin, with his brothers, ruleth both heaven and earth, and that Odin is his true name, and that he is the most mighty of all the gods."

HOW THE SONS OF BOR SLEW YMIR AND FROM HIS BODY MADE HEAVEN AND EARTH.

7. "Was there," asked Gangler, "any kind of equality or any degree of good understanding between these two races?"

"Far from it," replied Har; "for the sons of Bor slew the giant Ymir, and when he fell there ran so much blood from his wounds, that the whole race of Frost-giants was drowned in it, except a single giant, who saved himself with his household. He is called by the giants Bergelmir. He escaped by going on board his bark, and with him went his wife, and from them are descended the Frost-giants."

8. "And what became of the sons of Bor, whom ye look upon as gods?" asked Gangler.

"To relate this," replied Har, "is no trivial matter. They dragged the body of Ymir into the middle of Ginnungagap, and of it formed the earth. From Ymir's blood they made the seas and waters; from his flesh the land; from his bones the mountains; and his teeth and jaws, together with some bits of broken bones, served them to make the stones and pebbles."

"With the blood that ran from his wounds," added Jafnhar, "they made the vast ocean, in the midst of which they fixed the earth, the ocean encircling it as a ring, and hardy will he be who attempts to pass those waters."

"From his skull," continued Thridi, "they formed the heavens, which they placed over the earth, and set a dwarf at the corner of each of the four quarters. These dwarfs are called East, West, North, and South. They after wards took the wandering sparks and red hot flakes that had been cast out of Muspellheim, and placed them in the heavens, both above and below, to' give light unto the world, and assigned to every other errant coruscation a prescribed locality and motion. Hence it is recorded in ancient lore that from this time were marked out the days, and nights, and seasons."

"Such are the events that took place ere the earth obtained the form it now beareth."

"Truly great were the deeds ye tell me of!" exclaimed Gangler; "and wondrous in all its parts is the work thereby accomplished. But how is the earth fashioned?"

"It is round without," replied Har, "and encircled by the deep ocean, the outward shores of which were assigned for a dwelling to the race of giants. But within, round about the earth, they (the sons of Bor) raised a bulwark against turbulent giants, employing for this structure Ymir's eyebrows. To this bulwark they gave the name of Midgard They afterwards tossed Ymir's brains into the air, and they became the clouds, for thus we find it recorded.

"Of Ymir's flesh was formed the earth; of his sweat (blood), the seas; of his bones, the mountains; of his hair the trees; of his skull, the heavens; but with his eyebrows the blithe gods built Midgard for the sons of men, whilst from his brains the lowering clouds were fashioned."

9. "To make heaven and earth, to fix the sun and the moon in the firmament, and mark out the days and seasons, were, indeed, important labours," said Gangler; "but whence came the men who at present dwell in the world?"

"One day." replied Har, "as the sons of Bor were walking along the sea-beach they found two stems of wood, out of which they shaped a man and a woman. The first (Odin) infused into them life and spirit; the second (Vili) endowed them with reason and the power of motion; the third (Ve) gave them speech and features, hearing and vision. The man they called Ask, and the woman, Embla. From these two descend the whole human race whose assigned dwelling was within Midgard. Then the sons of Bor built in the middle of the universe the city called Asgard, where dwell the gods and their kindred, and from that abode work out so many wondrous things, both on the earth and in the heavens above it. There is in that city a place called Hlidskjalf, and when Odin is seated there on his lofty throne he sees over the whole world, discerns all the actions of men, and comprehends whatever he contemplates. His wife is Frigga, the daughter of Fjorgyn, and they and their offspring form the race that we call Æsir, a race that dwells in Asgard the old, and the regions around it, and that we know to be entirely divine. Wherefore Odin may justly be called All-father, for he is verily the father of all, of gods as well as of men, and to his power all things owe their existence. Earth is his daughter and his wife, and with her he had his first-born son, Asa-Thor, who is endowed with strength and valour, and therefore quelleth he everything that hath life."

10. "A giant called Njorvi," continued Har, "who dwelt in Jotunheim, had a daughter called Night (Nott) who, like all her race, was of a dark and swarthy complexion. She was first wedded to a man called Naglfari, and had by him a son named Aud, and afterwards to another man called Annar, by whom she had a daughter called Earth (Jord). She then espoused Delling, of the Æsir race, and their son was Day, (Dagr) a child light and beauteous like his father. Then took All-father, Night, and Day, her son, and gave them two horses and two cars, and set them up in the heavens that they might drive successively one after the other, each in twelve hours' time, round the world. Night rides first on her horse called Hrimfaxi, that every morn, as he ends his course, bedews the earth with the foam that falls from his bit. The horse made use of by Day is named Skinfaxi, from whose mane is shed light over the earth and the heavens."

11. "How doth All-father regulate the course of the sun and moon?" asked Gangler.

"There was formerly a man," replied Har, "named Mundilfari, who had two children so lovely and graceful that he called the male, Mani (moon), and the female, Sol (sun), who espoused the man named Glenur. But the gods being incensed at Mundilfari's presumption, took his children and placed them in the heavens, and let Sol drive the horses that draw the car of the sun, which the gods had made to give light to the world out of the sparks that flew from Muspellheim. These horses are called Arvak and Alsvid, and under their withers the gods placed two skins filled with air to cool and refresh them, or, according to some ancient traditions, a refrigerant substance called *isarnkul*. Mani was set to guide the moon in his course, and regulate his increasing and waning aspect. One day he carried off from the earth two children, named Bil and Hjuki, as they were returning from the spring called Byrgir, carrying between them the bucket called Saegr, on the pole Simul. Vidfinn was the father of these children, who always follow Mani (the moon), as we may easily observe even from the earth."

12. "But the sun," said Gangler, speeds at such a rate as if she feared that some one was pursuing her for her destruction."

"And well she may," replied Har, "for he that seeks her is not far behind, and she has no way to escape than to run before him."

"But who is he," asked Gangler, "that causes her this anxiety?"

"There are two wolves," answered Har; "the one called Skoll pursues the sun, and it is he that she fears, for he shall one day overtake and devour her; the other, called Hati, the son of Hrodvitnir, runs before her, and as eagerly pursues the moon that will one day be caught by him."

"Whence come these wolves?" asked Gangler.

"A hag," replied Har, "dwells in a wood, to the eastward of Midgard, called Jarnvid, (the Iron Wood,) which is the abode of a race of witches called Jarnvidjur. This old hag is the mother of many gigantic sons, who are all of them shaped like wolves, two of whom are the wolves thou askest about. There is one of that race, who is said to be the most formidable of all, called Managarm: he will be filled with the life-blood of men who draw near their end, and will swallow up the moon, and stain the heavens and the earth with blood. Then shall the sun grow dim, and the winds howl tumultuously to and fro."

13. "I must now ask," said Gangler, "which is the path leading from earth to heaven?"

"That is a senseless question," replied Har, with a smile of derision. "Hast thou not been told that the gods made a bridge from earth to heaven, and called it Bifrost? Thou must surely have seen it; but, perhaps, thou callest it the rainbow. It is of three hues, and is constructed with more art than any other work. But, strong though it be, it will be broken to pieces when the sons of Muspell, after having traversed great rivers, shall ride over it."

"Methinks," said Gangler, "the gods could not have been in earnest to erect a bridge so liable to be broken down, since it is in their power to make whatever they please."

"The gods," replied Har, "are not to be blamed on that account; Bifrost is of itself a very good bridge, but there is nothing in nature that can hope to make resistance when the sons of Muspell sally forth to the great combat."

THE GOLDEN AGE.

14. "What did All-father do after Asgard was made?" demanded Gangler.

"In the beginning," answered Har, "he appointed rulers, and bade them judge with him the fate of men, and regulate the government of the celestial city. They met for this purpose in a place called Idavoll, which is in the centre of the divine abode. Their first work was to erect a court or hall wherein are twelve seats for themselves, besides the throne which is occupied by All-father. This hall is the largest and most magnificent in the universe, being resplendent on all sides, both within and without, with the finest gold. Its name is Gladsheim. They also erected another hall for the sanctuary of the goddesses. It is a very fair structure, and called by men Vingolf. Lastly they built a smithy, and furnished it with hammers, tongs, and anvils, and with these made all the other requisite instruments, with which they worked in metal, stone and wood, and composed so large a quantity of the metal called gold that they made all their moveables of it. Hence that age was named the Golden Age. This was the age that lasted until the arrival of the women out of Jotunheim, who corrupted it."

15. "Then the gods, seating themselves upon their thrones, distributed justice, and bethought them how the dwarfs had been bred in the mould of the earth, just as worms are in a dead body. It was, in fact, in Ymir's flesh that the dwarfs were engendered, and began to move and live. At first they were only maggots, but by the will of the gods they at length partook both of human shape and understanding, although they always dwell in rocks and caverns.

"Modsognir and Durin are the principal ones. As it is said in the Voluspa—

"'Then went the rulers there,All gods most holy,To their seats aloft,And counsel together took,Who should of dwarfsThe race then fashion,From the livid bonesAnd blood of the giant.

Modsognir, chiefOf the dwarfish race,And Durin tooWere then created.And like to menDwarfs in the earthWere formed in numbersAs Durin ordered.'"

OF THE ASH YGGDRASILL, MIMIR'S WELL., AND THE NORNS OR DESTINIES.

16. "Where," asked Gangler, "is the chief or holiest seat of the gods?"

"It is under the ash Yggdrasill," replied Har, "where the gods assemble every day in council."

"What is there remarkable in regard to that place?" said Gangler.

" That ash," answered Jafnhar, "is the greatest and best of all trees. Its branches spread over the whole world, and even reach above heaven. It has three roots very wide asunder. One of them extends to the Æsir, another to the Frost-giants in that very place where was formerly Ginnungagap, and the third stands over Nifelheim, and under this root, which is constantly gnawed by Nidhogg, is Hvergelmir. But under the root that stretches out towards the Frost-giants there is Mimir's well, in which wisdom and wit lie hidden. The owner of this well is called Mimir. He is full of wisdom, because he drinks the waters of the well from the horn Gjoll every morning. One day All-father came and begged a draught of this water, which he obtained, but was obliged to leave one of his eyes as a pledge for it.

"The third root of the ash is in heaven, and under it is the holy Urdar-fount. 'Tis here that the gods sit in judgment. Every day they ride up hither on horseback over Bifrost, which is called the Æsir Bridge. These are the names of the horses of the Æsir. Sleipnir is the best of them; he has eight legs, and belongs to Odin. The others are Gladr, Gyllir, Glær, Skeidbrimir, Silfrintoppr, Synir, Gils, Falhofnir, Gulltoppr, and Lettfeti. Baldur's horse was burnt with his master's body. As for Thor, he goes on foot, and is obliged every day to wade the rivers called Kormt and OErmt, and two others called Kerlaung.

"Through these shall Thor wade every day, as he fares to the doomstead under Yggdrasill's ash, else the Æsir Bridge would be in flames, and boiling hot would become the holy waters." "But tell me," said Gangler, "does fire burn over Bifrost?"

"That," replied Har, "which thou seest red in the bow, is burning fire; for the Frost-giants and the Mountain-giants would go up to heaven by that bridge if it were easy for every one to walk over it. There are in heaven many goodly homesteads, and none without a celestial ward. Near the fountain, which is under the ash, stands a very beauteous dwelling, out of which go three maidens, named Urd, Verdandi, and Skuld. These maidens fix the lifetime of all men, and are called Norns. But there are, indeed, many other Norns, for, when a man is born, there is a Norn to determine his fate. Some are known to be of heavenly origin, but others belong to the races of the elves and dwarfs; as it is said—

"'Methinks the Norns were born far asunder, for they are not of the same race. Some belong to the Æsir, some to the Elves, and some are Dvalin's daughters."

"But if these Norns dispense the destinies of men," said Gangler, "they are, methinks, very unequal in their distribution; for some men are fortunate and wealthy, others acquire neither riches nor honours, some live to a good old age, while others are cut off in their prime."

"The Norns," replied Har, "who are of a good origin, are good themselves, and dispense good destinies. But those men to whom misfortunes happen ought to ascribe them to the evil Norns."

17. "What more wonders hast thou to tell me," said Gangler, "concerning the ash?"

"What I have further to say respecting it," replied Har, "is, that there is an eagle perched upon its branches who knows many things: between his eyes sits the hawk called Vedurfolnir. The squirrel named Ratatosk runs up and down the ash, and seeks to cause strife between the eagle and Nidhogg. Four harts run across the branches of the tree, and bite the buds. They are called Dainn, Divalinn, Duneyr, and Durathror. But there are so many snakes with Nidhogg in Hvergelmir that no tongue can recount them."

"It is also said that the Norns who dwell by the Urdar-fount draw every day water from the spring, and with it and the clay that lies around the fount sprinkle the ash, in order that its branches may not rot and wither away. This water is so holy that everything placed in the spring becomes as white as the film, within an eggshell. As it is said in the Voluspa—

"'An Ash know I standing,Named Yggdrasill,A stately tree sprinkledWith water the purest;

Thence come the dewdropsThat fall in the dales;Ever blooming, it standsO'er the Urdar-fountain.'"

"The dew that falls thence on the earth men call honey-dew, and it is the food of the bees. Two fowls are fed in the Urdar-fount; they are called swans, and from them are descended all the birds of this species."

18. "Thou tellest me many wonderful things of heaven," said Gangler, "but what other homesteads are to be seen there?"

"There are many other fair homesteads there," replied Har; "one of them is named Elf-home (Alfheim), wherein dwell the beings called the Elves of Light; but the Elves of Darkness live under the earth, and differ from the others still more in their actions than in their appearance. The Elves of Light are fairer than the sun, but the Elves of Darkness blacker than pitch. There is also a mansion called Breidablik, which is not inferior to any other in beauty; and another named Glitnir, the wall, columns and beams of which are of ruddy gold, and the roof of silver. There is also the stead called Himinbjorg, that stands on the borders where Bifrost touches heaven, and the stately mansion belonging to Odin, called Valaskjalf, which was built by the gods, and roofed with pure silver, and in which is the throne called Hlidskjalf. When All-father is seated on this throne, he can see over the whole world. On the southern edge of heaven is the most beautiful homestead of all, brighter than the sun itself. It is called Gimli, and shall stand when both heaven and earth have passed away, and good and righteous men shall dwell therein for everlasting ages."

"But what will preserve this abode when Surtur's fire consumes heaven and earth?" asked Gangler.

"We are told," replied Har, "that towards the south there is another heaven above this called Andlang, and again above this a third heaven called Vidblain. In this last, we think Gimli must be seated, but we deem that the Elves of Light abide in it now."

19. "Tell me," said Gangler, "whence comes the wind, which is so strong that it moves the ocean and fans fire to flame, yet, strong though it be, no mortal eye can discern it? wonderfully, therefore, must it be shapen."

"I can tell thee all about it," answered Har; "thou must know that at the northern extremity of the heavens sits a giant called Hræsvelgur, clad with eagles' plumes. When he spreads out his wings for flight, the winds arise from under them."

20. "Tell me further," said Gangler, "why the summer should be hot, and the winter cold."

"A wise man would not ask such a question, which every one could answer," replied Har; "but, if thou hast been so dull as not to have heard the reason, I will rather forgive thee for once asking a foolish question than suffer thee to remain any longer in ignorance of what ought to have been known to thee. The father of Summer is called Svasuth, who is such a gentle and delicate being that what is mild is from him called sweet. The father of Winter has two names, Vindloni and Vindsval. He is the son of Vasad, and, like all his race, has an icy breath, and is of a grim and gloomy aspect."

206

OF ODIN.

21. "I must now ask thee," said Gangler, "who are the gods that men are bound to believe in?"

"There are twelve gods," replied Har, "to whom divine honours ought to be rendered."

"Nor are the goddesses," added Jafnhar, "less divine and mighty."

"The first and eldest of the Æsir," continued Thridi, "is Odin. He governs all things, and, although the other deities are powerful, they all serve and obey him as children do their father. Frigga is his wife. She foresees the destinies of men, but never reveals what is to come. For thus it is said that Odin himself told Loki, 'Senseless Loki, why wilt thou pry into futurity, Frigga alone knoweth the destinies of all, though she telleth them never?'

"Odin is named Alfadir (All-father), because he is the father of all the gods, and also Valfadir (Choosing Father), because he chooses for his sons all of those who fall in combat. For their abode he has prepared Valhalla and Vingolf, where they are called Einherjar (Heroes or Champions). Odin is also called Hangagud, Haptagud, and Farmagud, and, besides these, was named in many ways when he went to King Geirraudr," forty-nine names in all.

"A great many names, indeed!" exclaimed Gangler; "surely that man must be very wise who knows them all distinctly, and can tell on what occasions they were given."

"It requires, no doubt," replied Har, "a good memory to recollect readily all these names, but I will tell thee in a few words what principally contributed to confer them upon him. It was the great variety of languages; for the various nations were obliged to translate his name into their respective tongues, in order that they might supplicate and worship him. Some of his names, however, have been owing to adventures that happened to him on his journeys, and which are related in old stories. Nor canst thou ever pass for a wise man if thou are not able to give an account of these wonderful adventures."

22. "I now ask thee," said Gangler, "what are the names of the other gods. What are their functions, and what have they brought to pass?"

"The mightiest of them." replied Har, "is Thor. He is called Asa-Thor and Auku-Thor, and is the strongest of gods and men. His realm is named Thrudvang, and his mansion Bilskirnir, in which are five hundred and forty halls. It is the largest house ever built."

"Thor has a car drawn by two goats called Tanngniost and Tanngrisnir. From his driving about in this car he is called Auku-Thor (Charioteer-Thor). He likewise possesses three very precious things. The first is a mallet called Mjolnir, which both the Frost and Mountain Giants know to their cost when they see it hurled against them in the air; and no wonder, for it has split many a skull of their fathers and kindred. The second rare thing he possesses is called the belt of strength or prowess (Megingjardir). When he girds it about him his divine might is doubly augmented; the third, also very precious, being his iron gauntlets, which he is obliged to put on whenever he would lay hold of the handle of his mallet. There is no one so wise as to be able to relate all Thor's marvellous exploits, yet I could tell thee so many myself that hours would be whiled away ere all that I know had been recounted."

OF BALDUR.

23. "I would rather," said Gangler, "hear something about the other Æsir."

"The second son of Odin," replied Har, "is Baldur, and it may be truly said of him that he is the best, and that all mankind are loud in his praise. So fair and dazzling is he in form and features, that rays of light seem to issue from him; and thou mayst have some idea of the beauty of his hair, when I tell thee that the whitest of all plants is called Baldur's brow. Baldur is the mildest, the wisest, and the most eloquent of all the Æsir, yet such is his nature that the judgment he has pronounced can never be altered. He dwells in the heavenly mansion called Breidablik, in which nothing unclean can enter."

24. "The third god," continued Har, "is Njord, who dwells in the heavenly region called Noatun. He rules over the winds, and checks the fury of the sea and of fire, and is therefore invoked by sea-farers and fisher men. He is so wealthy that he can give possessions and treasures to those who call on him for them. Yet Njord is not of the lineage of the Æsir, for he was born and bred in Vanaheim. But the Vanir gave him as hostage to the Æsir, receiving from them in his stead Hoenir. By this means was peace re-established between the Æsir and Vanir. Njord took to wife Skadi, the daughter of the giant Thjassi. She preferred dwelling in the abode formerly belonging to her father, which is situated among rocky mountains, in the region called Thrymheim, but Njord loved to reside near the sea. They at last agreed that they should pass together nine nights in Thrymheim, and then three in Noatun. One day, when Njord came back from the mountains to Noatun, he thus sang—

"'Of mountains I'm weary,Not long was I there,Not more than nine nights;

But the howl of the wolfMethought sounded illTo the song of the swan-bird.'

"To which Skadi sang in reply—

"'Ne'er can I sleepIn my couch on the strand,For the screams of the sea-fowl,The mew as he comesEvery morn from the mainIs sure to awake me.'

"Skadi then returned to the rocky mountains, and abode in Thrymheim. There, fastening on her snow-skates and taking her bow, she passes her time in the chase of savage beasts, and is called the Ondur goddess, or Ondurdis. As it is said—

"'Thrymheim's the landWhere Thjassi abodeThat mightiest of giants.But snow-skating SkadiNow dwells there, I trow,In her father's old mansion.'"

OF THE GOD FREY, AND THE GODDESS FREYJA.

25. "Njord had afterwards, at his residence at Noatun, two children, a son named Frey, and a daughter called Freyja, both of them beauteous and mighty. Frey is one of the most celebrated of the gods. He presides over rain and sunshine, and all the fruits of the earth, and should be invoked in order to obtain good harvests, and also for peace. He, moreover, dispenses wealth among men. Freyja is the most propitious of the goddesses; her abode in heaven is called Folkvang. To whatever field of battle she rides, she asserts her right to one half of the slain, the other half belonging to Odin. As it is said—

"'Folkvang 'tis calledWhere Freyja hath rightTo dispose of the hall seats

Every day of the slain,She chooseth the half,And half leaves to Odin.'

"Her mansion, called Sessrumnir, is large and magnificent; thence she sallies forth in a car drawn by two cats. She lends a very favourable ear to those who sue to her for assistance. It is from her name that women of birth and fortune are called in our language Freyjor. She is very fond of love ditties, and all lovers would do well to invoke her."

26. "All the gods appear to me," said Gangler, "to have great power, and I am not at all surprised that ye are able to perform so many great achievements, since ye are so well acquainted with the attributes and functions of each god, and know what is befitting to ask from each, in order to succeed. But are there any more of them besides those you have already mentioned?"

"Ay," answered Har, "there is Tyr, who is the most daring and intrepid of all the gods. 'Tis he who dispenses valour in war, hence warriors do well to invoke him. It has become proverbial to say of a man who surpasses all others in valour that he is *Tyr-strong*, or valiant as Tyr. A man noted for his wisdom is also said to be 'wise as Tyr.' Let me give thee a proof of his intrepidity. When the Æsir were trying to persuade the wolf, Fenrir, to let himself be bound up with the chain, Gleipnir, he, fearing that they would never afterwards unloose him, only consented on the condition that while they were chaining him he should keep Tyr's right hand between his jaws. Tyr did not hesitate to put his hand in the monster's mouth, but when Fenrir perceived that the Æsir had no intention to unchain him, he bit the hand off at that point, which has ever since been called the wolf's joint. From that time Tyr has had but one hand. He is not regarded as a peacemaker among men."

27. "There is another god," continued Har, "named Bragi, who is celebrated for his wisdom, and more especially for his eloquence and correct forms of speech. He is not only eminently skilled in poetry, but the art itself is called from his name *Bragr*, which epithet is also applied to denote a distinguished poet or poetess. His wife is named Iduna. She keeps in a box the apples which the gods, when they feel old age approaching, have only to taste of to become young again. It is in this manner that they will be kept in renovated youth until Ragnarok."

"Methinks," interrupted Gangler, "the gods have committed a great treasure to the guardianship and good faith of Iduna."

"And hence it happened," replied Har, smiling, "that they once ran the greatest risk imaginable, as I shall have occasion to tell thee when thou hast heard the names of the other deities.

28. "One of them is Heimdall, called also the White God. He is the son of nine virgins, who were sisters, and is a very sacred and powerful deity. He also bears the appellation of the Gold-toothed, on account of his teeth being of pure gold, and also that of Hallinskithi. His horse is called Gulltopp, and he dwells in Himinbjorg at the end of Bifrost. He is the warder of the gods, and is therefore placed on the borders of heaven, to prevent the giants from forcing their way over the bridge. He requires less sleep than a bird, and sees by night, as well as by day, a hundred miles around him. So acute is his ear that no sound escapes him, for he can even hear the grass growing on the earth, and the wool on a sheep's back. He has a horn called the Gjallar-horn, which is heard throughout the universe. His sword is called Hofud (Head).

29. "Among the Æsir," continued Har, "we also reckon Hodur, who is blind, but extremely strong. Both gods and men would be very glad if they never had occasion to pronounce his name, for they will long have cause to remember the deed perpetrated by his hand.

30. "Another god is Vidar, surnamed the Silent, who wears very thick shoes. He is almost as strong as Thor himself, and the gods place great reliance on him in all critical conjunctures.

31. "Vali, another god, is the son of Odin and Rinda, he is bold in war, and an excellent archer.

32. "Another is called Ullur, who is the son of Sif, and stepson of Thor. He is so well skilled in the use of the bow, and can go so fast on his snow-skates, that in these arts no one can contend with him. He is also very handsome in his person, and possesses every quality of a warrior, wherefore it is befitting to invoke him in single combats.

33. "The name of another god is Forseti, who is the son of Baldur and Nanna, the daughter of Nef. He possesses the heavenly mansion called Glitnir, and all disputants at law who bring their cases before him go away perfectly reconciled.

"His tribunal is the best that is to be found among gods or men.

OF LOKI AND HIS PROGENY.

34. "There is another deity," continued Har, "reckoned in the number of the Æsir, whom some call the caluminator of the gods, the contriver of all fraud and mischief, and the disgrace of gods and men. His name is Loki or Loptur. He is the son of the giant Farbauti. His mother is Laufey or Nal; his brothers are Byleist and Helblindi. Loki is handsome and well made, but of a very fickle mood, and most evil disposition. He surpasses all beings in those arts called Cunning and Perfidy. Many a time has he exposed the gods to very great perils, and often extricated them again by his artifices. His wife is called Siguna, and their son Nari.

35. "Loki," continued Har, "has likewise had three children by Angurbodi, a giantess of Jotunheim. The first is the wolf Fenrir; the second Jormungand, the Midgard serpent; the third Hela (Death). The gods were not long ignorant that these monsters continued to be bred up in Jotunheim, and, having had recourse to divination, became aware of all the evils they would have to suffer from them; their being sprung from such a mother was a bad presage, and from such a sire was still worse. All-father therefore deemed it advisable to send one of the gods to bring them to him. When they came he threw the serpent into that deep ocean by which the earth is engirdled. But the monster has grown to such an enormous size that, holding his tail in his mouth, he encircles the whole earth. Hela he cast into Nifelheim, and gave her power over nine worlds (regions), into which she distributes those who are sent to her, that is to say, all who die through sickness or old age. Here she possesses a habitation protected by exceedingly high walls and strongly barred gates. Her hall is called Elvidnir; Hunger is her table; Starvation, her knife; Delay, her man; Slowness, her maid; Precipice, her threshold; Care, her bed; and Burning Anguish forms the hangings of her apartments. The one half of her body is livid, the other half the colour of human flesh. She may therefore easily be recognized; the more so, as she has a dreadfully stern and grim countenance.

"The wolf Fenrir was bred up among the gods; but Tyr alone had the daring to go and feed him. Nevertheless, when the gods perceived that he every day increased prodigiously in size, and that the oracles warned them that he would one day become fatal to them, they determined to make a very strong iron fetter for him, which they called Læding. Taking this fetter to the wolf, they bade him try his strength on it. Fenrir, perceiving that the enterprise would not be very difficult for him, let them do what they pleased, and then, by great muscular exertion, burst the chain and set himself at liberty. The gods, having seen this, made another fetter, half as strong again as the former, which they called Dromi, and prevailed on the wolf to put it on, assuring him that, by breaking this, he would give an undeniable proof of his vigour.

"The wolf saw well enough that it would not be so easy to break this fetter, but finding at the same time that his strength had increased since he broke Læding, and thinking that he could never become famous without running some risk, voluntarily submitted to be chained. When the gods told him that they had finished their task, Fenrir shook himself violently, stretched his limbs, rolled on the ground, and at last burst his chains, which flew in pieces all around him. He then freed himself from Dromi, which gave rise to the proverb, 'to get loose out of Læding, or to dash out of Dromi,' when anything is to be accomplished by strong efforts.

223

BINDING THE WOLF FENIR

"After this, the gods despaired of ever being able to bind the wolf; wherefore All-father sent Skirnir, the messenger of Frey, into the country of the Dark Elves (Svartalfaheim) to engage certain dwarfs to make the fetter called Gleipnir. It was fashioned out of six things; to wit, the noise made by the footfall of a cat; the beards of women; the roots of stones; the sinews of bears; the breath of fish; and the spittle of birds. Though thou mayest not have heard of these things before, thou mayest easily convince thyself that we have not been telling thee lies. Thou must have seen that women have no beards, that cats make no noise when they run, and that there are no roots under stones. Now I know what has been told thee to be equally true, although there may be some things thou art not able to furnish a proof of."

"I believe what thou hast told me to be true," replied Gangler, "for what thou hast adduced in corroboration of thy statement is conceivable. But how was the fetter smithied?"

"This can I tell thee," replied Har, "that the fetter was as smooth and soft as a silken string, and yet, as thou wilt presently hear, of very great strength. When it was brought to the gods, they were profuse in their thanks to the messenger for the trouble he had given himself; and taking the wolf with them to the island called Lyngvi, in the Lake Amsvartnir, they showed him the cord, and expressed their wish that he would try to break it, assuring him at the same time that it was somewhat stronger than its thinness would warrant a person in supposing it to be. They took it themselves, one after another, in their hands, and after attempting in vain to break it, said, 'Thou alone, Fenrir, art able to accomplish such a feat.'

"'Methinks,' replied the wolf, 'that I shall acquire no fame in breaking such a slender cord; but if any artifice has been employed in making it, slender though it seems, it shall never come on my feet.'

"The gods assured him that he would easily break a limber silken cord, since he had already burst asunder iron fetters of the most solid construction. 'But if thou shouldst not succeed in breaking it,' they added, 'thou wilt show that thou art too weak to cause the gods any fear, and we will not hesitate to set thee at liberty without delay.'

"'I fear me much,' replied he wolf, 'that if ye once bind me so fast that I shall be unable to free myself by my own efforts, ye will be in no haste to unloose me. Loath am I, therefore, to have this cord wound round me; but in order that ye may not doubt my courage, I will consent, provided one of you put his hand into my mouth as a pledge that ye intend me no deceit.'

" The gods wistfully looked at each other, and found that they had only the choice of two evils, until Tyr stepped forward and intrepidly put his right hand between the monster's jaws. Hereupon the gods, having tied up the wolf, he forcibly stretched himself as he had formerly done, and used all his might to disengage himself, but the more efforts he made the tighter became the cord, until all the gods, except Tyr, who lost his hand, burst into laughter at the sight.

"When the gods saw that the wolf was effectually bound, they took the chain called Gelgja, which was fixed to the fetter, and drew it through the middle of a large rock named Gjoll, which they sank very deep into the earth; afterwards, to make it still more secure, they fastened the end of the cord to a massive stone called Thviti, which they sank still deeper. The wolf made in vain the most violent efforts to break loose, and opening his tremendous jaws endeavoured to bite them. The gods seeing this, thrust a sword into his mouth, which pierced his under-jaw to the hilt, so that the point touched the palate. He then began to howl horribly, and since that time the foam flows continually from his mouth in such abundance that it forms the river called Von. There will he remain until Ragnarok."

"Verily," said Gangler, "an evil progeny is that of Loki, yet most mighty and powerful; but since the gods have so much to fear from the wolf, why did they not slay him?"

"The gods have so much respect for the sanctity of their peace-steads," replied Har, "that they would not stain them with the blood of the wolf, although prophecy had intimated to them that he must one day become the bane of Odin."

OF THE GODDESSES.

36. "Tell me now," said Gangler, "which are the goddesses?"

"The first," replied Har, "is Frigga, who has a magnificent mansion called Fensalir. The second is Saga, who dwells at Sokkvabekk, a very large and stately abode. The third is Eir, the best of all in the healing art. The fourth, named Gefjon, is a maid, and all those who die maids become her hand-maidens. The fifth is Fulla, who is also a maid, and goes about with her hair flowing over her shoulders, and her head adorned with a gold ribbon. She is entrusted with the toilette and slippers of Frigga, and admitted into the most important secrets of that goddess. Freyja is ranked next to Frigga: she is wedded to a person called Odur, and their daughter, named Hnossa, is so very handsome that whatever is beautiful and precious is called by her name (*hnosir.*) But Odur left his wife in order to travel into very remote countries. Since that time Freyja continually weeps, and her tears are drops of pure gold. She has a great variety of names, for having gone over many countries in search of her husband, each people gave her a different name. She is thus called Mardoll, Horn, Gefn, and Syr, and also Vanadis. She possesses the necklace Brising. The seventh goddess is Sjofna, who delights in turning men's hearts and thoughts to love; hence a wooer is called, from her name, *Sjafni.* The eighth, called Lofna, is so mild and gracious to those who invoke her, that by a peculiar privilege which either All-Father himself or Frigga has given her, she can remove every obstacle that may prevent the union of lovers sincerely attached to each other. Hence her name is applied to denote love, and whatever is beloved by men. Vora, the ninth goddess, listens to the oaths that men take, and particularly to the troth plighted between man and woman, and punishes those who keep not their promises. She is wise and prudent, and so pentrating that nothing remains hidden from her. Syn, the tenth, keeps the door in the hall, and shuts it against those who ought not to enter. She presides at trials when any thing is to be denied on oath, whence the proverb, 'Syn (negation) is set against it,' when ought is denied. Hlina, the eleventh, has the care of those whom Frigga intends to deliver from peril. Snotra, the twelfth, is wise and courteous, and men and women who possess these qualities have her name applied to them. Gna, the thirteenth, is the messenger that Frigga sends into the various worlds on her errands. She has a horse that can run through air and water, called Hofvarpnir. Once, as she drove out, certain Vanir saw her car in the air, when one of them exclaimed,

"'What flieth there? What goeth there? In the air aloft what glideth?'

"She answered,

"'I fly not though I go, And glide through the air On Hofvarpnir, Whose sire's Hamskerpir, And dam Gardrofa.'

"Sol and Bil are also reckoned among the goddesses, but their nature has already been explained to thee.

37. "There are besides these a great many other goddesses, whose duty it is to serve in Valhalla; to bear in the drink and take care of the drinking-horns and whatever belongs to the table. They are named in Grimnismal, and are called Valkyrjor. Odin sends them to every field of battle, to make choice of

227

those who are to be slain, and to sway the victory. Gudur, Rota, and the youngest of the Norns, Skuld, also ride forth to choose the slain and turn the combat. Jord (earth), the mother of Thor, and Rinda, the mother of Vali, are also reckoned amongst the goddesses."

OF FREY AND GERDA.

38. "There was a man," continued Har, "named Gymir, who had for wife Aurboda, of the race of the Mountain-giants. Their daughter is Gerda, who is the most beautiful of all women. One day Frey having placed himself in Hlidskjalf, to take a view of the whole universe, perceived, as he looked towards the north, a large and stately mansion which a woman was going to enter, and as she lifted up the latch of the door so great a radiancy was thrown from her hand that the air and waters, and all worlds were illuminated by it. At this sight, Frey, as a just punishment for his audacity in mounting on that sacred throne, was struck with sudden sadness, insomuch so, that on his return home he could neither speak, nor sleep, nor drink, nor did any one dare to inquire the cause of his affliction; but Njord, at last, sent for Skirnir, the messenger of Frey, and charged him to demand of his master why he thus refused to speak to any one. Skirnir promised to do this, though with great reluctance, fearing that all he had to expect was a severe reprimand. He, however, went to Frey, and asked him boldly why he was so sad and silent. Frey answered, that he had seen a maiden of such surpassing beauty that if he could not possess her he should not live much longer, and that this was what rendered him so melancholy. 'Go, therefore,' he added, 'and ask her hand for me, and bring her here whether her father be willing or not, and I will amply reward thee.' Skirnir undertook to perform the task, provided he might be previously put in possession of Frey's sword, which was of such excellent quality that it would of itself strew a field with carnage whenever the owner ordered it. Frey, impatient of delay, immediately made him a present of the sword, and Skirnir set out on his journey and obtained the maiden's promise, that within nine nights she would come to a place called Barey, and there wed Frey. Skirnir having reported the success of his message, Frey exclaimed,

"'Long is one night,Long are two nights,But how shall I hold out three?Shorter hath seemedA month to me oftThan of this longing-time the half.'

" Frey having thus given away his sword, found himself without arms when he fought with Beli, and hence it was that he slew him with a stag's antlers."

"But it seems very astonishing," interrupted Gangler, "that such a brave hero as Frey should give away his sword without keeping another equally good for himself. He must have been in a very bad plight when he encountered Beli, and methinks must have mightily repented him of the gift."

"That combat," replied Har, "was a trifling affair. Frey could have killed Beli with a blow of his fist had he felt inclined: but the time will come when the sons of Muspell shall issue forth to the fight, and then, indeed, will Frey truly regret having parted with his falchion."

39. "If it be as thou hast told me," said Gangler, "that all men who have fallen in fight since the beginning of the world are gone to Odin, in Valhalla, what has he to give them to eat, for methinks there must be a great crowd there?"

"What thou sayest is quite true," replied Har, "the crowd there is indeed great, but great though it be, it will still increase, and will be thought too little when the wolf cometh. But however great the band of men in Valhalla may be, the flesh of the boar Sæhrimnir will more than suffice for their sustenance. For although this boar is sodden every morning he becomes whole again every night. But there are few, methinks, who are wise enough to give thee, in this respect, a satisfactory answer to thy question. The cook is called Andhrimnir, and the kettle Eldhrimnir. As it is said,—'Andhrimnir cooks in Eldhrimnir, Sæhrimnir.' 'Tis the best of flesh, though few know how much is required for the Einherjar."

"But has Odin," said Gangler, "the same food as the heroes?"

"Odin,' replied Har, 'gives the meat that is set before him to two wolves, called Geri and Freki, for he himself stands in no need of food. Wine is for him both meat and drink.

"Two ravens sit on Odin's shoulders and whisper in his ear the tidings and events they have heard and witnessed. They are called Hugin and Munin. He sends them out at dawn of day to fly over the whole world, and they return at eve towards meal time. Hence it is that Odin knows so many things, and is called the Raven's God. As it is said,—

'Hugin and MuninEach dawn take their flightEarth's fields over.

I fear me for Hugin,Lest he come not back,But much more for Munin.'"

40. "What have the heroes to drink," said Gangler, "in sufficient quantity to correspond to their plentiful supply of meat: do they only drink water?"

"A very silly question is that," replied Har; "dost thou imagine that All-Father would invite kings and jarls and other great men and give them nothing to drink but water! In that case, methinks, many of those who had endured the greatest hardships, and received deadly wounds in order to obtain access to Valhalla, would find that they had paid too great a price for their water drink, and would indeed have reason to complain were they there to meet with no better entertainment. But thou wilt see that the case is quite otherwise. For the she-goat, named Heidrun, stands above Valhalla, and feeds on the leaves of a very famous tree called Lærath, and from her teats flows mead in such great abundance that every day a stoop, large enough to hold more than would suffice for all the heroes, is filled with it."

"Verily," said Gangler, "a mighty useful goat is this, and methinks the tree she feeds on must have very singular virtues."

"Still more wonderful," replied Har, "is what is told of the stag Eikthyrnir. This stag also stands over Valhalla and feeds upon the leaves of the same tree, and whilst he is feeding so many drops fall from his antlers down into Hvergelmir that they furnish sufficient water for the rivers that issuing thence flow through the celestial abodes."

41. "Wondrous things are these which thou tellest me of," said Gangler, "and Valhalla must needs be an immense building, but methinks there must often be a great press at the door among such a number of people constantly thronging in and out?"

"Why dost thou not ask," replied Har, "how many doors there are, and what are their dimensions; then wouldst thou be able to judge whether there is any difficulty in going in and out. Know, then, that there is no lack of either seats or doors. As it is said in Grimnismal:—

"'Five hundred doorsAnd forty moreMethinks are in Valhalla.Eight hundred heroes through each doorShall issue forthAgainst the wolf to combat.'"

42. "A mighty band of men must be in Valhalla," said Gangler, "and methinks Odin must be a great chieftain to command such a numerous host. But how do the heroes pass their time when they are not drinking?"

"Every day," replied Har, "as soon as they have dressed themselves they ride out into the court (or field), and there fight until they cut each other to pieces. This is their pastime, but when meal-time approaches they remount their steeds and return to drink in Valhalla. As it is said:—

"'The Einherjar allOn Odin's plainHew daily each other,While chosen the slain are.From the fray they then ride,And drink ale with the Æsir.'

"Thou hast thus reason to say that Odin is great and mighty, for there are many proofs of this. As it is said in the very words of the Æsir:—

"'The ash YggdrasillIs the first of trees,As Skidbladnir of ships,Odin of Æsir,Sleipnir of steeds,Bifrost of bridges,Bragi of bards,Habrok of hawks,And Garm of hounds is.'

43. "Thou mad'st mention," said Gangler, "of the horse Sleipnir. To whom does he belong, and what is there to say respecting him?"

" Thou seemest to know nothing either about Sleipnir or his origin," replied Har, "but thou wilt no doubt find what thou wilt hear worthy of thy notice. Once on a time when the gods were constructing their abodes, and had already finished Midgard and Valhalla, a certain artificer came and offered to build them, in the space of three half years, a residence so well fortified that they should be perfectly safe from the incursion of the Frost-giants, and the giants of the mountains, even although they should have penetrated within Midgard. But he demanded for his reward the goddess Freyja, together with the sun and moon. After long deliberation the Æsir agreed to his terms, provided he would finish the whole work himself without ony one's assistance, and all within the space of one winter, but if anything remained unfinished on the first day of summer, he should forfeit the recompense agreed on. On being told these terms, the artificer stipulated that he should be allowed the use of his horse, called Svadilfari, and this, by the advice of Loki, was granted to him. He accordingly set to work on the first day of winter, and during the night let his horse draw stone for the building. The enormous size of the stones struck the Æsir with astonishment, and they saw clearly that the horse did one half more of the toilsome work than his master. Their bargain, however, had been concluded in the presence of witnesses, and confirmed by solemn oaths, for without these precautions a giant would not have thought himself safe among the Æsir, especially when Thor returned from an expedition he had then undertaken towards the east against evil demons.

"As the winter drew to a close the building was far advanced, and the bulwarks were sufficiently high and massive to render this residence impregnable. In short, when it wanted but three days to summer the only part that remained to be finished was the gateway. Then sat the gods on their seats of justice and entered into consultation, inquiring of one another who among them could have advised to give Freyja away to Jotunheim, or to plunge the heavens in darkness by permitting the giant to carry away the sun and moon. They all agreed that no one but Loki, the son of Laufey, and the author of so many evil deeds, could have given such bad counsel, and that he should be put to a cruel death if he did not contrive some way or other to prevent the artificer from completing his task and obtaining the stipulated recompense. They immediately proceeded to lay hands on Loki, who, in his fright, promised upon oath that let it cost him what it would, he would so manage matters that the man should lose his reward. That very night, when the artificer went with Svadilfari for building stone, a mare suddenly ran out of a forest and began to neigh. The horse being thus excited, broke loose and ran after the mare into the forest, which obliged the man also to run after his horse, and thus between one and the other the whole night was lost, so that at dawn the work had not made the usual progress. The man seing that he had no other means of completing his task, resumed his own gigantic stature, and the gods now clearly perceived that it was in reality a Mountain-giant who had come amongst them. No longer regarding their oaths, they, therefore, called on Thor, who immediately ran to their assistance, and lifting up his mallet Mjolnir paid the workman his wages, not with the sun and moon, and not even by sending him back to Jotunheim, for with the first blow he shattered the giant's skull to pieces, and hurled him headlong into Nifelhel. But Loki had run such a race with Svadilfari that shortly after he bore a grey foal with eight legs. This is the horse Sleipnir, which excels all horses ever possessed by gods or men."

OF THE SHIP SKIDBLADNIR.

44. "What hast thou to say," demanded Gangler, "of Skidbladnir, which thou toldst me was the best of ships? Is there no other ship as good or as large?"

"Skidbladnir," replied Har, "is without doubt the best and most artfully constructed of any, but the ship Nagffar is of larger size. They were dwarfs, the sons of Ivaldi, who built Skidbladnir, and made a present of her to Frey. She is so large that all the Æsir with their weapons and war stores find room on board her. As soon as the sails are set a favourable breeze arises and carries her to her place of destination, and she is made of so many pieces, and with so much skill, that when she is not wanted for a voyage Frey may fold her together like a piece of cloth, and put her in his pocket."

"A good ship truly, is Skidbladnir," said Gangler, " and many cunning contrivances and spells must, no doubt, have been used in her construction."

THOR'S ADVENTURES ON HIS JOURNEY TO THE LAND OF THE GIANTS.

45. "But tell me," he (Gangler) continued, "did it ever happen to Thor in his expeditions to be overcome either by spells or by downright force?"

"Few can take upon them to affirm this," replied Har, "and yet it has often fared hard enough with him; but had he in reality been worsted in any rencounter there would be no need to make mention of it, since all are bound to believe that nothing can resist his power."

"It would, therefore, appear," said Gangler, "that I have asked of you things that none of you are able to tell me of."

"There are, indeed, some such rumours current among us," answered Jafnhar, "but they are hardly credible; however, there is one sitting here can impart them to thee, and thou shouldst the rather believe him, for never having yet uttered an untruth, he will not now begin to deceive thee with false stories."

"Here then will I stand," said Gangler, "and listen to what ye have to say, but if ye cannot answer my question satisfactorily I shall look upon you as vanquished."

Then spake Thridi and said, "We can easily conceive that thou art desirous of knowing these tidings, but it behooves thee to guard a becoming silence respecting them. The story I have to relate is this:—

46. "One day the God Thor set out in his car drawn by two he-goats, and accompanied by Loki, on a journey. Night coming on, they put up at a peasant's cottage, where Thor killed his goats, and after flaying them, put them in the kettle. When the flesh was sodden, he sat down with his fellow-traveller to supper, and invited the peasant and his family to partake of his repast. The peasant's son was named Thjalfi, and his daughter Roska. Thor bade them throw all the bones into the goats' skins which were spread out near the fire-place, but young Thjalfi broke one of the shank bones with his knife to come to the marrow. Thor having passed the night in the cottage, rose at the dawn of day, and when he was dressed took his mallet Mjolnir, and lifting it up, consecrated the goats' skins, which he had no sooner done than the two goats re-assumed their wonted form, only that one of them now limped on one of its hind legs. Thor perceiving this, said that the peasant, or one of his family, had handled the shank bone of this goat too roughly, for he saw clearly that it was broken. It may readily be imagined how frightened the peasant was when he saw Thor knit his brows, and grasp the handle of his mallet with such force that the joints of his fingers became white from the exertion. Fearing to be struck down by the very looks of the god, the peasant and his family made joint suit for pardon, offering whatever they possessed as an atonement for the offence committed. Thor, seeing their fear, desisted from his wrath, and became more placable, and finally contented himself by requiring the peasant's children, Thjalfi and Roska, who became his bond-servants, and have followed him ever since.

'Leaving his goats with the peasant, Thor proceeded eastward on the road to Jotunheim, until he came to the shores of a vast and deep sea, which having passed over he penetrated into a strange country along with his companions, Loki, Thjalfi, and Roska. They had not gone far before they saw

237

before them an immense forest, through which they wandered all day. Thjalfi was of all men the swiftest of foot. He bore Thor's wallet, but the forest was a bad place for finding anything eatable to stow in it. When it became dark, they searched on all sides for a place where they might pass the night, and at last came to a very large hall with an entrance that took up the whole breadth of one of the ends of the building. Here they chose them a place to sleep in; but towards midnight were alarmed by an earthquake which shook the whole edifice. Thor, rising up, called on his companions to seek with him a place of safety. On the right they found an adjoining chamber, into which they entered, but while the others, trembling with fear, crept into the furthest corner of this retreat, Thor remained at the doorway with his mallet in his hand, prepared to defend himself, whatever might happen. A terrible groaning was heard during the night, and at dawn of day, Thor went out and observed lying near him a man of enormous bulk, who slept and snored pretty loudly. Thor could now account for the noise they had heard over night, and girding on his Belt of Prowess, increased that divine strength which he now stood in need of. The giant awakening, rose up, and it is said that for once in his life Thor was afraid to make use of his mallet, and contented himself by simply asking the giant his name.

"'My name is Skrymir, said the other, 'but I need not ask thy name, for I know thou art the God Thor. But what hast thou done with my glove?' And stretching out his hand Skrymir picked up his glove, which Thor then perceived was what they had taken over night for a hall, the chamber where they had sought refuge being the thumb. Skrymir then asked whether they would have his fellowship, and Thor consenting, the giant opened his wallet and began to eat his breakfast. Thor and his companions having also taken their morning repast, though in another place, Skrymir proposed that they should lay their provisions together, which Thor also assented to. The giant then put all the meat into one wallet, which he slung on his back and went before them, taking tremendous strides, the whole day, and at dusk sought out for them a place where they might pass the night under a large oak tree. Skrymir then told them that he would lie down to sleep. 'But take ye the wallet,' he added, 'and prepare your supper.'

"Skrymir soon fell asleep, and began to snore strongly, but incredible though it may appear, it must nevertheless be told, that when Thor came to open the wallet he could not untie a single knot, nor render a single string looser than it was before. Seeing that his labour was in vain, Thor became wroth, and grasping his mallet with both hands while he advanced a step forward, launched it at the giant's head. Skrymir, awakening, merely asked whether a leaf had not fallen on his head, and whether they had supped and were ready to go to sleep. Thor answered that they were just going to sleep, and so saying, went and laid himself down under another oak tree. But sleep came not that night to Thor, and when he remarked that Skrymir snored again so loud that the forest re-echoed with the noise, he arose, and grasping his mallet, launched it with such force that it sunk into the giant's skull up to the handle. Skrymir awakening, cried out—

"'What's the matter? did an acorn fall on my head? How fares it with thee, Thor?'

"But Thor went away hastily, saying that he had just then awoke, and that as it was only midnight there was still time for sleep. He however resolved that if he had an opportunity of striking a third blow, it should settle all matters between them. A little before daybreak he perceived that Skrymir was again fast asleep, and again grasping his mallet, dashed it with such violence that it forced its way into the giant's cheek up to the handle. But Skrymir sat up, and stroking his cheek, said—

"'Are there any birds perched on this tree? Methought when I awoke some moss from the branches fell on my head. What! Art thou awake, Thor? Methinks it is time for us to get up and dress ourselves; but you have not now a long way before you to the city called Utgard. I have heard you whispering to one another that I am not a man of small dimensions; but if you come into Utgard you will see there many men much taller than myself. Wherefore I advise you, when you come there, not to make too much of yourselves, for the followers of Utgard-Loki will not brook the boasting of such mannikins as ye are. The best thing you could do would probably be to turn back again, but if you persist in going on, take the road that leads eastward, for mine now lies northward to those rocks which you may see in the distance.'

"Hereupon, he threw his wallet over his shoulders and turned away from them, into the forest, and I could never hear that Thor wished to meet with him a second time.

47. "Thor and his companions proceeded on their way, and towards noon descried a city standing in the middle of a plain. It was so lofty that they were obliged to bend their necks quite back on their shoulders ere they could see to the top of it. On arriving at the walls they found the gateway closed with a gate of bars strongly locked and bolted. Thor, after trying in vain to open it, crept with his companions through the bars, and thus succeeded in gaining admission into the city. Seeing a large palace before them, with the door wide open, they went in and found a number of men of prodigious stature sitting on benches in the hall. Going further, they came before the king, Utgard-Loki, whom they saluted with great respect. Their salutations were however returned by a contemptuous look from the king, who, after regarding them for some time, said with a scornful smile—

"'It is tedious to ask for tidings of a long journey, yet if I do not mistake me, that stripling there must be Aku-Thor. Perhaps,' he added, addressing himself to Thor, 'thou mayst be taller than thou appearest to be. But what are the feats that thou and thy fellows deem yourselves skilled in, for no one is permitted to remain here who does not, in some feat or other, excel all other men.'

"'The feat I know,' replied Loki, 'is to eat quicker than any one else, and in this I am ready to give a proof against any one here who may choose to compete with me.'

"'That will indeed be a feat,' said Utgard-Loki, 'if thou performest what thou promisest, and it shall be tried forthwith.'

"He then ordered one of his men, who was sitting at the further end of the bench, and whose name was Logi, to come forward and try his skill with Loki. A trough filled with flesh meat having been set on the hall floor, Loki placed himself at one end, and Logi at the other, and each of them, began to eat as fast as he could, until they met in the middle of the trough. But it was found that Loki had only eaten the flesh, whereas his adversary had devoured both flesh and bone, and the trough to boot. All the company therefore adjudged that Loki was vanquished.

"Utgard-Loki then asked what feat the young man who accompanied Thor could perform. Thjalfi answered that he would run a race with any one who might be matched against him. The king observed that skill in running was something to boast of, but that if the youth would win the match he must display great agility. He then arose and went with all who were present to a plain where there was a good ground for running on, and calling a young man named Hugi, bade him run a match with Thjalfi. In the first course Hugi so much outstripped his competitor that he turned back and met him not far from the starting-place.

"'Thou must ply thy legs better, Thjalfi,' said Utgard-Loki, 'if thou wilt win the match, though I must needs say that there never came a man here swifter of foot than thou art.'

"In the second course, Thjalfi was a full bow-shot from the goal when Hugi arrived at it.

"'Most bravely dost thou run, Thjalfi,' said Utgard-Loki, 'though thou wilt not, methinks, win the match. But the third, course must decide.'

"They accordingly ran a third time, but Hugi had already reached the goal before Thjalfi had got half way. All who were present then cried out that there had been a sufficient trial of skill in this kind of exercise.

50. "Utgard-Loki then asked Thor in what feats he would choose to give proofs of that dexterity for which he was so famous. Thor replied, that he would begin a drinking match with any one. Utgard-Loki consented, and entering the palace, bade his cupbearer bring the large horn which his followers were obliged to drink out of when they had trespassed in any way against established usage. The cupbearer having presented it to Thor, Utgard-Loki said—

"'Whoever is a good drinker will empty that horn at a single draught, though some men make two of it, but the most puny drinker of all can do it at three.'

"Thor looked at the horn, which seemed of no extraordinary size, though somewhat long; however, as he was very thirsty, he set it to his lips, and without drawing breath pulled as long and as deeply as he could, that he might not be obliged to make a second draught of it; but when he set the horn down and looked in, he could scarcely perceive that the liquor was diminished.

"''Tis well drunken,' exclaimed Utgard-Loki, 'though nothing much to boast of; and I would not have believed had it been told me that Asa-Thor could not have taken a greater draught, but thou no doubt meanest to make amends at the second pull.'

"Thor, without answering, went to it again with all his might, but when he took the horn from his mouth it seemed to him as if he had drunk rather less than before, although the horn could now be carried without spilling.

"'How now, Thor,' said Utgard-Loki; 'thou must not spare thyself more in performing a feat than befits thy skill; but if thou meanest to drain the horn at the third draught thou must pull deeply; and I must needs say that thou wilt not be called so mighty a man here as thou art among the Æsir, if thou showest no greater prowess in other feats than, methinks, will be shown in this.'

"Thor, full of wrath, again set the horn to his lips, and exerted himself to the utmost to empty it entirely, but on looking in found that the liquor was only a little lower, upon which he resolved to make no further attempt, but gave back the horn to the cupbearer.

51. "'I now see plainly,' said Utgard-Loki, 'that thou are not quite so stout as we thought thee, but wilt thou try any other feat, though, methinks, thou art not likely to bear any prize away with thee hence.'

"'I will try another feat,' replied Thor, 'and I am sure such draughts as I have been drinking would not have been reckoned small among the Æsir; but what new trial hast thou to propose?'

"'We have a very, trifling game here,' answered Ut-gard-Loki, 'in which we exercise none but children. It consists in merely lifting my cat from the ground, nor should I have dared to mention such a feat to Asa-Thor if I had not already observed that thou art by no means what we took thee for.'

"As he finished speaking, a large grey cat sprung on the hall floor. Thor advancing put his hand under the cat's belly, and did his utmost to raise him from the floor, but the cat bending his back had, notwithstanding all Thor's efforts, only one of his feet lifted up, seeing which, Thor made no further attempt.

"'This trial has turned out,' said Utgard-Loki, 'just as I imagined it would; the cat is large, but Thor is little in comparison to our men.'

"'Little as ye call me,' answered Thor, 'let me see who amongst you will come hither now I am in wrath, and wrestle with me.'

"'I see no one here,' said Utgard-Loki, looking at the men sitting on the benches, 'who would not think it beneath him to wrestle with thee; let somebody, however, call hither that old crone, my nurse Elli, and let Thor wrestle with her if he will. She has thrown to the ground many a man not less strong and mighty than this Thor is.'

53. "A toothless old woman then entered the hall, and was told by Utgard-Loki to take hold of Thor. The tale is shortly told. The more Thor tightened his hold on the crone the firmer she stood. At length, after a very violent struggle, Thor began to lose his footing, and was finally brought down upon one knee. Utgard-Loki then told them to desist, adding that Thor had now no occasion to ask any one else in the hall to wrestle with him, and it was also getting late. He therefore showed Thor and his companions to their seats, and they passed the night there in good cheer.

54. "The next morning, at break of day, Thor and his companions dressed themselves and prepared for their departure. Utgard-Loki then came and ordered a table to be set for them, on which there was no lack either of victuals or drink. After the repast Utgard-Loki led them to the gate of the city, and, on parting, asked Thor how he thought his journey had turned out, and whether he had met with any men stronger than himself. Thor told him that he could not deny but that he had brought great shame on himself. 'And what grieves me most,' he added, 'is that ye will call me a man of little worth.'

55. "'Nay,' said Utgard Loki, 'it behooves me to tell thee the truth now thou are out of the city which so long as I live, and have my way, thou shalt never re-enter. And by my troth, had I known

beforehand that thou hadst so much strength in thee, and wouldst have brought me so near to a great mishap, I would not have suffered thee to enter this time. Know then that I have all along deceived thee by my illusions; first, in the forest, where I arrived before thee, and there thou wert not able to untie the wallet, because I had bound it with iron wire, in such a manner that thou couldst not discover how the knot ought to be loosened. After this, thou gavest me three blows with thy mallet; the first, though the least, would have ended my days had it fallen on me, but I brought a rocky mountain before me which thou didst not perceive, and in this mountain thou wilt find three glens, one of them remarkably deep. These are the dints made by thy mallet. I have made use of similar illusions in the contests ye have had with my followers. In the first, Loki, like hunger itself, devoured all that was set before him, but Logi was, in reality, nothing else than ardent fire, and therefore consumed not only the meat but the trough which held it. Hugi, with whom Thjalfi contended in running, was Thought, and it was impossible for Thjalfi to keep pace with that. When thou, in thy turn, didst try to empty the horn, thou didst perform, by my troth, a deed so marvellous, that had I not seen it myself I should never have believed it. For one end of that horn reached the sea, which thou wast not aware of, but when thou comest to the shore thou wilt perceive how much the sea has sunk by thy draughts, which have caused what is now called the ebb. Thou didst perform a feat no less wonderful by lifting up the cat, and to tell thee the truth, when we saw that one of his paws was off the floor, we were all of us terror-stricken, for what thou tookest for a cat was in reality the great Midgard serpent that encompassed the whole earth, and he was then barely long enough to inclose it between his head and tail, so high had thy hand raised him up towards heaven. Thy wrestling with Elli was also a most astonishing feat, for there was never yet a man, nor ever shall be, whom Old Age, for such in fact was Elli, will not sooner or later lay low if he abide her coming. But now as we are going to part, let me tell thee that it will be better for both of us if thou never come near me again, for shouldst thou do so, I shall again defend myself by other illusions, so that thou wilt never prevail against me.'

"On hearing these words, Thor, in a rage, laid hold of his mallet and would have launched it at him, but Utgard-Loki had disappeared, and when Thor would have returned to the city to-destroy it, he found nothing around him but a verdant plain. Proceeding, therefore, on his way, he returned without stopping to Thrudvang. But he had already resolved to make that attack on the Midgard serpent which afterwards took place. I trust," concluded Thridi, "that thou wilt now acknowledge that no one can tell thee truer tidings than those thou hast heard respecting this journey of Thor to Jotunheim."

HOW THOR WENT TO FISH FOR THE MIDGARD SERPENT.

56. "I find by your account," said Gangler, "that Utgard-Loki possesses great might in himself, though he has recourse to spells and illusions; but his power may be seen by his followers, being in every respect so skillful and dexterous. But tell me, did Thor ever avenge this affront?"

" It is not unknown," replied Har, "though nobody has talked of it, that Thor was determined to make amends for the journey just spoken of, and he had not been long at home ere he set out again so hastily that he had neither his car nor his goats, nor any followers with him. He went out of Midgard under the semblance of a young man, and came at dusk to the dwelling of a giant called Hymir. Here Thor passed the night, but at break of day, when he perceived that Hymir was making his boat ready for fishing, he arose and dressed himself, and begged the giant would let him row out to sea with him. Hymir answered, that a puny stripling like he was could be of no great use to him. 'Besides,' he added, 'thou wilt catch thy death of cold if I go so far out and remain so long as I am accustomed to do.' Thor said, that for all that, he would row as far from the land as Hymir had a mind, and was not sure which of them would be the first who might wish to row back again. At the same time he was so enraged that he felt sorely inclined to let his mallet ring on the giant's skull without further delay, but intending to try his strength elsewhere, he stifled his wrath, and asked Hymir what he meant to bait with. Hymir told him to look out for a bait himself. Thor instantly went up to a herd of oxen that belonged to the giant, and seizing the largest bull, that bore the name of Himinbrjot, wrung off his head, and returning with it to the boat, put out to sea with Hymir. Thor rowed aft with two oars, and with such force that Hymir, who rowed at the prow, saw with surprise, how swiftly the boat was driven forward. He then observed that they were come to the place where he was wont to angle for flat fish, but Thor assured him that they had better go on a good way further. They accordingly continued to ply their oars, until Hymir cried out that if they did not stop they would be in danger from the great Midgard serpent. Notwithstanding this, Thor persisted in rowing further, and in spite of Hymir's remonstrances was a great while before he would lay down his oars. He then took out a fishing-line, extremely strong, furnished with an equally strong hook, on which he fixed the bull's head, and cast his line into the sea. The bait soon reached the bottom, and it may be truly said that Thor then deceived the Midgard serpent not a whit less than Utgard-Loki had deceived Thor when he obliged him to lift up the serpent in his hand: for the monster greedily caught at the bait, and the hook stuck fast in his palate. Stung with the pain, the serpent tugged at the hook so violently, that Thor was obliged to hold fast with both hands by the pegs that bear against the oars. But his wrath now waxed high, and assuming all his divine power, he pulled so hard at the line that his feet forced their way through the boat and went down to the bottom of the sea, whilst with his hands he drew up the serpent to the side of the vessel. It is impossible to express by words the dreadful scene that now took place. Thor, on one hand, darting looks of ire on the serpent, whilst the monster, rearing his head, spouted out floods of venom upon him. It is said that when the giant Hymir beheld the serpent, he turned pale and trembled with fright and seeing, more over, that the water was entering his boat on all sides, he took out his knife, just as Thor raised his mallet aloft, and cut the line, on which the serpent sunk again under the water. Thor, however, launched his mallet at him, and there are some who say that it struck off the monster's head at the bottom of the sea, but one may assert with more certainty that he still lives and lies in the ocean. Thor then struck Hymir such a blow with his fist, nigh the ear, that the giant fell headlong into the water, and Thor, wading with rapid strides, soon came to the land again."

THE DEATH OF BALDUR THE GOOD.

57. "Verily," said Gangler, "it was a famous exploit which Thor performed on that journey, but did any other such events take place among the Æsir?"

"Ay," replied Har, "I can tell thee of another event which the Æsir deemed of much greater importance. Thou must know, therefore, that Baldur the Good having been tormented with terrible dreams, indicating that his life was in great peril, communicated them to the assembled Æsir, who resolved to conjure all things to avert from him the threatened danger. Then Frigga exacted an oath from fire and water, from iron, and all other metals, as well as from stones, earths, diseases, beasts, birds, poisons, and creeping things, that none of them would do any harm to Baldur. When this was done, it became a favourite pastime of the Æsir, at their meetings, to get Baldur to stand up and serve them as a mark, some hurling darts at him, some stones, while others hewed at him with their swords and battle-axes, for do they what they would none of therm could harm him, and this was regarded by all as a great honour shown to Baldur. But when Loki, the son of Laufey, beheld the scene, he was sorely vexed that Baldur was not hurt. Assuming, therefore, the shape of a woman, he went to Fensalir, the mansion of Frigga. That goddess, when she saw the pretended woman, inquired of her if she knew what the Æsir were doing at their meetings. She replied, that they were throwing darts and stones at Baldur without being able to hurt him.

"'Ay,' said Frigga, 'neither metal nor wood can hurt Baldur, for I have exacted an oath from all of them.'

"'What!' exclaimed the woman, 'have all things sworn to spare Baldur?'

"'All things,' replied Frigga, 'except one little shrub that grows on the eastern side of Valhalla, and is called Mistletoe, and which I thought too young and feeble to crave an oath from.'

"As soon as Loki heard this he went away, and, resuming his natural shape, cut off the mistletoe, and repaired to the place where the gods were assembled. There he found Hodur standing apart, without partaking of the sports, on account of his blindness, and going up to him, said, 'Why dost thou not also throw something at Baldur?"

"'Because I am blind,' answered Hodur, 'and see not where Baldur is, and have, moreover, nothing to throw with.'

"'Come then,' said Loki, 'do like the rest, and show honour to Baldur by throwing this twig at him, and I will direct thy arm, toward the place where he stands.'

58. "Hodur then took the mistletoe, and under the guidance of Loki, darted it at Baldur, who, pierced through and through, fell down lifeless. Surely never was there witnessed, either among gods or men, a more atrocious deed than this! When Baldur fell the Æsir were struck speechless with horror, and then they looked at each other, and all were of one mind to lay hands on him who had done the deed, but they were obliged to delay their vengeance out of respect for the sacred place (Peace-stead) where they were assembled. They at length gave vent to their grief by loud lamentations, though not one of

245

them could find words to express the poignancy of his feelings. Odin, especially, was more sensible than the others of the loss they had suffered, for he foresaw what a detriment Baldur's death would be to the Æsir. When the gods came to themselves, Frigga asked who among them wished to gain all her love and good will; 'For this,' said she, 'shall he have who will ride to Hel and try to find Baldur, and offer Hela a ransom if she will let him return to Asgard;' whereupon Hermod, surnamed the Nimble, the son of Odin, offered to undertake the journey. Odin's horse Sleipnir was then led forth, on which Hermod mounted, and galloped away on his mission.

59. "The Æsir then took the dead body and bore it to the seashore, where stood Baldur's ship Hringhorn, which passed for the largest in the world. But when they wanted to launch it in order to make Baldur's funeral pile on it, they were unable to make it stir. In this conjuncture they sent to Jotunheim for a certain giantess named Hyrrokin, who came mounted on a wolf, having twisted serpents for a bridle. As soon as she alighted, Odin ordered four Berserkir to hold her steed fast, who were, however, obliged to throw the animal on the ground ere they could effect their purpose. Hyrrokin then went to the ship, and with a single push set it afloat, but the motion was so violent that the fire sparkled from the rollers, and the earth shook all around. Thor, enraged at the sight, grasped his mallet, and but for the interference of the Æsir would have broken the woman's skull. Baldur's body was then borne to the funeral pile on board the ship, and this ceremony had such an effect on Nanna, the daughter of Nep, that her heart broke with grief, and her body was burnt on the same pile with her husband's. Thor then stood up and hallowed the pile with Mjolnir, and during the ceremony kicked a dwarf named Litur, who was running before his feet, into the fire. There was a vast concourse of various kinds of people at Baldur's obsequies. First came Odin, accompanied by Frigga, the Valkyrjor and his ravens; then Frey in his car drawn by a boar named Gullinbursti or Slidrugtanni; Heimdall rode his horse called Gulltopp, and Freyja drove in her chariot drawn by cats. There were also a great many Frost-giants and giants of the mountains present. Odin laid on the pile the gold ring called Draupnir, which afterwards acquired the property of producing every ninth night eight rings of equal weight. Baldur's horse was led to the pile fully capari soned, and consumed in the same flames on the body of his master.

BALDUR IN THE ABODE OF THE DEAD

60. "Meanwhile, Hermod was proceeding on his mission. For the space of nine days, and as many nights, he rode through deep glens so dark that he could not discern anything until he arrived at the river Gjoll, which he passed over on a bridge covered with glittering gold. Modgudur, the maiden who kept the bridge, asked him his name and lineage, telling him that the day before five bands of dead persons had ridden over the bridge, and did not shake it so much as he alone. 'But,' she added, 'thou hast not death's hue on thee, why then ridest them here on the way to Hel?'

"'I ride to Hel,' answered Hermod, 'to seek Baldur. Hast thou perchance seen him pass this way?'

"'Baldur,' she replied, 'hath ridden over Gjoll's bridge, but there below, towards the north, lies the way to the abodes of death.'

"Hermod then pursued his journey until he came to the barred gates of Hel. Here he alighted, girthed his saddle tighter, and remounting, clapped both spurs to his horse, who cleared the gate by a tremendous leap without touching it. Hermod then rode on to the palace, where he found his brother Baldur occupying the most distinguished seat in the hall, and passed the night in his company. The next morning he besought Hela (Death) to let Baldur ride home with him, assuring her that nothing but lamentations were to be heard among the gods. Hela answered that it should now be tried whether Baldur was so beloved as he was said to be.

" 'If therefore,' she added, 'all things in the world, both living and lifeless, weep for him, then shall he return to the Æsir, but if any one thing speak against him or refuse to weep, he shall be kept in Hel.'

"Hermod then rose, and Baldur led him out of the hall and gave him the ring Draupnir, to present as a keepsake to Odin. Nanna also sent Frigga a linen cassock and other gifts, and to Fulla a gold finger-ring. Hermod then rode back to Asgard, and gave an account of all he had heard and witnessed.

"The gods upon this dispatched messengers throughout the world, to beg everything to weep, in order that Baldur might be delivered from Hel. All things very willingly complied with this request, both men and every other living being, as well as earths and stones, and trees and metals, just as thou must have seen these things weep when they are brought from a cold place into a hot one. As the messengers were returning with the conviction that their mission had been quite successful, they found an old hag named Thaukt sitting in a cavern, and begged her to weep Baldur out of Hel.

"It was strongly suspected that this hag was no other than Loki himself who never ceased to work evil among the Æsir."

THE FLIGHT AND PUNISHMENT OF LOKI.

61. "Evil are the deeds of Loki truly," said Gangler; "first of all in his having caused Baldur to be slain, and then preventing him from being delivered out of Hel. But was he not punished for these crimes?"

" Ay," replied Har, "and in such a manner that he will long repent having committed them. When he perceived how exasperated the gods were, he fled and hid himself in the mountains. There he built him a dwelling with four doors, so that he could see everything that passed around him. Often in the daytime he assumed the likeness of a salmon, and concealed himself under the waters of a cascade called Franangursfors, where he employed himself in divining and circumventing whatever stratagems the Æsir might have recourse to in order to catch him. One day, as he sat in his dwelling, he took flax and yarn, and worked them into meshes in the manner that nets have since been made by fishermen. Odin, however, had descried his retreat out of Hlidskjalf, and Loki becoming aware that the gods were approaching, threw his net into the fire, and ran to conceal himself in the river. When the gods entered the house, Kvasir, who was the most distinguished among them all for his quickness and penetration, traced out in the hot embers the vestiges of the net which had been burnt, and told Odin that it must be an invention to catch fish. Whereupon they set to work and wove a net after the model they saw imprinted in the ashes. This net, when finished, they threw into the river in which Loki had hidden himself. Thor held one end of the net, and all the other gods laid hold of the other end, thus jointly drawing it along the stream. Notwithstanding all their precautions the net passed over Loki, who had crept between two stones, and the gods only perceived that some living thing had touched the meshes. They therefore cast their net a second time, hanging so great a weight to it that it everywhere raked the bed of the river. But Loki, perceiving that he had but a short distance from the sea, swam onwards and leapt over the net into the waterfall. The Æsir instantly followed him, and divided themselves into two bands. Thor, wading along in mid-stream, followed the net, whilst the others dragged it along towards the sea. Loki then perceived that he had only two chances of escape, either to swim out to sea, or to leap again over the net. He chose the latter, but as he took a tremendous leap Thor caught him in his hand. Being, however, extremely slippery, he would have escaped had not Thor held him fast by the tail, and this is the reason why salmons have had their tails ever since so fine and thin.

"The gods having thus captured Loki, dragged him without commiseration into a cavern, wherein they placed three sharp-pointed rocks, boring a hole through each of them. Having also seized Loki's children, Vali and Nari, they changed the former into a wolf, and in this likeness he tore his brother to pieces and devoured him. The gods then made cords of his intestines, with which they bound Loki on the points of the rocks, one cord passing under his shoulders, another under his loins, and a third under his hams, and afterwards transformed these cords into thongs of iron. Skadi then suspended a serpent over him in such a manner that the venom should fall on his face, drop by drop. But Siguna, his wife, stands by him and receives the drops as they fall in a cup, which she empties as often as it is filled. But while she is doing this, venom falls upon Loki, which makes him howl with horror, and twist his body about so violently that the whole earth shakes, and this produces what men call earthquakes. There will Loki lie until Ragnarok,"

OF RAGNAROK, OR THE TWILIGHT OE THE GODS, AND THE CONFLAGRATION OF THE UNIVERSE.

63. "I have not heard before of Ragnarok," said Gangler; "what hast thou to tell me about it?"

"There are many very notable circumstances concerning it," replied Har, "which I can inform thee of. In the first place will come the winter, called Fimbul-winter, during which snow will fall from the four corners of the world; the frosts will be very severe, the wind piercing, the weather tempestuous, and the sun impart no gladness. Three such winters shall pass away without being tempered by a single summer. Three other similar winters follow, during which war and discord will spread over the whole globe. Brethren for the sake of mere gain shall kill each other, and no one shall spare either his parents or his children.

64. "Then shall happen such things as may truly be accounted great prodigies. The wolf shall devour the sun, and a severe loss will that be for mankind. The other wolf will take the moon, and this too will cause great mischief. Then the stars shall be hurled from the heavens, and the earth so violently shaken that trees will be torn up by the roots, the tottering mountains tumble headlong from their foundations, and all bonds and fetters be shivered in pieces. Fenrir then breaks loose, and the sea rushes over the earth, on account of the Midgard serpent turning with giant force, and gaining the land. On the waters floats the ship Naglfar, which is constructed of the nails of dead men. For which reason great care should be taken to die with pared nails, for he who dies with his nails unpared, supplies materials for the building of this vessel, which both gods and men wish may be finished as late as possible. But in this flood shall Naglfar float, and the giant Hrym be its steersman.

"The wolf Fenrir advancing, opens his enormous mouth; the lower jaw reaches to the earth, and the upper one to heaven, and would in fact reach still farther were there space to admit of it. Fire flashes from his eyes and nostrils. The Midgard serpent, placing himself by the side of the wolf, vomits forth floods of poison which overwhelm the air and the waters. Amidst this devastation heaven is cleft in twain, and the sons of Muspell ride through the breach. Surtur rides first, and both before and behind him flames burning fire. His sword outshines the sun itself. Bifrost, as they ride over it, breaks to pieces. Then they direct their course to the battlefield called Vigrid. Thither also repair the wolf Fenrir and the Midgard serpent, and also Loki, with all the followers of Hel, and Hrym with all the Hrimthursar. But the sons of Muspell keep their effulgent bands apart on the field of battle, which is one hundred miles long on every side.

65. "Meanwhile Heimdall stands up, and with all his force sounds the Gjallar-horn to arouse the gods, who assemble without delay. Odin then rides to Mimir's well and consults Mimir how he and his warriors ought to enter into action. The ash Yggdrasill begins to shake, nor is there anything in heaven or earth exempt from fear at that terrible hour. The Æsir and all the heroes of Valhalla arm themselves and speed forth to the field, led on by Odin, with his golden helm and resplendent cuirass, and his spear called Gungnir. Odin places himself against the wolf Fenrir; Thor stands by his side, but can render him no assistance, having himself to combat with the Midgard serpent. Frey encounters Surtur, and terrible blows are exchanged ere Frey falls; and he owes his defeat to his not having that trusty sword he gave to Skirnir. That day the dog Garm, who had been chained in the Gnipa cave,

breaks loose. He is the most fearful monster of all, and attacks Tyr, and they kill each other. Thor gains great renown for killing the Midgard serpent, but at the same time, recoiling nine paces, falls dead upon the spot suffocated by the floods of venom which the dying serpent vomits forth upon him. The wolf swallows Odin, but at that instant Vidar advances, and setting his foot on the monster's lower jaw, seizes the other with his hand, and thus tears and rends him till he dies. Vidar is able to do this because he wears those shoes for which stuff has been gathering in all ages, namely, the shreds of leather which are cut off to form the toes and heels of shoes, and it is on this account that those who would render a service to the Æsir should take care to throw such shreds away. Loki and Heimdall fight, and mutually kill each other.

" After this, Surtur darts fire and flame over the earth, and the whole universe is consumed."

66. "What will remain," said Gangler, "after heaven and earth and the whole universe shall be consumed, and after all the gods, and the heroes of Valhalla, and all mankind shall have perished? For ye have already told me that every one shall continue to exist in some world or other, throughout eternity."

"There will be many abodes," replied Thridi, "some good, others bad. The best place of all to be in will be Gimli, in heaven, and all who delight in quaffing good drink will find a great store in the hall called Brimir, which is also in heaven in the region Okolni. There is also a fair hall of ruddy gold called Sindri, which stands on the mountains of Nida, (Nidafjoll). In those halls righteous and well-minded men shall abide. In Nastrond there is a vast and direful structure with doors that face the north. It is formed entirely of the backs of serpents, wattled together like wicker work. But the serpents' heads are turned towards the inside of the hall, and continually vomit forth floods of venom, in which wade all those who-commit murder, or who forswear themselves."

67. "Will any of the gods survive, and will there be any longer a heaven and an earth?" demanded Gangler.

"There will arise out of the sea," replied Har, "another earth most lovely and verdant, with pleasant fields where the grain shall grow unsown. Vidar and Vali shall survive; neither the flood nor Surtur's fire shall harm them. They shall dwell on the plain of Ida, where Asgard formerly stood. Thither shall come the sons of Thor, Modi and Magni, bringing with them their father's mallet Mjolnir. Baldur and Hodur shall also repair thither from the abode of death (Hel). There shall they sit and converse together, and call to mind their former knowledge and the perils they underwent, and the fight of the wolf Fenrir and the Midgard serpent. There too shall they find in the grass those golden tablets (orbs) which the Æsir once possessed. As it is said,—

"'There dwell Vidar and ValiIn the gods' holy seats,When slaked Surtur's fire isBut Modi and MagniWill Mjolnir possess,And strife put an end to.'

"Thou must know, moreover, that during the conflagration caused by Surtur's fire, a woman named Lif (Life), and a man named Lifthrasir, lie concealed in Hodmimir's forest. They shall feed on morning dew, and their descendants shall soon spread over the whole earth.

"But what thou wilt deem more wonderful is, that the sun shall have brought forth a daughter more lovely than herself, who shall go in the same track formerly trodden by her mother.

"And now," continued Thridi, "if thou hast any further questions to ask, I know not who can answer thee, for I never heard tell of any one who could relate what will happen in the other ages of the world. Make, therefore, the best use thou canst of what has been imparted to thee."

Upon this Gangler heard a terrible noise all around him: he looked everywhere, but could see neither palace nor city, nor anything save a vast plain. He therefore set out on his return to his own kingdom, where he related all that he had seen and heard, and ever since that time these tidings have been handed down by oral tradition.

ÆGIR'S JOURNEY TO ASGARD.

68. Ægir, who was well skilled in magic, once went to Asgard, where he met with a very good reception. Supper time being come, the twelve mighty Æsir,—Odin, Thor, Njord, Frey, Tyr, Heimdall, Bragi, Vidar, Vali, Ullur, Hoenir and Forseti, together with the Asynjor,—Frigga, Freyja, Gefjon, Iduna, Gerda, Siguna, Fulla and Nanna, seated themselves on their lofty doom seats, in a hall around which were ranged swords of such surpassing brilliancy that no other light was requisite. They continued long at table, drinking mead of a very superior quality. While they were emptying their capacious drinking horns, Ægir, who sat next to Bragi, requested him to relate something concerning the Æsir. Bragi instantly complied with his request, by informing him of what had happened to Iduna.

IDUNA AND HER APPLES.

69. "Once," he said, "when Odin, Loki, and Hoenir went on a journey, they came to a valley where a herd of oxen were grazing, and being sadly in want of provisions did not scruple to kill one for their supper. Vain, however, were their efforts to boil the flesh; they found it, every time they took off the lid of the kettle, as raw as when first put in. While they were endeavouring to account for this singular circumstance a noise was heard above them, and on looking up they beheld an enormous eagle perched on the branch of an oak tree. 'If ye are willing to let me have my share of the flesh,' said the eagle, 'it shall soon be boiled;' and on their assenting to this proposal, it flew down and snatched up a leg and two shoulders of the ox—a proceeding which so incensed Loki, that he laid hold of a large stock, and made it fall pretty heavily on the eagle's back. It was, however, not an eagle that Loki struck, but the renowned giant Thjassi, clad in his eagle plumage. Loki soon found this out to his cost, for while one end of the stock stuck fast to the eagle's back, he was unable to let go his hold of the other end, and was consequently trailed by the eagle-clad giant over rocks and forests, until he was almost torn to pieces. Loki in this predicament began to sue for peace, but Thjassi told him that he should never be released from his hold until he bound himself by a solemn oath to bring Iduna and her apples out of Asgard. Loki very willingly gave his oath to effect this object, and went back in a piteous plight to his companions.

70. "On his return to Asgard, Loki told Iduna that, in a forest at a short distance from the celestial residence, he had found apples growing which he thought were of a much better quality than her own, and that at all events it was worth while making a comparison between them. Iduna, deceived by his words, took her apples, and went with him into the forest, but they had no sooner entered it than Thjassi, clad in his eagle-plumage, flew rapidly towards them, and catching up Iduna, carried her treasure off with him to Jotunheim. The gods being thus deprived of their renovating apples, soon became wrinkled and grey; old age was creeping fast upon them, when they discovered that Loki had been, as usual, the contriver of all the mischief that had befallen them. They therefore threatened him with condign punishment if he did not instantly hit upon some expedient for bringing back Iduna and her apples to Asgard. Loki having borrowed from Freyja her falcon-plumage, flew to Jotunheim, and finding that Thjassi was out at sea fishing, lost no time in changing Iduna into a sparrow and flying off with her; but when Thjassi returned and became aware of what had happened, he donned his eagle-plumage, and flew after them. When the Æsir saw Loki approaching, holding Iduna transformed into a sparrow between his claws, and Thjassi with his outspread eagle wings ready to overtake him, they placed on the walls of Asgard bundles of chips, which they set fire to the instant that Loki had flown over them; and as Thjassi could not stop his flight, the fire caught his plumage, and he thus fell into the power of the Æsir, who slew him within the portals of the celestial residence. When these tidings came to Thjassi's daughter, Skadi, she put on her armour and went to Asgard, fully determined to avenge her father's death; but the Æsir having declared their willingness to atone for the deed, an amicable arrangement was entered into. Skadi was to choose a husband in Asgard, and the Æsir were to make her laugh, a feat which she flattered herself it would be impossible for any one to accomplish. Her choice of a husband was to be determined by a mere inspection of the feet of the gods, it being stipulated that the feet should be the only part of their persons visible until she had made known her determination. In inspecting the row of feet placed before her, Skadi took a

fancy to a pair which she flattered herself, from their fine proportions, must be those of Baldur. They were however Njord's, and Njord was accordingly given her for a husband, and as Loki managed to make her laugh, by playing some diverting antics with a goat, the atonement was fully effected. It is even said that Odin did more than had been stipulated, by taking out Thjassi's eyes, and placing them to shine as stars in the firmament.

THE ORIGIN OF POETRY.

71. Ægir having expressed a wish to know how poetry originated, Bragi informed him that the Æsir and Vanir having met to put an end to the war which had long been carried on between them, a treaty of peace was agreed to and ratified by each party spitting into a jar. As a lasting sign of the amity which was thenceforward to subsist between the contending parties, the gods formed out of this spittle a being to whom they gave the name of Kvasir, and whom they endowed with such a high degree of intelligence that no one could ask him a question that he was unable to answer. Kvasir then traversed the whole world to teach men wisdom, but was at length treacherously murdered by the dwarfs, Fjalar and Galar, who, by mixing up his blood with honey, composed a liquor of such surpassing excellence that whoever drinks of it acquires the gift of song. When the Æsir inquired what had become of Kvasir, the dwarfs told them that he had been suffocated with his own wisdom, not being able to find any one who by proposing to him a sufficient number of learned questions might relieve him of its superabundance. Not long after this event, Fjalar and Galar managed to drown the giant Gilling and murder his wife, deeds which were avenged by their son Suttung taking the dwarfs out to sea, and placing them on a shoal which was flooded at high water. In this critical position they implored Suttung to spare their lives, and accept the verse-inspiring beverage which they possessed as an atonement for their having killed his parents. Suttung having agreed to these conditions, released the dwarfs, and carrying the mead home with him, committed it to the care of his daughter Gunnlauth. Hence poetry is indifferently called Kvasir's blood, Suttung's mead, the dwarf's ransom, etc.

72. Æsir then asked how the gods obtained possession of so valuable a beverage, on which Bragi informed him that Odin being fully determined to acquire it, set out for Jotunheim, and after journeying for some time, came to a meadow in which nine thralls were mowing. Entering into conversation with them, Odin, offered to whet their scythes, an offer which they gladly accepted, and finding that the whetstone he made use of had given the scythes an extraordinary sharpness, asked him whether he was willing to dispose of it. Odin, however, threw the whetstone in the air, and in attempting to catch it as it fell, each thrall brought his scythe to bear on the neck of one of his comrades, so that they were all killed in the scramble. Odin took up his night's lodging at the house of Suttung's brother, Baugi, who told him that he was sadly at a loss for labourers, his nine thralls having slain each other. Odin, who went under the name of Baulverk, said that for a draught of Suttung's mead he would do the work of nine men for him. The terms agreed on, Odin worked for Baugi the whole summer, but Suttung was deaf to his brother's entreaties, and would not part with a drop of the precious liquor, which was carefully preserved in a cavern under his daughter's custody. Into this cavern Odin was resolved to penetrate. He therefore persuaded Baugi to bore a hole through the rock, which he had no sooner done than Odin, transforming himself into a worm, crept through the crevice, and resuming his natural shape, won the heart of Gunnlauth. After passing three nights with the fair maiden, he had no great difficulty in induc ing her to let him take a draught out of each of the three jars, called Odhroerir, Bodn, and Son, in which the mead was kept. But wishing to make the most of his advantage, he pulled so deep that not a drop was left in the vessels. Transforming himself into an eagle, he then flew off as fast as his wings could carry him, but Suttung becoming aware of the stratagem, also took upon himself an eagle's guise, and flew after him. The Æsir, on seeing him approach Asgard, set out in the yard all the jars they could lay their hands on, which Odin filled by discharging through his beak the wonder-working liquor he had drunken. He was however, so near being caught by Suttung, that some of the liquor escaped him by an impurer vent, and as no care was taken of this it fell to the share of the poetasters. But the liquor discharged in the jars was kept for the gods, and for those men who have sufficient wit to make a right use of it. Hence poetry is also called Odin's booty, Odin's gift, the beverage of the gods, &c, &c.

Made in the USA
Lexington, KY
21 May 2019